On his first day at state university, freshman Johnny Darling rues his decision to enroll. He's 150 miles from his family and friends and terribly homesick. But when he's assigned Ben Stonecipher as a roommate, Johnny's life brightens. Ben's a handsome guy from a wealthy family, but he's emotionally troubled, and for good reason. He's responsible for his twin brother's recent death.

A liquor-fueled night in the dorm room leads to personal confessions and intimacy. In the days that follow, an intense affair blossoms between Johnny and Ben, one that must weather the threat of a love triangle neither boy is prepared to deal with.

I Love You, Johnny Darling

Jere' M. Fishback

A NineStar Press Publication

Published by NineStar Press
P.O. Box 91792,
Albuquerque, New Mexico, 87199 USA.
www.ninestarpress.com

I Love You, Johnny Darling

Printed in the USA
First Edition
September, 2018

Print ISBN: 978-1-949340-79-2

Also available in eBook, ISBN: 978-1-949340-75-4

Warning: This book contains sexual content, which may only be suitable for mature readers, discussion of past incestuous acts (between cousins) and sex between high school student/teacher, and infidelity.

Chapter One

MY FRESHMAN YEAR of college was about to start, and I felt certain I was screwed.

I lay alone in my fourth-floor dormitory room that resembled a prison cell: cinder-block walls painted taupe, asphalt tile floor, two twin beds, two Formica bureaus, two metal desks with chairs, and two closets. The showers and toilets were down the hall. Outside, a misty rain fell from a sky the color of dishwater. Weak light entered the room through a pair of casement windows framed by plastic drapes. The windows offered a view of a parking lot and a row of dumpsters.

I didn't know a single soul on campus nor in the city of Gainesville where my school was located.

I could have felt sorry for myself, but what good would it do? I put myself in the situation—*I* made the choice to come there. Instead of staying at home and attending community college, I enrolled at the University of Florida, and now it was too late to change my mind. My mom had left me there two hours before—that was right after we unloaded my things from her car—and by now, she was probably halfway back to St. Petersburg Beach.

Great.

I'm Johnny Darling, and that's *not* a nickname by the way. Darling is my legal name, and you can only imagine the shit I've taken ever since I reached seventh grade, and guys started getting cruel about qualities that made someone different in any way.

"Want to suck my dick, Darling? I'll bet you'd *love* to."

"Do you wear panties under your chinos, Darling?"

"Hey, Darling, will you be my homecoming date? I'll buy you a corsage."

And so on.

I was always slender, so it wasn't like I could stop the taunts by slugging some guy who outweighed me by thirty pounds. I'd never even thrown a punch—I wouldn't have known how to—so all the way through junior high and into early high school, I endured the crap.

I am also queer as a flamingo; I figured that out the first time I viewed a television show called *Flipper* when I was thirteen. The series starred a bottle-nosed dolphin and a sinewy blond boy named Luke Halpin who frequently appeared shirtless in the show. Mostly he wore only a skimpy pair of cutoff blue jeans. Luke had a washboard stomach, shoulders that bulged like softballs, and a chest that looked like it was carved from marble. The first time I saw him I grew so excited I thought I might bust through the zipper on my shorts. After that, I never missed an episode of *Flipper* during the three years it aired because—and I'll freely admit this—I was insanely in love with Luke Halpin. He became my go-to fantasy whenever I lay in my bed at night and touched myself under the sheets.

Oh, Luke...

But I digress.

This was 1969, and the world I dwelled in was not kind to faggots. The only way I could survive was to hide my urges and pretend to be straight. That way, I wouldn't get my teeth knocked out. My sex life—and this was pathetic—was a tube of jelly and my right hand. In high school, I actually went on dates with girls to the prom and all, but never felt anything sexual when I held a girl's hand or put my arm around her waist. Even then, I knew marriage to a woman wasn't going to work for me.

Now, in the dorm room, I lay on the bed closest to the windows and wove my fingers behind my neck. I stared at the plaster ceiling, then at a cobweb waving in one corner. My hang-up clothes were stored in one of the room's closets, while my folded clothes rested in a bureau. My manual Olivetti typewriter—it weighed twenty pounds—hulked on the desk I'd chosen to use.

Cool air wafted from a ceiling register, so at least the room was climate-controlled. I'd heard some dorms on campus didn't even have air-conditioning and I figured the rooms in those buildings must have felt like ovens right then, so I had *something* to be grateful for. I wasn't sweating and—

Someone rapped on my door, and my body jerked in response. *Who could it be?*

I turned my gaze to the door and hollered, "Come in."

When the door swung open, three people stood in the hallway, peering into my room. Two were a middle-aged couple. The third was a slender guy my age. All three carried cardboard boxes.

"Hi," the younger guy said. "I'm Ben Stonecipher, and I guess we're roommates. Mind if we come in?"

I swung my feet to the floor and rose. Then I shook Ben's hand after he put down his boxes. His grip felt firm and warm.

After I introduced myself, he pointed to the couple behind him. "These are my folks, Will and Sarah Stonecipher."

Will Stonecipher looked like a doctor in a TV series: tall, with salt-and-pepper hair, a trim waist, and an easy smile. He wore dress slacks, a Banlon shirt, and leather slip-ons.

After he set down his boxes, he shook my hand. "Pleased to meet you, Johnny," he said in a gentle baritone flavored with a Florida drawl. Then he pointed at his son. "Don't let that guy give you any trouble this year, understand?"

Sarah Stonecipher looked at her husband and pursed her lips while shaking her head. Then she took my hand in hers. "You shouldn't listen a word my husband says," she said with a grin on her pretty face. Her prematurely gray hair was cut short like my mom's, and she wore minimal makeup. Her yellow sleeveless blouse, white capris, and sandals flattered her slim figure.

"I'm sure you and Ben will get along just fine, as long as you don't mind a little snoring," she said.

When I glanced at Ben, he rolled his emerald eyes.

Will asked where I was from.

"St. Petersburg Beach," I said, right after I released Sarah's hand. "My mom drove me up here this morning."

Will nodded while he looked around the room. "We're from Merritt Island, on the opposite coast. Ever been there?"

I shook my head. In fact, I'd never even *heard* of Merritt Island.

"It's not a tourist destination like your town," Will said, "but it's our home."

All three Stoneciphers left the room to retrieve more of Ben's belongings. They returned with clothing on hangers, an electric typewriter, a desk lamp, and a tennis racket in a wooden press, held together with thumbscrews. When they finished hanging the clothes in Ben's closet, I felt a little embarrassed that Ben's wardrobe was twice the size of mine. He even owned a navy-blue sports jacket with brass buttons.

Okay, I also owned a sports jacket, but it was a houndstooth number my mom had bought at a church thrift store, and it didn't look good on me because the sleeves were too short.

Ben also owned a portable stereo record player, a Magnavox model, along with an entire boxful of vinyl LP records. He set up the player on a folding metal TV tray he'd brought. The player resembled a small suitcase. When Ben opened it up, the player displayed two speakers and a turntable.

"Well," Sarah said to Ben with her hands on her hips, "I think that's everything from the car. We have a three-hour drive ahead of us, so I guess we'll be going."

Ben nodded and his mom hugged him. Ben and his dad shook hands; then Will shook mine too.

"I'm very pleased to have met you, Johnny, and good luck in school."

"You'll have to visit us sometime," Sarah said to me.

I nodded, but then I asked myself how Ben and I would even get to wherever Merritt Island was. Freshman at UF were not allowed to have cars, so we wouldn't have transportation. We would be, in a sense, captives on campus for the year.

After his parents left, Ben started unpacking boxes. Some contained books; others held things like toiletries, socks, underwear, and T-shirts.

I sat on my bed, watching.

Ben was good-looking by anyone's standards, an inch or so taller than me, probably six feet, fair-skinned with thick eyebrows, a turned-up nose, and full crimson lips. He parted his dark hair on the side. His voice was deeper than mine, also flavored with a drawl like his dad's. He wore blue jeans, penny loafers, and a button-up shirt with the shirttail untucked and the sleeves rolled to his elbows.

I rubbed the tip of my nose with a knuckle. "When I picked up my room key, the lady behind the desk said we'll need to get our sheets and towels from the linen room downstairs. They close at five."

Ben nodded and glanced at his wristwatch—a gold model with a band made from alligator hide. "I'll be unpacked in another half hour. Why don't we go after that?"

"Sounds good," I said. "Which bed do you want?"

He pointed to the bed I wasn't sitting on, the one closest to the door. "I'll take that one if it's okay with you."

"It's fine," I said while I cracked my knuckles.

After Ben arranged his typewriter and lamp on the desk I hadn't selected, he fished a framed photo from a box and placed it on his desk as well, a studio portrait of four people: Ben's parents and two boys who were dressed identical and looked like younger versions of Ben, maybe age sixteen.

"Are you on the meal plan?" Ben asked.

"Yeah, are you?"

Ben nodded while he placed a few books on his desk: a dictionary, a Bible, and what looked like a high school yearbook. "I wonder if the food's any good. I guess we can eat as much as we want, so I hope it's decent."

After Ben finished unpacking, I helped him carry all his empty boxes down a stairwell, where we tossed them into one of the dumpsters we had seen from our room. By now, the rain had stopped, and Ben checked his wristwatch again.

"It's only two thirty," he said. "Feel like taking a walk around campus before we get our linens?"

I nodded. "My first class tomorrow morning is in a building called Peabody Hall. I checked a school map; it's located in the northeast part of campus. Let's see if we can find it."

Our dorm was in the southwest corner of campus, and the first buildings we passed were pretty austere, built of red brick with awning-style windows and few architectural features. But everywhere huge trees soared thirty or forty feet: longleaf pines, multi-trunked live oaks festooned with Spanish moss, magnolias, sabal palms, and a Shumard oak with a rutted trunk so wide two grown men couldn't wrap their arms around it. The sidewalk we trod on snaked through expanses of damp Bahia grass. Azalea and camellia shrubs hugged the flanks of most buildings we encountered.

I asked Ben where Merritt Island was located.

"Do you know the Kennedy Space Center?" he replied.

I nodded. "Some friends and I drove over there to watch the moon-landing launch, back in July. The night before liftoff we slept in my car in Titusville."

"The space center is actually a part of Merritt Island, at its north end. Our property is close to the middle of the island and a short drive from the Atlantic. My dad's family has lived there since the Civil War; we own citrus groves and also a beef cattle ranch. It was a great place to grow up."

I thought of the little two-bedroom cottage my mom had raised me and my sister in, and the fact I had no idea where my father was or even if he was still alive. Clearly, Ben and I had come from very different backgrounds.

My last two years of high school, I'd worked at a gas station. Four nights a week, five hours per night, I pumped gas, checked engine oil levels, fixed flat tires, and performed oil changes. I drove a rusty Ford Fairlane to school, one I bought from a station customer for a hundred bucks. My cuticles, the free edges of my fingernails, and the whorls on the pads of my fingers all stayed perpetually black no matter how much I scrubbed them with Lava soap. My beat-up work boots looked like I'd dunked them in a grease vat, and the coveralls I wore to work were oil and sweat stained.

I could only imagine what Ben would have thought had he seen me back then. And what would he think of me in the days and weeks ahead, when he learned I didn't have a pedigree like his?

As we approached the northeast section of campus, the buildings looked older and statelier, with mullioned windows and pitched roofs rimmed by battlements. Some were covered in ivy. Peabody Hall was a small building, really, just four stories with a gabled tile roof. Its western flank faced a broad and grassy plaza shaded by longleaf pines.

I glanced at my Timex wristwatch and realized it had taken us fifteen minutes to walk there from the dorm. My first class the next morning was at 8:00, so I'd need to leave the dorm no later than 7:45, maybe 7:40 to be safe. I didn't want to be late the first day of school, now did I?

"Have you bought your books yet?" Ben asked while he studied the buildings around us.

"Not yet; I guess I will after classes end tomorrow. What about you?"

Ben nodded. "My mom drove me over here last week to buy them from the campus bookstore, and get this: when I checked out at the register, the cashier tried to sell me a *beanie*."

"A what?"

"It's a silly little orange-and-blue cap that male freshmen are expected to wear their first quarter."

I made a face. "I don't understand. Why?"

"So upperclassmen can pick on them—it's a tradition here."

"Did you buy one?"

Ben shook his head. "It's not required, so why invite that sort of treatment from guys? I have more respect for myself than that."

I decided not to buy a beanie either.

BACK AT THE dorm, we had to sign a card for our linens: three towels, two bedsheets, and a pillowcase, all tattooed as university property. The little woman behind the laundry room counter had a moustache and a mole on her cheek the size of an M&M. Speaking with a drawl as thick as molasses, she told us we could exchange our dirty linens for clean ones every Thursday. If we lost anything, a towel or whatever, we'd have to pay to replace it.

Just before we made up our beds, Ben cued up a record on his stereo, an album I knew well, *Surrealistic Pillow* by the Jefferson Airplane, a San Francisco-based band. My favorite song on the album was "Somebody to Love."

While we put sheets on our beds, Ben asked me about St. Petersburg Beach.

"I like it there," I told him. "We live in a section called Pass-a-Grille. The homes there are older and our neighbors are nice. The beach is real pretty; the sand looks like table sugar and the water's clear. I spend a lot of time at the shore when I'm not at school or working."

"Working?"

I explained about the gas station.

Ben spread a sheet out on his mattress and tucked the edges under. "I've never had a job like that. Instead, I work for my dad in the groves or helping out with the cattle. He pays me a buck fifty an hour. It's not bad, except in summer when the weather gets hot and the mosquitoes swarm."

I shook my pillow into my pillowcase. "I know what you mean. Summers at the gas station were brutal 'cause I normally worked in the daytime when I wasn't in school. The pumps weren't shaded by a canopy, so I roasted while servicing customers."

When Ben asked about my family, I wasn't sure what to say. How to explain?

"It's just me, my mom, and my sister, Tricia. My dad...doesn't live with us."

"Your parents are divorced?"

I nodded, then pointed at the framed photo on Ben's desk. "I guess you have a twin brother?"

Ben lowered his gaze and rubbed his lips together. He held his pillow to his chest and fingered one corner while he spoke. "I did, but not any longer. He died in a boating accident last February."

Shit.

"I'm sorry," I said. "That must've been tough for you and your parents."

Ben worked his jaw from side to side. Then he looked up at me. "The whole thing was a nightmare. It nearly killed my parents—they're still not over it—and to be honest, I'm not either."

I couldn't think of anything to say, so I asked, "What was your brother's name?"

"Charles but we always called him Chuck."

"I guess you guys were close?"

"We did everything together. When he died, it felt really strange, like I'd lost a limb or something."

Again, I didn't know what to say, so I busied myself with spreading a cotton blanket on my bed. I'd brought the blanket from home. I tried to imagine losing my sister—we were pretty close—but I couldn't even bear to think of it.

Ben cleared his throat. "Let's talk about something else, okay?"

"Sure," I replied, but neither of us spoke again for several minutes, and the silence that hung between us seemed as thick as tar.

Chapter Two

OUR FIRST WEEK of classes had ended, and my head spun like whirligig in a gale. Most days I only attended three hours of class, but then I had so many reading assignments that I was usually at my desk with my nose in a book at least five more hours a day. For the most part, the material wasn't too difficult with the exception of my physical science course.

Science and I had never gotten along; I always struggled with it in high school. Now, at the university, I could stare at the same page in my physical science text for a half hour or more, but nothing sunk in. My brain didn't want to comprehend what I was reading or the diagrams I looked at, and it was frustrating.

Ben and I seemed to get along well. Like me, he didn't know a single person at the university. Each day, we ate breakfast and dinner together at the cafeteria connected to our dorm. The food was okay. Most weeknights, we spent an hour in the lounge on our dorm floor, where we shot pool or watched a little TV. Ben had a subscription to the *Orlando Sentinel*, and after we both read an issue, we discussed the events of the day.

Right then, Richard Nixon was trying to appoint an ultra-conservative guy named Clement Haynsworth to the US Supreme Court, but the Democratic-controlled senate was balking at the appointment. It looked like the New York Mets might actually win the National League pennant, something no one had anticipated when the season began. And activist students were trying to organize a nationwide "moratorium" on college campuses to protest the Vietnam War, so a lot was going on.

This will sound perverted—I know—but the best part of my day came when Ben took his evening shower. In our room beforehand, he undressed completely, and when his briefs came off, I stole glances at his private areas while my mouth turned pasty and my crotch tingled. Once he was naked, he wrapped a towel around his waist and left for the shower room with his toiletry kit in hand. Fifteen minutes later, I was done jerking off into a tissue and Ben was back, smelling of soap and shampoo. He'd peel off his towel and reach into a bureau drawer for a fresh pair of briefs while I stole more glances.

Aye-yi-yi.

I'd never lived with another guy, so I hadn't been exposed to male nudity on a daily basis like that. In high school, I'd taken one mandatory year of PE, which involved showering with my classmates, but that was in a smelly locker room with a bunch of sweaty guys and the whole thing was nasty.

With Ben, it was different. It was just him and me in our room, so the situation felt...intimate.

And Ben was so damned sexy. I loved the way his body tapered from his broad shoulders to his narrow waist. I liked the dark hairs on his calves that reminded me of raindrops tumbling toward his ankles. His genitals enchanted me, of course, but his best feature was his butt—two cream-colored melons as smooth as porcelain. When I walked to classes, I often found myself thinking about Ben's body, and sometimes I'd go stiff in my chinos—no joke.

Every evening, usually around nine, Ben's mother called him on our room's wall-mounted phone. She did most of the talking and Ben spoke to her with a gentle tone. He always reassured her that everything with him was good, that school was going well, and he and I were getting along fine.

One evening, after one of those phone calls, Ben lay down on his bed. He stared up at the ceiling with his hands joined behind his neck. Then he drew a breath and let it out.

I was at my desk and looked up from my American Institutions text.

"Is something wrong?" I asked.

Ben wore briefs—that was all—and his genitals bulged beneath the cotton. "I wish my mom wouldn't worry so much about me. I know why she does—it's because of my brother. She's afraid she's going to lose me, too, that I'll get run over by a bus or something. I know she means well—I try to be understanding—but sometimes, I feel suffocated."

I didn't know what to say. My mom had never been the clingy type. Even as a child, I'd had more freedom than most kids my age. I made my own decisions on everything, from whether to attend church to what clothing I wore to school.

Since arriving at the university, I hadn't even spoken to my mom. Long-distance calls were expensive, especially on weekdays, so Mom and I had agreed that she would call me at 8:00 p.m. every Sunday, when rates were the cheapest.

"It's probably tough on your mom, having you live away from home for the first time," I said. "But after a while, I'm sure she'll get used to it."

Ben looked at me and scowled. "Not her."

An hour later, we were getting ready for bed. Both of us brushed our teeth down the hall at a row of sinks. After Ben rinsed his mouth out, he pulled an orange plastic bottle from his shaving kit. He uncapped the bottle and dropped a pale-yellow tablet into the palm of his hand. Then he placed the tablet on his tongue and bent to gulp water from the tap.

I'd seen Ben do this several times and was curious what the pills were for.

One day when Ben wasn't around, I did something sneaky. I unzipped his shaving kit and plucked out the bottle. The label had Ben's name on it and also the logo of a Merritt Island pharmacy. The name of the drug Ben took was called imipramine.

BEN'S VOICE WOKE me. "I'm sorry, Chuck. I'm so sorry."

I opened my eyelids. Our room was dark, but outside a three-quarter moon shone in an inky sky, offering a bit of light. I turned to check the alarm clock on the nightstand. The time was 2:30 in the morning.

"I didn't mean to," Ben said, but he wasn't even awake. He talked in his sleep, babbling incoherent stuff that sort of dribbled out of his mouth. He thrashed around under his bedcovers like he wrestled a demon.

After I pulled my covers aside and rose, I grabbed Ben's shoulder and shook it. "Hey, wake up."

Ben settled onto his back, and his eyelids fluttered open. At first, it seemed like he didn't know where he was. His gaze flitted here and there, and then he looked at me.

"What is it?" he asked.

"I think you were having a bad dream."

"Was I?"

"You were talking to your brother."

"What did I say?"

"You kept telling him you were sorry for something. That's all I could understand anyway."

Ben tossed his tangled covers aside and sat up on his mattress. He planted his feet on the floor. Bathed in moonlight, he yawned and scratched his head. "What time is it?"

When I told him, he frowned and shook his head.

"Are you okay?" I asked.

"Yes and no."

I sat down on my bed. "What does *that* mean?"

Ben cocked his head to one side while he studied his bare feet. Then he looked at me. "It means I'm not dying, but the inside of my head is terribly fucked up right now."

Huh?

"I don't understand what you're saying."

Ben rubbed his jaw with the flat of his hand. "I killed my brother."

"You mean Chuck?"

Ben nodded.

"How is that possible? You said he died in a boating accident."

"But the accident was my fault. There were four of us guys in the boat, and I was at the helm. We were all drinking beer and acting stupid. I wasn't watching where we were going. I hit a channel marker, the boat flipped, and Chuck...drowned."

When Ben uttered those last two words, his voice broke like a twelve-year-old's. Then he started crying, and I mean *sobbing* out of control. His shoulders shook. He curled up into the fetal position on his bed while he continued to wail. Moonlight reflected in the tears streaming down his cheeks and nose. His face was contorted; he didn't even look like himself right then, but more like some tormented soul in a crazy house.

I got up and sat next to Ben on his bed. I put my hand on his shoulder and felt him tremble. I'd never seen a person so shaken up and I honestly didn't know how to handle the situation.

"Tell me what I can do," I said.

He didn't answer my question right away, but only after his sobs diminished to whimpers.

"There's nothing you can do," he finally said. "It's too late for anybody to do anything. Chuck is gone and it's my fault. My folks pretend that they don't blame me, but I know they do—everyone does. I'm just a miserable fuckup, Johnny, and now I have to live with that for the rest of my life."

Say something.

"I don't think you're a fuckup. In fact, I think you're a really decent guy. You shouldn't hate yourself because you made a mistake. That's what people do—they make mistakes."

"But mine was a huge one."

"I *know* but—"

"Chuck is dead because of me. How am I supposed to go through life with that on my conscience?"

LATER THAT MORNING, when we dressed for class, Ben apologized to me for his emotional meltdown.

"It's okay," I said. "Anytime you want to talk about Chuck, just let me know."

Ben nodded.

"Thanks, Johnny—I'll do that."

A FEW DAYS later, right after we shared dinner in the cafeteria, Ben and I took a walk to Lake Alice, maybe a half mile west of our dorm. Rain had fallen earlier and now everything around us was damp, the trees and shrubs and the ground we trod on. It all had a loamy smell. The sky was overcast, the air was still and heavy with moisture, and the lake's surface looked like a mirror. A little way from shore, two wood ducks paddled around in a stand of cattails.

"I always thought I was a strong person," Ben told me. "I've never been one to cry or feel sorry for myself. But this whole thing with Chuck has turned me into jelly. I'm a mess these days."

"You have a right to be," I said.

Ben looked at me and raised an eyebrow. "Can I tell you something I've never told anyone? And if I do, will you keep it to yourself?"

"Of course."

Ben stopped walking and I did as well. His hands were in the front pockets of his blue jeans, and he lowered his chin for a moment. Then he drew a breath and looked at me.

"Back in July, I decided to kill myself. I couldn't stand the guilt I felt over Chuck any longer. My dad owns shotguns for quail hunting. One afternoon, I took a gun from his case, loaded it, and brought it with me in my mom's car. I drove to one of our orange groves, way off where no one would see me."

"Jesus, Ben."

"Looking back, I know it was a stupid thing to do, but at the time, suicide seemed to make sense. I sat there in my car, holding the shotgun in my lap and thinking about how much I missed Chuck and how I'd feel better if I were dead. Plus, I figured if I shot myself it might partially make up for my mistake."

"But you didn't. What happened?"

Ben shrugged. "I chickened out—I didn't have the balls to stick the gun in my mouth and pull the trigger. I couldn't even get that right."

"You'd have only made things worse for your folks if you had died."

He looked at me and his eyes glistened. "You don't think they secretly hate me?"

"Your parents?"

He nodded.

"They don't hate you. If they did, then your mom wouldn't call you every night. Think about that for a minute."

Ben rubbed the tip of his index finger against the pad of his thumb, and I could almost hear his brain fluids churn. Meanwhile, I was close to going nuts. When I had first met Ben, he seemed so self-assured and smooth, like a guy cruising through life effortlessly. But clearly he wasn't. I tried to imagine him sitting in the orange grove and holding the shotgun in his lap, and a shudder ran through me. I'd felt bad at times in my life, but never *that* bad. What must it have felt like?

"Listen," I said, "I'm sure glad you didn't kill yourself. I'm glad you're here today."

Ben looked at me and crinkled his forehead. "Are you?"

"I am. Now what do you say we get back to the dorm? I have a ton of reading to do."

Chapter Three

SOMETIME IN LATE September, around eight at night, a knock sounded on our dorm room's door. A pair of attractive guys wearing fraternity jerseys and blue jeans stood in the hallway. One was blond with some muscle on him, the other slender and dark-haired. The dark-haired guy knew Ben from class and they shook hands. He introduced Ben to the blond guy, and then Ben introduced me to the fraternity guys.

It seemed our dark-haired visitor was also a freshman. He had pledged the fraternity. The blond guy was a brother in charge of recruiting new members, and he spoke to Ben in a self-assured tone.

"Alpha Tau Omega is one of the best fraternities on campus. Our membership standards are high. We want pledges with good looks, excellent grades, and leadership skills." He pointed to the dark-haired guy who sat beside him on Ben's bed. "Craig seems to think you'd fit right in at ATO, so we're here to ask you to join us for dinner this Friday. You can meet the brothers and see the house. What do you think?"

Ben was seated on my bed, facing them. I still sat in my desk chair. I tried to concentrate on the text before me, but it was hard with the conversation going on. I glanced over my shoulder at Ben. His elbows rested on his knees, and his hands were joined before him. He took a few seconds before he spoke.

"Sure," he said, "I'll come for dinner."

After the fraternity boys left, I asked Ben if he'd seriously consider joining ATO.

He looked at me for a second before he lowered his gaze and shrugged. "Maybe."

Hours later, Ben and I lay in our respective beds in the darkness. Ben snored softly. I was wide awake, lying on my side and facing Ben so I could study his face and hair. I felt all stirred up. Partly because our visitors had shown zero interest in *me*, other than saying goodbye when they left, but mostly because I felt threatened by the possibility Ben might accept a pledge bid. If he did, I was pretty sure the fraternity would consume most of Ben's free time, and then I'd be without the only friend I had at school.

In my mind's eye, I envisioned Ben wearing an ATO jersey, and I winced at the thought.

FRIDAY NIGHT ARRIVED. After Ben took his evening shower, he combed his damp hair. Then he put on dress slacks, penny loafers, and a pressed Oxford-cloth shirt.

A Beatles album, *Sgt. Pepper's Lonely Hearts Club Band*, played on Ben's stereo. My favorite song, "Eleanor Rigby," was on right then. It always made me feel a little sad.

"Are you nervous?" I asked Ben.

He looked at my reflection in his mirror. "A little. Craig told me ATO has over one hundred members. That's a lot of people to meet at one time."

That night I ate dinner alone in the cafeteria, among scores of chattering students. For company, I read the *Orlando Sentinel*. My food tasted like cardboard, and I felt so blue I wanted to cry. I had never been so lonely. When I finished eating, I took a long walk around campus. Light had faded from the sky, and a few stars had already appeared in the eastern horizon. Crickets chirped in the trees I trod under. Clumps of male students passed by me, laughing and cracking jokes, headed for the student union where guys went to bowl or play ping-pong.

I strolled with my hands in my pockets and my chin lowered most of the time. My loafers scuffed the concrete sidewalk. I felt a lot like I had the day Mom dropped me off at school, and I lay alone in the dorm, ruing my enrollment at the university. It amazed me how quickly those feelings had returned now that I knew it was possible my friendship with Ben would wither. I wasn't the kind of guy who made friends easily—I never had been—so it was unlikely I'd find someone to take Ben's place, not anytime soon.

I thought of my friends back in south Pinellas County, my high school buddies I'd spent all my free time with before coming up to Gainesville, and now I realized how much I missed them. Most were enrolled at St. Petersburg Junior College, a two-year school. They continued to live in their parents' homes, and I suspected they were a lot happier than I was right then because they got to see one another constantly.

I decided to visit my academic advisor the following week. He was a nice guy who'd helped me create a classroom schedule before school began, when I visited campus for freshman orientation. I would explain my unhappiness with living at the university and ask about the possibility of a transfer to St. Petersburg Junior College. And maybe I'd have a chat with my mom about returning to live with her in St. Petersburg Beach.

I figured sometimes you had to face the consequences of a poor choice you'd made. And then you did what was necessary to change your situation—you had to act.

Right?

BEN ARRIVED BACK at our dorm room around 9:00 p.m.

I lay on my bed, reading a collection of short stories assigned by my English professor. The story I read was Jack London's *The Whale Tooth*, a tale taking place in Fiji. London was a good writer; I liked him. He had the ability to describe a place so well I could see it inside my head.

Ben undressed while we talked.

"So, how was it?" I asked. Then I held my breath.

Ben unbuttoned his shirt. "I liked it, I guess. The food was good and the guys were friendly—they offered me a pledge pin." Ben reached into his shirt pocket and showed me a shiny little brass thing he placed atop his bureau.

Shit.

"Did you accept the offer?"

Ben peeled off his shirt and tossed it into his hamper, then unbuckled his belt. "I told them I'd think about it. But before I make a decision, I want to talk about pledging with you, to see what you think."

I set aside my book and rose to a sitting position. This was an important moment.

"Look, it seems like a good fraternity and a real opportunity if it's what you want—being part of an organization."

Ben kicked off his shoes, then lowered his pants to his ankles and stepped out of them. He talked while he draped the pants over a coat hanger. "It's a huge commitment. I'd be expected over there for lunch and dinner every day. On weekends, there are pledge work parties—yard maintenance, housecleaning, that sort of thing. And then I'd have to study the fraternity's history, memorize all the brothers' names and their hometowns. I worry my grades might suffer."

I didn't say anything.

After Ben placed his pants and shoes in his closet, he sat on his bed, facing me. He rested his elbows on his knees, made a steeple with his arms and hands, and looked at me.

"And then there's us. Right now, you're my best friend and I think we understand each other very well. If I join ATO, things will change. I won't have the time to spend with you that I do now, and I'm not sure I want that to happen. I'd like to hear your view of the situation."

I heard my pulse pound inside my head. "I don't want to get in the way of your opportunity, but I should tell you something." I lowered my gaze and shifted my ass on my mattress, then looked back at Ben. "If our friendship fizzles—and it will if you pledge—then after Christmas, I'll probably transfer to junior college in St. Pete. I felt so shitty eating dinner by myself tonight, and I don't want to experience that every day. But that's *my* problem. You aren't obligated to take care of me."

Ben squinted. "That's not true. I need to look out for you because you've certainly taken care of *me* since I got here."

"How?"

"You've seen those pills I take each night before bed?"

I nodded.

"I suffer from depression—I'm in a very dark place right now. My shrink believes my condition is related to my brother's death. He says I feel guilty because Chuck's gone and I'm still alive. The pills help some, but having a close friend—a guy I can talk to honestly about my feelings—is very important to me right now. And I don't think I'd find someone like you at the ATO house."

Ben's knees crackled when he rose. He strode to his bureau and seized the pledge pin in his fingertips, then walked to his desk and dropped the pin into his metal wastebasket. The pin made a noise when it struck the basket's bottom.

Twang.

Chapter Four

THE THIRD WEEK of October arrived, and Gainesville's weather had cooled. I wasn't dripping sweat when I walked across campus. Some mornings, I wore a sweater. Midterm exams had been given that week, and I thought I did well with the exception of physical science. I'd be happy with a C on that one.

On Friday night, Ben and I didn't have to study; we could relax.

Back in August, just before I'd left St. Petersburg Beach for school, one of my regular gas station customers gave me a bottle of rum as a going-away gift. It had sat unopened on my closet shelf ever since I arrived in Gainesville.

Now, Ben and I decided we would mix Cuba Libres and get ourselves a bit drunk as a way of celebrating the end of midterms. Earlier, we had purchased a six-pack of cola, and since we didn't have a fridge, we had no ice. We would have to drink the Cuba Libres at room temperature, but that was okay with us.

The Cuba Libres were sweet and fizzy. I wasn't much of a drinker, and after I drained my first glass, I already felt a bit woozy. Ben and I sat on our respective beds, facing each other. I wore jeans and a T-shirt. Ben wore jeans but no shirt, and I found myself stealing glances at the thin line of hair that descended from his navel and dribbled into the waistband of his jeans.

A Simon & Garfunkel album, *Bookends*, played on Ben's stereo. My favorite song on the album was titled "America," and I wasn't sure why because it always made me feel a little lonely when I listened to it.

Ben talked about the sport of surfing and how much he liked it.

"Brevard County is Florida's surfing capital, and this time of year the waves fire. My friends and I always surfed three or four days a week during October, and right now, I find myself missing that."

I nodded. "I miss the Gulf breezes and the smell of saltwater, also the sound of waves hitting the shore. Sometimes, Gainesville feels terribly confining to me because it's landlocked."

Ben bobbed his chin. "We should plan a trip to Merritt Island, maybe next weekend. We can ride the bus over there on Friday afternoon, and my folks can bring us back here on Sunday. I'm sure they wouldn't mind."

We had both finished our first drink, and now we mixed two more. We clinked the rims of our glasses and each took a gulp.

After I burped, I asked Ben, "Are you feeling anything yet?"

"I'm a little light-headed. How about you?"

"The same."

We talked about the next day's home football game we'd attend together. The Gators would play North Carolina, and people were excited because so far the Gators were undefeated and they could possibly win the SEC championship. Our quarterback, John Reaves, and his favorite receiver, Carlos Alvarez, had chalked up big passing yardage every game.

Our glasses were empty again, and when I rose to mix two more drinks, I felt unsteady on my feet. I spilled soda on my desktop when I made the next round. Then I tottered back to my bed and handed Ben his drink.

Ben raised his glass. "To our friendship. We're lucky to be roommates, don't you think?"

I nodded. We clinked glasses again, and each of us took a healthy gulp from his drink.

A thought entered my head. Ben had shared serious private information with me since we'd lived together, about his mental illness and his brother's death and also his near-suicide attempt. But I had shared nothing personal about myself with Ben. Should that change?

Probably so, Darling. Go on—tell him.

I shifted my weight on my mattress and brought my gaze to Ben's. I stared into his emerald eyes.

"If I tell you something personal about myself—it's something no one else knows—will you promise to keep it a secret?"

"Of course, you know you can trust me."

I drew a breath and let it out.

"I'm gay—I like men."

Ben lowered his gaze while he rubbed his lips together. Then he looked up at me.

"How long have you known that?"

"Since seventh grade. I've just never felt anything for girls."

Ben blinked. "Have you ever...?"

"What?"

"Touched another guy?"

I shook my head, and we both took another gulp from our drinks.

Ben's gaze drilled into mine. "Be honest, Johnny—do you ever think about touching me?"

I lowered my gaze and nodded. Then I looked at Ben again. "Does that offend you?"

"Not at all. In fact, I've thought about touching you that way myself, but I wasn't sure how you'd feel about it, so I didn't tell you. But now..."

My heart banged against my rib cage. Was the rum screwing with my head, or was this really happening?

Ben reached across the gap between our beds; he stroked my cheek with a fingertip. "Let's lock the door and close the drapes. We can move our beds together so they're like a double."

Ten minutes later, we lay naked in semidarkness; the only light came from a desk lamp Ben had draped with a towel. We touched each other's private places while our lips smacked and our tongues dueled. Tendrils of electricity snaked through my limbs.

This, of course, was my first sexual experience.

Not so for Ben.

He knew what he was doing in bed with another guy. He used his mouth, tongue, and fingers in creative ways that made my heart chug like an eighteen-wheeler. I savored the scent of Ben's skin; it reminded me of how damp oak leaves smelled. When he suggested we pleasure each other simultaneously, we shifted positions and I took Ben into my mouth. I worked him with my tongue and lips while Ben did the same to me.

Exhilaration bubbled inside me.

It didn't take long before I unloaded, and when I did, I felt like I was levitating. My body jerked over and over. Ben reached orgasm as well, and I swallowed his sour-tasting seed like it was ambrosia.

Who'd have guessed I'd like guzzling another guy's jizz?

When our breathing slowed, we changed positions so I lay on my back with my head on two pillows. Ben's cheek rested on my sternum. I ran my fingers through his dark hair while my chest rose and fell. Ben's arm draped my belly.

"Did you like the sex?" he asked.

"It was amazing, probably the best thing that's ever happened to me."

"My junior year of high school, I had a friend named Andy. We used to do this all the time, mostly at his house when his folks weren't around. Then he moved to Vero Beach and I went nuts."

"You were in love with him?"

"I guess, if that's possible between two guys."

I toyed with Ben's ear while I talked. "In high school, I felt attracted to one of my best friends in a major way. His name is Steve, a beautiful guy who used to spend the night at my house on a regular basis—we even slept in the same bed—but I never told him about my feelings. I feared he might end our friendship if I did."

Ben drew a breath. "The only person I ever told about Andy was my brother, Chuck. I had to tell *somebody* when Andy moved away. Like I said, I went crazy from the loss."

"What did Chuck say?"

"He was surprised, of course. But he told me it was okay, that he didn't think any less of me because I liked Andy in a sexual way."

Go on, ask him.

"Do you like me that way?"

Ben looked at me and kissed my shoulder. Then he returned his cheek to my sternum. "Of *course* I do. But this is not just about sex—not for me anyway. You're nice looking, but you're also my best friend, someone who looks after me and cares how I'm feeling. What more could I ask for?"

My throat constricted and my eyes itched. This whole thing seemed too good to be true, but it was for real, it was happening. In the course of one night, Ben and I had moved beyond friendship and on to something much deeper.

Unbelievable.

Chapter Five

ON A FRIDAY evening, around 6:00 p.m., a week after my first sexual encounter with Ben, I sat beside him on a Greyhound bus with our knees and shoulders touching. A few hours before, we'd caught another bus that took us from Gainesville to Orlando. Then we switched to the bus we were presently on, headed westward on the Bee Line Expressway.

Late-afternoon sunshine slanted through the windows, reflecting in the lenses of an old man's horn-rimmed eyeglasses. He sat across the aisle from us. He read a *Life* magazine with a stylized photo of Vietnam War protesters on the cover, and I wondered how he must feel about people my age who rebelled against the values his generation believed in. And what would he think of me and Ben if he knew about our private life?

Yes, we had a private life, a very intense one.

Every morning, I woke up next to Ben. Usually, he was holding me, since we always went to sleep spoon-style, with Ben's hips pressed to my butt and his chest touching my shoulder blades. His nose would nestle in my hair, and his breath would tickle the back of my neck. Of course, we always slept naked, and it felt so natural having Ben's warm skin touching mine, as if it were something meant to be.

The fourth time we had sex—it was on the previous Monday—Ben produced a bottle of hand lotion from his bureau drawer, and when I asked him what the lotion was for, a grin crept across his handsome face.

"I want you to fuck me, Johnny."

Well.

I guess I'd never thought about two guys having butt sex, much less me and Ben doing it. But when I penetrated Ben, I felt the warmth of his gut and the clench of his muscle and it felt so amazing that I groaned like some kind of zoo animal. The backs of Ben's knees rested on my shoulders and I gazed into his eyes while I thrust inside him. When I came, it seemed like someone had stuck me with a cattle prod. My vision blurred and my body jerked, and I felt the orgasm in every part of my body.

After Ben came—also an explosive and noisy event—I laid my sweaty forehead on his collarbone, and for a reason I still don't fully understand, I *wept*. I totally lost control, feeling like a guy saved from execution by a last-minute pardon from the governor.

Ben stroked my hair while I cried.

"S-h-h-h. It's okay, Johnny."

I stayed inside Ben for the longest time, listening to him breathe and marveling at just how wonderful I felt despite my silly blubbering. I could have remained where I was for an eternity.

Thereafter, each night in our room, we moved our beds together and rearranged the blankets and sheets. Then, each morning, we restored things to their normal positions so the custodian didn't suspect what we'd been up to.

I had never been so relaxed. I felt completely comfortable in my own skin for the first time in my life. I knew who I was and what I required to be happy. All I needed was Ben. Even when we occupied separate places, I heard his voice inside my head. I felt his lips touch mine and his fingers stroke my flesh.

I'd heard the term "walking on air" many times, and now *I* felt that way as I moved through my school days. I felt almost drugged, and in a sense I *was*.

Ben was my drug.

Now, on the bus, I sat in an aisle seat while Ben sat next to the window, dozing. His chin rested on his sternum and his eyes were shut. Beyond the window, the Kissimmee River meandered through a broad plain studded with sabal palm islands. Late-afternoon sunlight reflected off the river's shimmering surface. Cattle stood in knee-deep water, looking stupefied and out of place.

I felt apprehensive about the weekend. I'd already met Ben's parents, but that was at the dormitory and our encounter was brief. This time, I would spend two nights under their roof and we'd share meals. They would likely ask me questions about my family and my past, and also there might be awkward moments if Ben's brother, Chuck, was mentioned.

And then there was the budding romance between me and Ben. Earlier, Ben had told me there were two full-size beds in his bedroom and that was where we'd both sleep. "I'll lock the door and you can move to my bed after lights out. It'll be a tight fit, but so what?"

When I asked Ben how his parents might react if they knew I was his lover, Ben grimaced.

"I don't think they'd be too happy about what we're doing, but it's our life not theirs, right?"

I'd nodded my assent.

In some ways, Ben seemed supremely confident, and I liked that. Despite the depression he struggled with and his angst regarding Chuck, he had a grasp of life that I didn't come close to possessing. He saw things clearly and logically. He knew what he wanted from the world, and it seemed that included me now.

On the bus, a half hour went by before we reached the bridge crossing the Indian River. The river was broad, and the bridge arced fifty feet into the air before we descended into Merritt Island. Lush vegetation abounded: sabal palms, mangroves, Brazilian pepper, Australian pines, and sea grape trees. Flowering hibiscuses of every hue bloomed: canary yellow, fire-engine red, pink, and orange.

Downtown was mostly one-story brick storefronts with crenellated trims and plate-glass windows. There wasn't a bus station, just a Greyhound office with two benches and a counter. Ben's mom waited for us on one of the benches when we exited the bus. She wore a blouse with a flower motif, dark slacks, and sandals, and a smile lit up her face when she rose to greet us. She hugged Ben for at least fifteen seconds, before shaking my hand.

"It's so good to see you again, Johnny."

She led us to her curb-parked car, a shiny cream-colored Oldsmobile convertible with the top presently lowered and caramel-colored upholstery—rolled and pleated leather. Ben took the passenger seat while I sat in the rear, and once we got moving, the wind rushing through the car fluttered my hair. After we left downtown, there wasn't much to see. We passed one-story homes, some frame, others cinder block. A shopping center with a Piggly-Wiggly, a Rexall drugstore, and a JC Penney was the island's most prominent architecture. Mostly the land was undeveloped and junglelike until we reached the Stoneciphers' property, perhaps five miles from town.

Ben's home was a large one-story ranch-style dwelling with a columned front porch, a cupola on the concrete tile roof, and green shutters at the awning-style windows. The grass was emerald, mowed and edged as neatly as pie slices. Lush azalea shrubs hugged the stucco walls, and a huge live oak shaded much of the yard.

To the north of the house, a citrus grove went on as far as I could see, acres and acres of trees planted in neat rows. To the south was a cattle pasture surrounded by a barbed-wire fence. It also seemed to go on forever. Off in the distance, scores of beef cattle stood around in clumps like folks at a cocktail party. In back of the house a large barnlike structure loomed, and when I exited the car, a pungent aroma made me crinkle my nose.

Ben later told me the smell was horse shit.

By then, the sun had halfway disappeared at the western horizon and clouds there boiled in shades of pink, gold, and green. A light breeze from the east stirred the fronds on a sabal palm next to the driveway. Then I smelled something else—saltwater and its familiar aroma that made my heart flutter.

I asked Ben how far we were from the Atlantic.

"About a ten-minute drive. We'll go there tomorrow."

Inside, the house was cool and quiet. My shoes sunk into cut pile carpet. The place looked like something out of *Good Housekeeping* magazine with its tasteful furnishings. The smell of roasting meat wafted from the kitchen. Ben led me down a hallway to his bedroom, where I tossed my overnight bag onto the bed he designated as mine. In addition to the beds, the room was furnished with a mirrored bureau, a desk and chair, and a bookcase with a dozen sports trophies sitting atop it. All the furniture matched. The room's wallpaper had an equestrian theme, and the bedspreads, wallpaper, and drapes did as well.

Ben's framed high school diploma from Merritt Island High School hung on one wall. A sticker on the diploma said Ben had graduated with honors. A taxidermic fish, a red drum that had to be two feet long, hung on another wall. When I asked Ben about the fish, he told me he'd caught it at the mouth of the Indian River.

"I was about to turn eleven years old. My dad got the fish stuffed as a birthday gift to me."

Ben even had his own private bath with gleaming fixtures and a tiled shower with a glass door.

I felt a bit overwhelmed by my opulent surroundings and wondered what Ben and his mom might say if they could see my modest little house in St. Petersburg Beach with its sandy yard and cypress flitch siding.

Sarah stuck her head through the doorway. "Your dad'll be home in a half hour and dinner will be ready by then. In the meantime, why don't you show Johnny around?"

I followed Ben back down the hallway, and when we passed another bedroom that looked like a duplicate of Ben's—same furnishings and wallpaper, same bedspreads and drapes—I knew without asking whose room it had been. I tried to imagine how hurtful it must have felt for Ben and his folks to look into that room every day and know they would never see Chuck again.

Ben led me outdoors, to the barn in back of the house. By then, the sky was almost dark, and after we entered the barn, Ben flicked a light switch on. Several ceiling fixtures hung from the barn's exposed rafters; the fixtures illuminated the place like a theater stage. A half-dozen horses stood in separate stalls. Some stared at us and twitched their pointy ears, while others didn't even seem to notice our presence.

Ben approached one of the larger horses, a black stallion with a shiny coat. "Hey, Midnight," Ben said while he petted the stallion's muzzle. "Meet my boyfriend, Johnny, from school."

A shiver ran up my spine when I heard the word boyfriend. Was that what I was now, Ben's boyfriend?

Aye-yi-yi.

The horse nickered and pawed his stall floor with a hoof.

Ben looked at me. "Tomorrow morning, we'll take a ride around the property. Ever been in a saddle?"

I shook my head.

"You'll get the hang of it quickly. Horseback riding is a great way to see the groves and ranch."

I wasn't so sure about *that*. The horses were huge, and I couldn't imagine myself sitting atop one. What if my mount decided to gallop? Would I fall off and make a fool of myself?

At the dinner table, Ben's dad (he insisted I call him Will) talked with his wife about the dozens of migrant workers who would soon arrive to help harvest oranges and grapefruits that ripened in the groves. It seemed there were barracks on the Stoneciphers' property where the migrants lived while they worked there. Some had already arrived, but most of the barracks would need to be readied and linens for the bunk beds distributed to new arrivals.

Our meal was delicious: roast beef, mashed potatoes with gravy, and steamed green beans. I helped myself to a basket of cornbread slices and a butter dish. A monogrammed silver pitcher of iced tea sat on a cork coaster, and vanilla-scented candles burned in a pair of silver candlesticks. A cabinet with glass doors held a china service for at least twelve people, along with serving platters and paper-thin wineglasses. We sat at a lacquered pecan table surrounded by ten chairs, also pecan with upholstered seats. The tablecloth was linen and utterly spotless. An oil painting of a warship under sail hung on one wall in a gilded frame.

But there was something odd in the room: an extra place setting—plate, napkin, silverware, and water glass—

directly across the table from me. Nobody else seemed to notice the extra setting, and I didn't ask about it because I was pretty sure who it was there for. Just looking at it gave me the creeps.

I knew little of citrus farming, cattle, or horses, so I didn't have much to say. I just listened to the Stoneciphers discuss these subjects. Ben seemed to have a deep understanding of his family's business. He asked all sorts of incisive questions about the groves and cattle, and his dad answered at length.

Then, about twenty minutes into our meal, Will looked at Ben and Sarah. "Listen to the three of us. Here we are, prattling on about oranges and cows, and poor Johnny hasn't had a chance to say a thing." Will swung his gaze to me. "Sorry, Johnny. Tell us how school's going?"

I talked about my classes and my midterm grades.

"All were As and Bs except for a C in physical science. So I think things are going well. Of course, I'm still adjusting to living away from my family, and I miss the Gulf Coast."

Will said, "Met any pretty girls on campus yet?"

I felt heat in my cheeks when I shook my head.

Will turned to Ben. "How about you? Gone on a date yet?"

Ben shook his head, and I knew what he was thinking. He was wondering what his dad would say if he could see us in bed together each night in our dorm room, doing the things we loved to do with each other.

"You boys need to get busy up there," Will said while his gaze flitted between Ben and me. "College isn't just about learning; it's about finding the right girl."

"Dad," Ben said in a slightly annoyed tone of voice, "I think Johnny and I can take care of ourselves."

Will looked at Sarah, then back at Ben. "All right, son. Just make time for fun once in a while, will you?"

Ben lowered his gaze and nodded.

AFTER DINNER, BEN and I took a walk through the citrus groves. A crescent moon shone, and because no streetlights burned nearby, we saw a thousand stars twinkling in the night sky. Crickets chirped in the trees. The air was cool, and both of us wore sweatshirts with the university's seal on the chests. The trees we passed were laden with fruit, oranges mostly, but also grapefruits. Somewhere close by an owl hooted. I was thinking about home and wondering what my mom and sister were doing that night when Ben snatched me from my reverie.

"Hey," he whispered.

When I looked at him, he was standing still with a mischievous grin on his handsome face. "What is it?"

"We're alone. How about a kiss?"

Seconds later, our hips and chests touched. Our lips smacked and our tongues rubbed and my hand rested on the Ben's nape while both his hands met at the small of my back. His breath steamed my upper lip, and when we finally separated, my vision was blurry and my knees seemed weak.

"I've never kissed another boy on my family's property," Ben said. "It felt awfully good."

I nodded while wiping spittle from my lips with the back of my hand. "Who'd have thought making out in an orange grove could be so sexy?"

Ben chuckled at my remark. He took my hand in his and we kept on walking. Our sneaker soles scraped the sandy soil while crickets and the owl serenaded us. I lifted my chin and studied the silvery moon while I pondered just how much my life had changed over the course of the past week. Before our Cuba Libre Night, as we'd dubbed it, I had been a lonely virgin—I'd never experienced intimacy—but now I felt like Ben and I were a single living organism.

Before Ben and I became lovers, I had worried constantly about my public image, about what people thought of me and the way I behaved and how I dressed and what I said. But now, I didn't care about any of that. I only cared about the life I shared with Ben and what *he* thought of me.

We came to a small wooden building with a corrugated tin roof. Ben opened the building's door, and the hinges screeched like those in a spook house. I followed him inside, squinting until my eyes adjusted to the darkness. Moonlight entered through a double-hung window, revealing the shapes of agricultural equipment. The room smelled of gasoline and fertilizer.

Ben pulled me to him so our hips and chests touched again. He kissed me on the mouth and our tongues rubbed. Then he sank to his knees before me, popped the button at the waistband of my jeans, and lowered my zipper. Moments later, my jeans and briefs were pooled at my ankles and Ben slurped away while chills crawled up my spine. Ben's warm mouth felt like heaven, and it didn't take long before my hips bucked. I unloaded while a groan burst from my throat.

Ben guzzled my come. He stayed on his knees while my pulse slowed. Our breathing and the crickets outside were the only sounds I heard. After I withdrew from Ben's mouth, I looked down at him.

He smiled at me and patted my bare thigh. "You can return the favor in my room later on tonight. Sound good?"

In the shadows, I grinned and nodded.

Chapter Six

SATURDAY MORNING I woke up in Ben's bed. His arm draped my chest and his hips pressed against my butt. I listened to his soft snoring as sunlight poured through a window on the room's eastern wall. I studied trophies on Ben's bookcase: tennis, baseball, and rodeo. A dozen Hardy Boys novels occupied the lowest shelf. There were James Bond novels by Ian Fleming and also *The Carpetbaggers* by Harold Robbins, a smutty book all the guys at school had read a couple of years ago. And a full set of the *World Book Encyclopedia* filled two other shelves.

I flipped over so I faced Ben. Then I kissed the bridge of his nose just as his eyelids fluttered open. His hair was in tangles and his morning breath was stale, but I didn't care. He still looked beautiful to me.

"Hey," he whispered. "How'd you sleep?"

"Like a sack of rocks."

"Me too. Ready to get up?"

We showered together in Ben's private bath, taking turns scrubbing each other with a soapy washcloth. Then we shampooed each other's hair. We hadn't done this before and it was kind of fun. Ben looked so cute with water streaming down his limbs.

We shared breakfast with Ben's folks at the Stoneciphers' kitchen table. Will read the *Orlando Sentinel* while Sarah sipped from her coffee cup. Ben and I drank fresh-squeezed orange juice so tangy my taste buds jangled.

We munched on Cheerios, and in between spoonfuls, Ben talked to me about the day ahead. "I thought this morning we'd tour the property on horseback. Then this afternoon, we can drive over to the coast."

He turned to Sarah. "Could we borrow your car?"

Sarah nodded. "I filled the tank yesterday."

After breakfast, we entered the barn. The morning was cool and sunny, and we both wore flannel shirts and blue jeans. The barn smelled of horse shit and hay.

Ben equipped Midnight and another horse named Penny with blankets, saddles, and bridles. Penny was a brown mare and a bit smaller than Midnight, but still plenty big.

"She's even-tempered," Ben told me while he adjusted the belt on Penny's saddle. "The two of you will get along just fine."

Ben showed me how to put my left foot in the stirrup on Penny's left side. Then I swung my right leg over Penny's back and settled into the saddle's seat. Suddenly, I was five feet above the ground. Ben adjusted both my stirrups to fit the length of my legs while I rested my hands on my saddle's horn. Penny nickered and shifted her weight beneath me, and I felt the power of her bulk.

Ben climbed onto Midnight's saddle as easily as he might climb into a car seat. He explained how to use Penny's reins to turn her left or right, and to make her go and stop.

"She's a smart girl," he said. "She'll know just what you want her to do."

Ben clucked his tongue and jiggled his reins, and Midnight loped forward. Penny and I followed Midnight and Ben out the barn door and into the sunshine. Above us, the sky was cloudless and bright blue. I came alongside Ben, and we walked the horses into the citrus groves, between the rows of trees.

A picking crew, a dozen or so black men, harvested oranges in one section of the grove, and we stopped to watch them for a few minutes. The pickers perched on ladders, plucked oranges from tree limbs, and dropped them into burlap sacks that hung from the men's shoulders like a postman's bag. Once a picker's sack was full, he emptied the contents into a wooden crate, then returned to his ladder to pick more fruit.

"During summer, they're up in New England harvesting blueberries, cherries, and apples, crops like that," Ben explained. "They also harvest tobacco in the Carolinas. Then they move south when the weather cools. In Florida, they pick citrus from November through January. Then they harvest strawberries in February and March, mostly over near Lakeland and Tampa."

We passed on through the rows of trees. I rocked from side to side as Penny's massive body moved, and my saddle squeaked. Already I was pretty sure the horse was getting used to me.

"Certain varieties of oranges ripen earlier than others," Ben said. "Those men are harvesting navel oranges right now. Later, they'll harvest the Parson and blood oranges. And then there are grapefruits to be picked as well. A month from now, we'll have sixty men or more working these groves from dawn till dusk."

Because I was high above the ground, I saw everything around me. The groves seemed to go on forever, row after row of trees with their waxy, forest green leaves and heavy fruit.

"Will all this property be yours one day?" I asked Ben.

Ben nodded as we loped along. "Until last February, we all thought Chuck and I would own this place together; that we'd run it as a team once my parents surrender control. But now it's just me and I'll have a whole lot of responsibility whenever that day comes."

I tried to imagine Ben in that position, maybe twenty years from now.

"Do you think you'll ever get married?" I asked him.

He looked at me and shrugged. "My parents expect it—you heard my dad at the table—but I'm not sure I could carry it off. I don't feel physical attraction to girls, never have. So how could I possibly make a woman happy?"

I responded while we continued to ride between the rows of trees. "When my friends in high school started dating, I couldn't understand their interest in girls. I thought maybe I was a late bloomer, that eventually I'd feel an urge. But now I know it's not going to happen."

After our tour of the groves, we visited the cattle ranch, which was basically acres and acres of cleared land where animals grazed on Bahia grass in groups of ten or twelve. All were either mature females or calves of both sexes. The cows were huge creatures with numbered ear tags. Most had black or rust-colored coats, and many had white faces. Their slender tails flicked back and forth.

Bulls were kept in a separate, fenced area, huge, thick-necked creatures that looked ominous when their gazes met mine. I sensed their strength and hair-trigger tempers, and knew I wouldn't want to spend time inside the bull pen.

"Most bulls are slaughtered for meat before the age of three," Ben explained. "Only the best are allowed to fully mature. Those we use for breeding."

Ben pointed to a palmetto and pine forest at the edge of the cleared land. "That's also our property. Those trees are slash pines—they grow pretty quickly. In another ten years or so a lumber company will harvest them, and then we'll replant seedlings."

I was coming to realize that the Stoneciphers' property was a living thing with organs that performed their assigned tasks smoothly. The land, trees, and animals all produced products people needed to live. They provided work and income for Ben's family and the folks they employed.

We visited the barracks where migrant workers lived when they labored there, a half-dozen single-story frame structures with pitched roofs and double-hung windows. Another building was a kitchen and dining hall where a woman in an apron prepared a hot lunch for the guys working in the groves. I smelled ground beef frying and coffee percolating. Steam rose from a cooking pot as big as a five-gallon bucket.

Only one barrack was presently occupied. After we hitched our horses to a pine tree, Ben showed me the inside of the barrack. We entered through a screened door. The rooms had no ceiling; the rafters were exposed, and the building's plywood sub-roof loomed above us. The floor was a concrete slab. There were two rows of wooden bunk beds, all neatly made up with sheets, blankets, and pillows, and between each set were two double bureaus stacked with workers' belongings: magazines, Royal Crown hair pomade, cigarette packs, electric razors, and portable radios. A bathroom offered toilets, sinks, and tiled shower stalls. Bath towels hung from wall hooks. An oil-burning space heater sat in the center of the barrack with a chimney that passed through the roof.

"When Chuck and I were kids, sometimes we'd spend the night in one of these barracks when they weren't in use. We'd hang out in our underwear, smoke cigars, listen to music, and play cards until midnight. It was fun stuff at the time."

I tried to imagine ten-year-old Ben puffing on a stogie while he played gin rummy with his brother, and the vision in my mind's eye made me grin. But then the grin disappeared when I tried to imagine just how badly Ben must miss Chuck. A whole part of Ben's past had been wiped out in only a few seconds of carelessness.

No wonder Ben was depressed.

After lunch, we climbed into Sarah Stonecipher's convertible in the Stoneciphers' three-car garage that also housed a shiny Cadillac Sedan DeVille. Ben occupied the driver's seat. He lowered the top, and then we cruised down the county road, flying past the groves. Wind fluttered our hair. The day had warmed up, and we both wore T-shirts and Bermuda shorts. Ben switched on the radio; we listened to a local AM rock station, WKKO. At the moment, it played a Blood, Sweat, & Tears song, "Spinning Wheel."

Ben reached for my left hand; he held it in his as we cruised along, and the feel of his palm pressed against mine made my heart sing. I had never felt so happy and carefree. I bathed in the sunshine and fresh air, feeling almost weightless.

Ben turned his gaze from the road to me. He gave me a wink while he squeezed my hand, and a grin spread across his face.

After I grinned back at him, Ben returned his gaze to the county road.

"You know, if you're not careful, I'll fall in love with you, Mr. Darling. I hope that's okay."

My heart leapt into my throat. For a few seconds, I couldn't speak, and when I did, my voice sounded squeaky. "Of course it's okay."

He squeezed my hand again but kept his gaze fixed on the windshield. "Right now, because of my depression, it's hard to feel totally happy like I used to. There's always sadness lurking in the back of my head. But when I'm around you, that sadness fades to the point I almost feel like my old self again. With you in my life, I'm not walking around with a twenty-pound weight on my shoulders."

Ben looked at me again. "Thank you for that, Johnny."

I didn't know what to say, so I didn't say anything. I just savored the feel of Ben's hand holding mine.

When we reach the Bee Line, Ben turned west, and we crossed the Banana River on an arcing concrete bridge. We reached the bridge's apex, and I saw the ocean's blue expanse, a new experience for me. Even though it was only 150 miles from St. Petersburg Beach, I had never seen the Atlantic before, and my pulse quickened when I thought that in only minutes I could dip my foot into a body of water that stretched from Florida all the way to Europe and Africa.

We reached the barrier island and entered the town of Cape Canaveral, a municipality that had not existed, Ben told me, until our late President Kennedy declared, back in 1960, that our country would put a man on the moon's surface by the decade's end. The Space Race had ensued, and the northern portion of Merritt Island was selected as a suitable place for rocket assemblies and launches. Thousands of people moved to Brevard County to work for NASA and its subcontractors and they needed someplace to live, so developers created entire neighborhoods for them, the kind we passed by. The homes were one-story, cinder-block structures with few architectural features. They squatted on treeless yards, baking in the afternoon sun. We passed strip centers occupied by hair salons, pizza parlors, and pawn shops. There were gas stations, mini-marts, tackle shops, and mom-and-pop motels.

We visited the Cocoa Beach Pier, where Ben fed dimes into a parking meter. After we slipped off our shoes and stowed them in the car, we walked barefooted through rust-colored sand to the ocean's edge, and then we waded ankle-deep along the shore. The water wasn't even cold, really. It felt good on my skin. A light breeze cooled my brow, and the sun was high in the sky.

A hundred yards offshore, a dozen guys sat astride their surfboards; they rose and fell as waves passed beneath them. The noses of their boards pointed skyward.

"Why aren't they surfing?" I asked Ben.

"They're waiting for a good wave, one that will break at just the right time. Let's watch them for a minute."

We stopped walking and studied the surfers, visoring our eyes with our hands and looking eastward. Sunlight glittered on the ocean's surface. Off in the distance, a brown pelican dive-bombed a pod of fish and came up with a catch in his gullet.

"There's a set coming in now," Ben said, pointing, and I saw them, a group of three waves approaching the lineup of surfers. Four guys turned the noses of their boards toward shore. They lay on their board decks and paddled furiously, chopping at the water with their hands. The first wave lifted them as its lip began to break.

One guy tried to get on his feet, but he slipped and fell off his board. Another guy simply failed to catch the wave properly, and it passed underneath him, leaving him behind. But the other two surfers had caught the wave. They popped up into a crouch with their left feet in front and their right feet trailing. They crouched and extended their arms for balance, and then they *glided* along the face of the wave. They almost looked like they were flying. Sunlight reflected off their wet shoulders and the tops of their heads.

I looked at Ben and shook my head in disbelief. "Do you really know how to do that?"

He nodded. "When Ron Jon's opened up two years ago, Chuck and I bought boards from them. Then one of the owners gave us lessons, right here at the pier. Surfing's not something you pick up overnight. It takes a lot of practice, plus you have to learn how to read waves so you know which ones to paddle for."

"What's Ron Jon's?"

"A surf shop right down the street, very cool. We'll visit there if you'd like."

I nodded and we walked on, both of us with our hands in the hip pockets of our shorts. We passed beneath the pier, a wooden structure extending maybe a quarter-mile into the ocean, resting on substantial wooden pilings covered in barnacles. The sounds of waves breaking against the shore echoed off the pier's underside.

"When's the last time you surfed?" I asked Ben.

He cleared his throat while lowering his chin. "I haven't since Chuck died. I kind of lost interest—I'm not sure why—but I'll return to it, maybe over Thanksgiving weekend. It's time I got my board wet again."

I thought about Chuck's empty bedroom.

I told Ben, "It's got to be tough, adjusting to losing your brother like that."

Ben kept his gaze on the sand before him. "The past nine months have been pure hell. That's the only way I can describe it."

"I kind of expected Chuck's name to come up in conversation during dinner last night, but that didn't happen. Is it always like that?"

Ben nodded.

"How come?"

Ben looked at me and then returned his gaze to the sand. "My grandma on my mom's side has her birthday in July. We had her over for dinner and a cake. After she blew out the candles, my mom asked her what she wished for, and Grandma said, 'I wished that Chuck were still alive. I miss him.'"

Ben shook his head. "Right away, my mom broke down and started sobbing. Then *I* started crying, and then my dad and grandma fell apart too. It was an awful moment. After that, no one in my family mentions Chuck's name in conversation. It hurts too much."

While I pondered the scene Ben had just described, *my* eyes went foggy and I had to clear my throat before I could speak. "Does it bother you when I bring up Chuck's name? Should I not do that anymore?"

"No, it's okay, Johnny, but...don't do it around my parents, understand?"

RON JON'S SURF shop was a one-story cinder-block building with a red-and-white sign and a crushed-shell parking lot and a fifties station wagon with real wood siding perched on the roof. Inside, a shirtless guy with a suntan and blond hair sat behind a glass counter. He looked straight out of the movie *Endless Summer*. He raised a palm and went back to reading a surfing magazine.

The walls of the shop were lined with new and used surfboards standing on end with their noses pointing at the ceiling. Shelves held stacks of surfing baggies. The glass counter offered cakes of surfboard wax and cheap sunglasses. Ben approached a circular rack holding T-shirts on hangers, and I followed along. The shirts were adorned with surfing logos.

"Pick one out," Ben said, "and I'll buy it for you—a souvenir of your first visit here."

When I protested, Ben pointed a finger at my nose. "Don't argue with me."

I chose a brown T-shirt with a yellow Hang Ten logo on the chest. It was made of heavy cotton fabric that was soft to the touch. Already I knew that each time I wore the shirt I'd remember this weekend. I liked Brevard County; it had a different feel than the Gulf Coast, and the air seemed fresher.

We returned to Sarah's Stonecipher's convertible, and Ben drove us southward on the A-1-A Highway. He pointed to a freestanding cinder-block building with a plate-glass storefront and a huge sign that read "Stonecipher Groves."

"That's our retail outlet. It'll open December first and close at the end of April. The shop does big business during tourist season."

When I asked Ben where we were headed next, he said, "I'm taking us to Sebastian Inlet at the county's southern border. It's the best surfing spot in Florida—sometimes, the waves there get huge."

We passed by Patrick Air Force Base, and then through beach communities like Satellite Beach, Indialantic, and Melbourne Beach. Huge swaths of ocean-front property were undeveloped and covered by vegetation: runty live oaks, sabal palms, and sea grape trees.

When we reached Sebastian Inlet, we parked on the road shoulder and followed a foot path that wound through thick vegetation until we emerged at the shore, on the north side of the inlet. The inlet's banks were fortified by huge blocks of granite that formed two jetties extending maybe fifty or seventy-five yards from shore.

"The inlet is man-made, dug in the 1920s," Ben told me. "Those jetties keep the tides from eroding the banks."

Just to the left of the northern jetty, several surfers bobbed on their boards in the ocean, waiting for waves. Unlike the muddy sea water in Cocoa Beach, the water at the inlet was clear and aquamarine. The sand was rust-colored. A nice breeze ruffled my bangs while we watched a guy catch a wave that looked taller than him. He popped up onto his feet and turned his board into the face of the wave.

Ben put a hand on my shoulder, and when I looked at him, he grinned at me and winked. "Pretty cool, eh?"

SATURDAY NIGHT, WE had our meal in the dining room—me, Ben, Sarah, Will, and Will's mother, Abigail. An extra place setting appeared, but no one mentioned it. Dinner was fresh shrimp sautéed with onion, garlic, green pepper, and tomatoes, served over pasta, accompanied by a tossed salad and garlic bread. The meal was one of the best I'd ever eaten, and when I told Sarah that, she beamed.

"The shrimp came out of the Indian River this afternoon," she told me. "They're right off the docks."

Abigail Stonecipher was a slender, gray-haired woman. When Ben had introduced me to her, I shook her hand and her palm felt like she'd just dunked it in ice water. Over dinner, I kept catching her staring at me with narrowed eyes, and I sensed she didn't like me for some reason. Or maybe she didn't like anybody.

She lived in an old folks' home in Melbourne where she said, "The staff is full of thieves. Peoples' valuables disappear all the time, but management won't do anything about it." The food there "tastes like cardboard." The cleaning people are "hit and miss. My venetian blinds are covered in dust."

After dinner, Ben and I took another walk through the orange groves. The moon was a little bigger than the previous night's. Off in the distance, where the migrant barracks were located, a radio station played Motown music. Crickets sang and men's laughter echoed through the trees.

"I'm sorry about Grandma Stonecipher," Ben told me. "She's sour on life."

I'll say.

"Has she always been that way?" I asked.

"Ever since I can remember. And my grandfather—her husband—was the same. They never had much positive to say. Honestly, I don't know how my dad turned out as normal as he is."

"I barely know my moms' parents," I said. "They live in Pittsburgh and only visit Florida once every year or two, to get away from the cold. I met my dad's parents just once, but I was so young I can barely recall their faces."

We walked in silence for a bit, and then I asked Ben about the extra place setting at dinner.

Ben drew a breath, let it out. "It's for Chuck, of course. My mom can't accept the fact he's gone. I think she somehow believes he's going to walk through our front door, healthy and alive, and she wants to be ready when he does. She even changes the sheets on his bed once a week."

I made a face. "Was there a funeral?"

"A *huge* one at First Methodist. Over two hundred people attended. There were so many flowers that Chuck's coffin looked like a Mardi Gras float. But if a funeral is supposed to bring peace to the dead person's family, Chuck's service didn't work for ours. We're all still a wreck, just a goddamned mess."

The more Ben told me about his family's grief, the more I realized just how emotionally wounded they were. In a sense, they were only going through the motions of living, putting one foot in front of the other and doing their best to pretend that everything was just as it always was.

But of course, it wasn't.

Did people ever recover from a loss like the Stoneciphers had suffered?

Chapter Seven

I WAS HOME for the first time in almost three months, to celebrate Thanksgiving with my family, and everything looked different than it had before I'd left for Gainesville. My sister wore her hair a new way. Instead of teasing it into a dome and dousing it with hairspray, she parted it in the middle and let it stream to her shoulders. Mom had replaced our old living room sofa with a faux-leather love seat, and she'd even switched brands of toilet paper.

Without consulting me?

My bedroom had turned into a sort of storage closet. Cardboard boxes were stacked on the floor, and a pile of clothing destined for our church's thrift store lay on my bed.

When I protested, Mom said, "Put the clothes in the trunk of my car. You'll just have to maneuver past the boxes. Sorry, but I don't have any place else to put them."

I put my hands on my hips and hissed, "Am I just an afterthought now?"

She shrugged.

I had ridden down there that afternoon with a guy I met through a ride-share kiosk at the student union. He drank beer all the way from Gainesville to Pinellas Park, driving eighty miles per hour on I-75. He kept swerving between other vehicles like a madman and blaring his eight-track stereo system so loudly I couldn't even talk with him. I was pretty sure he played an album, *In the Court of the Crimson King,* four times during the drive, which gave me a raging headache. Already, I'd decided to take the Greyhound bus to Gainesville on Sunday.

But it was good to be back in St. Petersburg Beach. I loved the scent of the salt-laden air, the sound of waves slapping the shore, and the way breeze sang in the needles of an Australian pine outside my bedroom windows. I even liked the way tires hissed on asphalt when a car passed on Gulf Way.

This was home.

Over dinner, I told Mom and my sister about my visit to Brevard County with Ben. I talked about the citrus and cattle and the surfers, about my classes at the university and what it was like eating in a cafeteria seven days a week.

Later on, I phoned a few of my buddies from high school, and we made plans to gather at my home Friday night. My mom and sister were going to see a Barbra Streisand movie, so my friends and I would have the place to ourselves for a few hours.

I told each of them to bring beer.

THANKSGIVING DAY DAWNED sunny and a bit chilly. Mom had our furnace lit.

I know some families enjoyed their Thanksgiving meal at noon, but mine always dined around 6:00 p.m., one of our holiday traditions. By midmorning, my mom and sister banged pots and pans around in the kitchen, getting stuffing ready for the turkey so it could go in the oven. The scent of sautéing celery, garlic, and onions made my stomach growl.

Mom asked me to trim the hedges in front of our house and to dig up weeds growing in our sandy front yard, using a hoe. So, I put on some old work clothes and my work boots from the gas station and got to work. I used manual clippers to shape the hedges—it was easy work—and then I raked up the clippings and dropped them into a garbage can.

Hoeing weeds had always been a detestable activity to me. The weeds at our property were stubborn and numerous, and it took me over an hour to rid the yard of all of them. Then I raked the sand again so it looked neat. Mom, I knew, would be pleased when she saw the results of my labors.

After lunch, I took a walk on the beach. Few people were down there because of the cold. I walked northward, right along the water's edge. A breeze blew in my face and the grayish Gulf water churned. Waves crashed against the shore, making a roaring sound. The breeze fluttered my hair and blew my bangs into my eyes, and it occurred to me that I hadn't had a haircut since late August. Now my hair covered the tops of my ears, and when I wore a button-up shirt, my hair draped the back of the collar. I was surprised my mom hadn't told me I needed a trim, but since she hadn't I decided to let my hair keep on growing. A lot of guys at the university wore their hair longer, and I kind of liked the look.

Still, I'd ask Ben if he minded me wearing my hair long. I wanted him to be proud of my appearance, and if he wanted me to get it cut, I would.

I thought back to Tuesday night, when Ben and I had last shared sex. Our beds were pushed together and a towel draped Ben's desk lamp. The buttery light from the lamp reflected in Ben's emerald eyes while I worked my hips and our lungs pumped. Ben kept making little grunts each time I thrust inside him, and in the middle of it all, he told me something that sent a chill up my spine.

"We won't be able to do this the next four nights. How will I stand it?"

I didn't speak; I only nodded while I kept on thrusting.

Now, at the beach, I found myself yearning for Ben's touch. I wanted to feel his lips pressed to mine, to hear his voice and smell his damp oak leaves scent that always made my heart race when we were intimate.

God, how I missed Ben.

FRIDAY NIGHT MY friends and I gathered at my house, five of us, and we all drank beer from aluminum cans with pop-tops. We tossed the tabs into an ashtray that was getting close to full. These were guys I had been close to in high school. Back then we did everything together: went to the beach, bowled, attended our school's football and basketball games, all those sorts of activities.

One was Steve, the boy I'd told Ben about. I'd had a deep crush on Steve my senior year. Steve was a year younger than me, so he was a junior at the time. He often spent the night at my house on weekends—we shared my bed—and when we undressed in my bedroom, my mouth grew sticky when I looked at Steve in his briefs. I studied the curve of his ass and the bulge in the pouch of his briefs, and after lights out, I lay beside him and imagined exploring his private places.

At the time, I'd never had a sexual experience, so I wasn't quite sure what sort of acts two boys could perform in bed, but it didn't matter. Just thinking about touching Steve made me stiff between my legs.

And my feelings for Steve were not just about sex. From the beginning of our friendship, we'd developed a closeness I'd never had with someone outside of my immediate family. We met in Geometry class—Steve sat next to me—and though he was only a sophomore, he seemed far more mature than fifteen. He had a way of listening to whatever I had to say as though it were terribly important.

I could still remember the first time we did something together outside of school. I picked Steve up at his family's home in south St. Petersburg and drove him to my house in St. Petersburg Beach. It was a warm Saturday in mid-October, and after we changed into swim trunks we swam in the Gulf and took a long walk along the shore.

I talked about my family and my nonexistent father and how I'd grown up feeling somewhat inferior to other guys because I was the only one who didn't live with his dad.

Steve talked about how inadequate he'd felt as a boy, due to his short stature in grade school and junior high.

"They called me all the usual names: shrimp, half-pint, midget, you name it. And I couldn't play sports worth a damn, which only made things worse. In Little League, I struck out every time I went to the plate. I was always the last guy picked when we formed teams during PE at school. Then in ninth grade, I hit a growth spurt, shot up four inches. And I finally found a sport I could excel at—cross-country. It helped my self-confidence a lot."

I had never met someone so easy to talk with about personal matters, no matter how private or embarrassing. But I never discussed my sexual desire for boys with Steve. That, I felt pretty certain, would put distance between us or might even end our friendship altogether.

My senior year of high school, when I caught mononucleosis and missed six weeks of school, Steve brought my assignments to my house every weekday afternoon. Then he took my completed work to my teachers.

When Steve spent two weeks convalescing after hernia repair surgery, I came to see him at his home every day.

Weekdays, we did our homework together in his bedroom. Weekends, we'd play chess or gin rummy while jawing about kids at school or what we hoped to do with our futures.

Now, seated in my living room, I studied Steve when he wasn't looking in my direction. A couple of inches shorter than me, he had dark hair, aquamarine eyes, and eyelashes as long as a girl's. He was slender and narrow in the hips, with a dazzling smile and a silky voice I found enchanting. He wore blue jeans and a button-up, long-sleeved shirt with the tails untucked. When I looked at him, all those feelings I'd had for him my senior year came rushing back at me and my belly did a few flip-flops.

Steve, of course, was a high school senior now, but the other guys were attending community college, and as I heard them talk about their day-to-day lives, it seemed to me that not much had changed. They might as well have still been in high school. They lived with their parents and ate dinner with their families most every night. They pursued the same activities we always had last school year. That fall, they had even attended our high school's home football games.

I was glad to see them, of course, but I realized something as the evening wore on: I had grown in maturity since leaving for Gainesville in September. I was on my own up there; I could take care of myself. I was going to school with kids from all over the state, students who were smart and inquisitive. And then there was Ben and what he and I had together, something none of these four guys could possibly understand, and it occurred to me that I was a bit of an outsider in this group now, someone who had moved on in life. I wasn't treading water.

When the evening wound down and guys got up to leave, Steve remained in his chair. He looked at me and spoke in his syrupy voice. "It's late and I drank a lot of beer, so I probably shouldn't try driving home. Mind if I spend the night?"

Right away my pulse raced, and my voice sounded a bit funny when I answered, "It's fine."

Fifteen minutes later, we undressed in my bedroom with the door closed and locked. I had a queen-size bed with a nightstand and a table lamp next to it. Steve hung his shirt on a wall hook and did the same with his jeans. The bulge in the pouch of his briefs looked more prominent than it had the previous school year.

Steve continued to run cross-country at our high school, and his body was lean and defined. He lay down on the same side of the bed he'd always slept on when he spent the night with me. Then he wove his fingers behind his neck with his elbows jutting, showing his dark armpit hair.

"Tonight," he said, "you didn't mention whether you're dating anyone at school. Are you?"

The beers I'd consumed earlier gave me the courage I needed to be honest with Steve. After I finished undressing, I sat on my side of the bed.

Go on, tell him.

"I'm involved with someone. I'll tell you about it if you promise to keep things between you and me. I don't want the other guys to know."

Steve's gaze met mine. "I can keep a secret."

I told him about Ben, about our Cuba Libre Night, and all that had transpired between us since then. I explained how we slept together every night.

When I was done, Steve asked, "Are you in love with this guy?"

I licked my lips. "I think so."

Steve moved to a lotus position. He rested his forearms on his knees and looked at me. "When you were in high school, did you have sex with boys?"

I shook my head. "I was too scared someone might find out, and then the whole damned school would know. I couldn't take the chance."

"Did you ever think about...?"

"What?"

"Having sex with me?"

I lowered my gaze and worked my jaw from side to side. I should have known Steve would ask me that question once I told him I was gay. I returned my gaze to him and spoke in a voice that quivered.

"Please don't hate me for telling you this, but yeah I did. Last school year, all that time we spent together and the nights you spent with me in this room, I wanted to touch you so badly my stomach hurt. I know that may sound strange, but—"

"It's okay, Johnny."

Steve gazed into his lap for a moment before he looked at me again. "Would you like to touch me right now?"

What?

An explosion went off inside my head. *He's offering himself to you, idiot. Say something.*

I opened my mouth to speak, but nothing came out. I sat there gazing into Steve's aquamarine eyes while my chest rose and fell.

Steve switched off the lamp on the nightstand, so we dwelled in semidarkness. The glow from a nearby streetlight stole into the room, offering faint illumination. Steve lay back down. Again, he joined his fingers behind his neck and his elbows jutted. He crossed his legs at his ankles. His briefs were a swath of white, and even in the dim light, I saw he was stiff.

When I placed a hand on his thigh, his skin felt warm.

"You're okay with this?" I asked.

"Sure."

I slid my hand over to Steve's crotch. Using my index finger, I stroked his erection through the cotton. Then I tugged at the waistband of his briefs.

"Lift your hips for a second."

I peeled the briefs down his legs and over his feet, and now he was naked. His dark pubic bush contrasted with his fair skin. I seized his erection and took it into my mouth. My lips made smacking sounds while I bobbed my head.

Meanwhile, my thoughts churned. I didn't really know what to think about the situation. I'd never imagined Steve would let me do something like that, but it was happening— it was real—and I felt thrilled by the situation. Steve was such a beautiful guy, and we'd been close friends for about two years. Now we were even closer, but where would this lead to?

Steve ran his fingers through my hair. Then he whispered so softly I barely heard him over my sucking.

"Johnny, take your briefs off—let's do a sixty-nine."

Aye-yi-yi.

Moments later, we both slurped. Little pulses of electricity traveled up and down my spine as Steve worked me with his tongue and lips. He was good at male/male sex. Clearly he had done it before—but with whom?

He answered that question twenty minutes later when we lay together and our pulses slowed. His cheek rested on my sternum, and my nose was buried in his dark hair. The taste of his semen lingered in my mouth.

"Nash taught me a couple of years ago. We were tent camping and both of us were horny. It just kind of *happened.*"

Nash was Steve's brother, a year older than me, a real outdoorsman and hyper-masculine. He'd captained our high school's swim team his senior year, and all the girls were crazy about him.

"Are you gay? Is Nash?"

"Nash is definitely not—that was a one-time thing—but I guess I'm mostly gay. I like certain girls, but the right guy can satisfy me so much more."

Holy shit.

Beyond the windows, two cats made sounds like a pair of babies crying. A fight was brewing. Out on Gulf Way a bus roared by. The lightest of breezes entered through the window above us and cooled my brow.

"So you've done this with someone other than Nash?"

"Yeah, but if I say who it is, you can't let anyone else know."

"All right."

Steve drew a breath and let it out. He rearranged his legs on the mattress. "My cross-country coach, Pete Castleman, has done this with me ever since I turned eighteen. Certain nights, I visit him at his apartment after I study at the city library."

Castleman?

I had a recollection of the guy, a lean and handsome man who'd taught my driver's education class. I spent a good deal of time in a car with him and three other classmates, and never once suspected he might have an interest in boys. Now, in my bedroom, I tried to imagine Castleman and Steve having sex, but it was hard for me to conjure up the vision. Steve was an adult as far as age of consent went, so I guessed what they were doing wasn't illegal but it still seemed strange.

"Does Castleman fuck you?"

"In the ass?"

"Yeah."

"I wouldn't let him do that—I'm not a girl."

I twirled a lock of Steve's hair around my finger while I explained how I shared butt sex with Ben most every night and how amazing it felt.

"Ben's not girlish at all; he just likes it when I'm inside him."

Moments passed before Steve spoke again.

"I might be willing to give it a try before you go back to Gainesville. I mean, if you'd like that."

My heart skipped a beat when I thought about what Steve had just proposed. Things between us were happening so quickly I couldn't digest them all. An hour ago, I'd considered Steve a straight boy who'd never let me touch him. Now he was offering me the ultimate act of male submission.

My thoughts turned to Ben. What would he think if he saw me and Steve right then? Would he grow jealous and angry, or would he laugh and tell me it was about time I finally got inside Steve's pants?

Should I even tell Ben about this?

STEVE CAME OVER Saturday afternoon while my mom and sister Christmas shopped. We sat beside each other on the love seat, making small talk for five minutes or so. Then, after Steve put a hand on my knee, he looked into my eyes.

"How much time do we have?"

"At least an hour."

Steve left his hand on my knee. He lowered his chin and rubbed his lips together. Then his gaze met mine.

"When you have sex with Ben, do you guys kiss each other?"

"Always."

"Do you want to kiss me?"

I nodded and brought my hand to the back of Steve's neck. I pulled him to me and our mouths met. Our lips parted and our tongues rubbed. Right away, I got stiff. I put my hand between Steve's thighs and squeezed his boner while we slobbered. My heart pounded so hard my pulse echoed inside my head.

Minutes later, we lay naked in my bedroom. I'd placed a hand towel and a tube of K-Y Jelly on the nightstand. Afternoon sunlight passed between the slats on the room's venetian blinds, casting bars of light onto the walls. Seabirds cried at the shore, and the occasional car passed on Gulf Way.

We pleasured each other with our mouths, as before. This went on for ten minutes or so before Steve lifted his chin from my groin.

"Hey," he said.

"What?"

"Are you going to...?"

"Is it what you want?"

He nodded.

After I stacked two pillows at the head of the bed, I told Steve to lie on his back and hold his legs aloft by wrapping his arms around the backs of his knees. Then I used jelly to lube him up.

"You okay?" I asked while working my fingers in and out.

"Yeah, I'm fine."

I looked into Steve's eyes. "Are you ready?"

Steve moistened his lips. "Sure, go ahead."

I knelt before Steve, hoisted his legs, and adjusted them until the backs of his knees rested on my shoulders. Then I drove my hips forward.

He groaned when I entered him. The warmth of his gut felt amazing. Once I was all the way in, I squeezed jelly onto Steve's erection and spread it around. Sunlight coming into the room reflected in his rigid flesh.

I worked my hips and got a rhythm going. So did Steve. He pumped his fist. The bedsprings sighed and we both sweated. The jelly made smacking sounds. I ran my fingers through Steve's dark hair while our chests heaved, and it didn't take long before I felt a tingling between my legs. Then a shiver ran through my body as I unloaded.

When Steve came, he groaned so loudly I had to place my hand over his mouth to silence him because the next-door neighbors had their windows open. The two of us stayed put like that—me inside Steve and rigid and Steve's knees resting on my shoulders. My forehead was pressed to his shoulder.

After a few minutes passed, Steve said, "Hey."

I turned my head and gazed into his eyes. "What?"

His lips parted into a smile. "That was pretty damned amazing."

It sure was, I thought, *but where will things go from here?*

Chapter Eight

WE WERE BACK in Gainesville, me and Ben. The second week of December arrived, and certain trees on campus had lost their leaves. My breath steamed in the chilly air when I walked to my earliest class. My cheeks stung when the wind blew out of the north, and many mornings the sky was overcast.

On a Wednesday evening, Ben and I studied for final exams in our dorm room. The day before, I had received a tin of Christmas cookies from my mom, and I munched on an oatmeal raisin item that was *real* tasty. Ben also nibbled on a cookie—his, a chocolate chip.

Crunching sounds filled the room.

The time was around six thirty. Darkness had fallen and our desk lamps were lit. Ben and I had eaten dinner in the cafeteria a little while before—beef stew, green beans, and fresh-baked rolls, a pretty good meal. I didn't know if it was due to the food the cafeteria served, but I had put on ten pounds since starting school in September. The muscles in my arms, chest, and shoulders had grown and become more defined.

Ben pushed back from his desk and his chair legs scraped the linoleum floor. He snatched another cookie—this one a Russian tea cake—before kissing my cheek.

"Your mom's quite the baker. We should send her a thank-you note."

I smiled and bobbed my chin.

"Or maybe I can thank her in person," Ben said. "I was thinking I could pay you a visit in St. Petersburg Beach during Christmas break. I can borrow one of my folks' cars and drive over, maybe spend a few days. What do you think?"

I lowered my gaze while my thoughts swirled. I thought about the opulence of the Stoneciphers' home and the vastness of their property and then about my little beach house. What would Ben think if he saw my family's modest circumstances?

"Is something wrong?" Ben asked.

I looked up at him and blinked, not really knowing what to say.

"What is it, Johnny?"

I shrugged while holding his gaze. "My family doesn't have the kind of money yours does. You'd probably feel sorry for us if you saw how we live."

A vertical crease appeared between Ben's eyebrows while he kept his gaze fixed on mine.

"That's silly. I don't care how big your house is or how much money your mom makes at her job. You've met my family, and now I want to meet yours. We're boyfriends, and I think it's important, don't you?"

Ben's remarks evoked a warm feeling inside me. He wasn't just trying to be nice; he'd really meant what he said. The disparity between his family's wealth and my family's lack of it didn't matter.

"All right then," I told him. "You can come over whenever you want to, and you can stay as long as you like. It'll be nice having you there."

Ben kissed me again, this time on my lips that were dusted with cookie crumbs.

"Perfect," he said, gazing into my eyes.

Then he kissed me again, only this time he pried my lips apart and rubbed his tongue against mine.

My heart thumped like a pile driver.

Chapter Nine

I WAS BACK in St. Petersburg Beach after a brutal week of final exams in Gainesville. The previous day, when my mom had picked me up at my dormitory, I tossed my dirty laundry into the passenger seat, then climbed into the back seat and immediately fell asleep. I didn't wake up until we got to our house and she roused me. But I thought I'd done well on my exams, and now it was time to relax and enjoy our island home.

My mom and sister had decorated a live Christmas tree, a blue spruce, and the tree's fragrance filled the house. Gifts lay under the tree, wrapped in shiny paper and ribbons.

On Sunday morning, I had just risen from bed. I wore a flannel robe and was barefooted as I strolled into the kitchen and poured myself a mug of coffee from our electric percolator. Outside, the sun shone and the air was cool. All the windows in the house were open, and traffic buzzed past on Gulf Way. My mom and sister were at church, so I had the place to myself. I sat in the living room's easy chair and studied headlines in the *St. Petersburg Times* while waiting for my coffee to cool.

The Vietnam War raged on. What had ever happened to Nixon's "secret plan" to end the war, the one he claimed to have up his sleeve when he campaigned? If anything, the war seemed to be expanding.

Our desk phone rang, and my knees crackled when I rose to answer the call. After lifting the receiver and saying hello, a familiar voice made my stomach flip-flop.

"Johnny?"

"Hi, Ben, what's up?"

"Nothing really. I just wanted to talk with you 'cause right now I'm missing you like all hell."

I thought back to Friday, to the hour just before Ben's parents picked him up in Gainesville. We had lain on Ben's bed, holding each other after a sweet round of sex. My head rested on Ben's chest, and I listened to his heart beat and wondered just how hard it was going to be spending two weeks apart from him.

Now, standing in my living room, I told Ben, "I dreamed about you last night."

"Was it a good dream?"

"Of course. We were walking in the groves on Merritt Island. It was nighttime and we held hands, and I don't remember what we were talking about but we were both laughing. Then, when I woke up this morning, I thought I was still in our dorm room. I turned to reach for you, but then I realized you weren't there and I felt kind of...*empty* inside."

"I know what you mean. I'd drive over there today if I could, but my dad needs help with the cattle right now. I'll be on horseback all day."

I ran my fingers through my hair. "When *can* you come over?"

"The day after Christmas. I'll stay three days, if that's okay."

"Of course it is. Or stay longer if you want to."

"We'll see," Ben said.

SUNDAY AFTERNOON'S WEATHER was cool and sunny. I washed my mom's car in our driveway when a Volkswagen engine muttered as it drew near. I looked up from my work just as Steve pulled to the curb in front of my house.

I walked to his car and poked my head through the passenger door window. "What's up?" I asked.

Steve looked great. He wore a crew-neck sweater and blue jeans, and when he smiled at me, his teeth glistened.

"I came to see if you'd like to go for a drive," he said.

Twenty minutes later, we cruised northward on Gulf Boulevard. Traffic was light. I was dressed similar to Steve, only I wore my UF sweatshirt. On the radio, Peter, Paul & Mary sang "Leaving on a Jet Plane," a song that usually made me sad when I heard it but not that day because I was with Steve and I knew what he wanted from me.

"My aunt Ruth lives in Redington Beach," he said while we idled at a stoplight. "Last week, she flew up to Richmond for the holidays, and she asked me to water her houseplants a few times while she's gone."

After reaching under his driver's seat, Steve produced a tube of jelly. He dropped it into my lap, looked at me, and winked.

"We'll have her place to ourselves."

His remark made a shiver run through me as I turned my gaze back to the windshield.

Steve's aunt's house was single story, stucco over cinder block with a cement tile roof. The lawn was emerald and healthy hibiscus shrubs hugged the walls. The blooms on the shrubs were the color of apricot flesh. Shiny fronds on a swayback coconut palm reflected sunlight. Steve found a house key under a flower pot, and we entered. Inside, things were as quiet as a tomb. Our sneakers squeaked on the polished oak floor. Plants were everywhere: philodendrons and coleuses perched on windowsills. Corn plants and rubber plants grew in large pots that sat on the floor. The living room's eastern windows overlooked the Intracoastal Waterway and a dock with davits.

While Steve filled a plastic pitcher with water from the kitchen tap, he told me about his aunt. "She was married to an airline executive in Richmond for twenty years or so. This was their vacation home. When they divorced, Aunt Ruth got it in the settlement, and now she lives here full-time."

"It's nice," I said. "Waterfront living has to be the best."

After Steve finished his watering, he strolled to the front door to engage the lock and deadbolt. Then he pointed to a hallway.

"The master bedroom's over there. Want to have some fun?"

I nodded while my pulse accelerated.

Steve led the way, carrying the jelly tube. His butt moved in the seat of his jeans, and I licked my lips in anticipation of what was to come.

The bedroom windows had venetian blinds that were partially closed, so the light in the room was diffused. The king-size bed had a down comforter and two stacks of pillows. After Steve placed the jelly on the nightstand, he wrapped his arms around my waist, and I did the same to him. Our mouths met and our lips parted and Steve's tongue rubbed against mine. I sifted my fingers through the hair on the back of Steve's neck—it was as soft as corn silk—and Steve's erection pressed against my thigh.

He insisted on removing my clothing himself. Then I returned the favor. After he lowered the comforter and top sheet, we fell to the mattress. Moments later, we pawed at each other like the two horny boys we were. We used our mouths and fingers to caress tender flesh.

Steve lifted his head from between my legs, and when I looked at him, he gripped my erection and rocked it from side to side.

"You know what I want, right?"

There was no way I'd refuse an invitation like that, and moments later, Steve was on his back with his legs slung over my shoulders. He clenched his teeth when I entered him but handled my penetration like a champ. I commenced thrusting my hips, and a strong scent of sex filled the room. The bedsprings twanged and the headboard drummed the wall.

Even in the cool December air, we sweated.

When I reached orgasm, I looked into Steve's pretty eyes. My body jerked three or four times when I unloaded.

Steve scattered sticky pearls across his chest while his lungs heaved and he groaned.

After our pulses slowed and I withdrew from Steve, we cleaned ourselves at a bathroom sink. Then, back in the bedroom, we lay side by side on the sheet, staring at the plaster ceiling. We listened to the clockwork of our bodies tick.

"I can't believe how much I enjoy doing this with you," Steve said while his chest rose and fell. "It seems so... natural, doesn't it?"

And it did, but there was a problem, a big one.

The problem was Ben.

I belonged to him and he belonged to me. We had shared our deepest secrets. Ben counted on me for emotional support that he needed to fight his depression. And his companionship at school was the bedrock of my life up there.

And then there was my physical relationship with Ben. My tongue had traveled over every inch of his body. For the past two months, I had fallen asleep in his arms most every night. I loved Ben like I've never loved anyone before, and I suspected he would be deeply hurt if he knew what I was up to at that very moment.

Steve, of course, had been my closest friend in Pinellas County ever since I'd met him. Now we were even closer, and in a major way. So what did Steve expect from me in the days and weeks ahead? And where did I want things to go between me and him?

ON DECEMBER TWENTY-THIRD, I Christmas-shopped at the Sears & Roebuck store in west St. Petersburg, amid throngs of holiday shoppers. Over the store's PA system, an orchestra played a jazzy version of "Santa Claus is Coming to Town." I'd already bought gifts for my family: a nice blouse for my mom and a Beatles album titled *Abbey Road* that I knew my sister would like.

In the men's clothing department, I shopped for Ben's gift. He already had so many material things. What could I buy him? I settled on a Fred Perry pique polo shirt, a dark-blue one with white stripes on the banded sleeves. With his fair skin and dark hair, Ben would look good in the shirt. A grin crossed my face when I decided that at school I would insist he wear it once a week.

And the thought I would see Ben three days from now got my heart racing every time I thought about it.

When I'd asked Mom if it would be okay for Ben to visit for a few days, she said, "Of course, but I guess he'll have to sleep on the living room love seat and that won't be too comfortable."

I tried to keep my voice steady when I responded to her remark.

"Mom, at school, Ben and I share a small dorm room—we're used to tight quarters. He can sleep in my room, and we'll share my bed like Steve and I used to. It's no big deal."

Mom shrugged and said, "That's fine with me if it's okay with you and Ben."

And I thought, *oh, y-e-a-h...*

HOURS AFTER MY shopping excursion and just after my sister and I had finished the dinner dishes, Steve called.

"What are you doing tonight?" he asked.

"Not much. I have three gifts to wrap. Then I guess I'll watch the *Andy Williams Christmas Special* on TV. Exciting stuff, eh?"

"Why don't I come out to the beach around eight?" Steve asked. "We could pay another visit to my aunt's place."

I felt a stirring in my briefs while I flexed my fingers against the phone receiver. Would I be disloyal to Ben if I said yes? Were things with Steve going too far too fast?

"Johnny?"

"H-m-m-m?"

"Should I come out there or not?"

Go on, idiot.

"Sure," I said. "Let's do it."

CHRISTMAS EVE MORNING, I woke to the sound of thunder. Rain clattered in puddles outside my bedroom windows. I lifted a venetian blind slat and studied the murky sky. There wouldn't be much I could do that day, not with the lousy weather. I couldn't walk on the beach or play tennis or basketball with my buddies in town.

What about a movie?

I slipped into blue jeans and a T-shirt, combed my unruly hair that grew to my shoulders, and headed for the bathroom. Ten minutes later, I sat at our dining table, munching on corn flakes and studying movie listings in the newspaper. A film called *Easy Rider*, which had come out last summer, was showing at a cheesy local theater that only screened second-run films.

Most every guy my age had seen *Easy Rider*, but not me, probably because I was working full-time at the gas station last summer and wasn't available when my friends all saw the movie. I knew this much about *Easy Rider*—it starred Peter Fonda, Dennis Hopper, and another actor named Jack Nicholson who I'd never heard of until the film was released. Nicholson had received an Oscar nomination for his role as an alcoholic ACLU lawyer who Fonda and Hopper meet in a jail cell.

I thought about calling Steve to see if he wanted to see the movie a second time, but then I hesitated.

The previous night, at Steve's aunt's house, Steve and I had showered together in the master bath, right after sex. I tongue-kissed Steve while warm water pounded my upper back, and it felt so good that I tore my mouth from his. I shouted something crazy and nonsensical, just to hear my voice echo off the tiles.

Our sex had been amazing. Steve had an eager mouth during foreplay and was verbal during intercourse. He didn't hesitate to use bad language while I thrust inside him, and I adored the nasty words he employed. They got me all excited.

But now I wasn't sure I should phone Steve about the movie. The more I saw of him during Christmas break, the stronger my desire for him became. And I knew the feeling was mutual because while driving me home the previous night, Steve had spoken of our future together while he held my hand in his. He said if he attended UF the next year, we should share a dorm room.

I didn't say anything in response to his suggestion, but I *probably* should have said something like: "You don't understand, Ben and I are boyfriends—we have a commitment to each other—and I'll most certainly live with him next year."

But I didn't want to spoil the moment, not after what Steve and I had just shared, so I kept my mouth shut and savored the feel of Steve's warm palm pressed to mine.

Now, as rain continued to fall at my house, I studied the *Easy Rider* ad again.

Should I go with Steve or without him?

Things were getting so...complicated.

Chapter Ten

CHRISTMAS MORNING, NOT long after my family opened our presents, my sister and I cleaned up after breakfast in the kitchen. In the living room, a blaze in the fireplace crackled, and the pleasant scent of burning pine wafted through our home.

I wore sweatpants, a T-shirt, and house slippers. My sister was still in her PJs and robe. She played *Abbey Road* on the stereo for the third time that morning, and right then "Here Comes the Sun" was on, one of my favorites on the album. But in truth, I liked every song, even Ringo's silly "Octopus's Garden."

When the phone rang in the living room, my mom answered before calling to me.

"Johnny, it's your friend Ben."

I took the call in Mom's bedroom, on the extension line with the door closed. I sat on the bed while I lifted the receiver and waited for my mom to hang up.

"Hey," I said, "Merry Christmas."

"Merry Christmas, Johnny."

Just hearing Ben's voice made my toes flex and my knees wag.

"Did you get any cool gifts?" Ben asked.

"Some nice clothes, stuff for cold weather that I'll need this winter. How about you?"

"Clothes mostly, but something else—something much better."

"What?"

"A Pontiac GTO, a '67. Can you believe it?"

I twisted the spirally receiver cord around my finger while trying to fathom what it might feel like to be eighteen years old and own the kind of car most guys my age would kill for. At my high school, during my senior year, only one kid—he was a surgeon's son—had driven a GTO.

"What color?" I asked.

"Metallic midnight blue—it's just beautiful. I'll drive it over to your place tomorrow, and I should get there around noon, if that's okay."

"That's great," I said. "I have yard work I'll take care of in the morning. Then I'm free to do whatever."

When I asked Ben how his folks were doing, a few seconds passed before he answered.

"I think they're a little sad right now. This is our first Christmas without Chuck and..."

"What?"

Ben's voice shook. "It's hard—very tough on all three of us. Chuck was always the family Christmas nut, singing carols in the shower and wearing a Santa cap around the house. It's not the same without him."

"I'm sorry," I said.

Ben whimpered for a few seconds and sniffled a time or two. "Shit. I didn't think it would be this difficult. Honestly, I can't wait for this day to end so we can put goddamned Christmas behind us. I know that sounds terrible, but it's how I feel."

"I don't blame you. Don't get all guilty about it."

We talked a few more minutes before Ben said he had to go.

"I can't wait to see you," he said.

After my sister and I finished the dishes, I asked her to join me and Mom in the living room so we could talk about Ben. I sat in our easy chair. My mom and Tricia took the love seat. I rested my forearms on my knees while I told them about Ben's brother, Chuck, and how Ben and his parents were going through a terrible time. I told them about Ben's problems with depression and the medication he took for it.

"How awful," Mom said. "No family deserves tragedy like that."

I pursed my lips and nodded. "Please keep what I've told you to yourselves. I'm sure it's embarrassing for Ben, what he's going through, so be extra nice to him. I want him to enjoy his visit here."

Mom and Tricia nodded.

ON OUR PACKED-SHELL driveway, the GTO's engine ticked as it cooled from the three-hour drive Ben had just completed. I walked around the car in circles, admiring its gleaming flanks and stacked headlights. The air scoop on the hood made the car look as though it breathed like a living creature. A tachometer rose from the hood as well, facing the windshield and very cool. Sunlight reflected off the GTO's hefty chrome bumpers.

"My dad bought it off a guy in Daytona Beach, a retired GM executive who didn't drive it all that much. The odometer only has 12,000 miles on it."

The day was sunny and cool, and Ben looked princely in a sweater, a pair of corduroy jeans, and penny loafers. If I could have, I would've wrapped him in a bear hug when he'd arrived, just minutes before, but a hug would have to wait for a more private setting.

We shook hands instead.

After Ben grabbed his suitcase from the GTO's back seat, we went inside the house, and I introduced Ben to my sister, who looked at him like he was a movie star. My mom was at work, so Ben would have to wait until that evening to meet her.

In my bedroom, Ben stowed his suitcase in a corner. He glanced here and there before his gaze met mine.

"Where will I sleep?"

I pointed to my bed. "Right there with me."

When he raised his eyebrows, I shrugged in response. "I ran it past Mom and she didn't bat an eye."

Ben pointed at the door. "Does it lock?"

"Sure does."

Ben's gaze drilled into mine. "Perfect."

WE CRUISED IN the GTO, heading northward on Gulf Boulevard, and I was reminded of the drives I'd taken with Steve to Redington Beach. Only somehow this felt different, and I thought I knew why. Although Steve was a close friend, he was still only that—a friend. Ben, on the other hand, was my *boy*friend, and it felt so right to hold his hand. Wind rushed through the car. The GTO's engine rumbled as we passed motels, restaurants, and strip centers. Here and there, when we passed gaps between the buildings to our left, the Gulf of Mexico glittered.

The GTO's interior was amazing. The dashboard before the driver's seat, the part where the dials were, and the center console, where the shift knob was located, were faux wood. The front seats were vinyl buckets.

When we stopped at a traffic light, a carload of high school girls pulled alongside us in the outside lane. One girl, a babe with blonde hair growing past her shoulders, poked her head out a window.

She looked at me and shouted, "Nice car."

I gave her a smile and a wave.

"We're going to the A&W drive-in on Treasure Island," she hollered. "Why don't you guys join us?"

When I glanced at Ben, he rolled his eyes.

"Sorry," I told the girl while I squeezed Ben's hand. "We already have plans."

The light changed and Ben accelerated, pulling away from the girls.

I snickered and shook my head. "Now that you own this car, you'd better get used to that sort of thing."

Ben shrugged. "I'm an expert at shaking off girls. I don't want to sound conceited, but they were always after me in high school, not because of my looks but because my family has money."

Go on, ask.

"Speaking of money…"

"What?"

"Now that you've seen my house, what do you think? Are you surprised by how small it is?"

Ben kept his gaze fixed on the windshield. "It's just a house, Johnny. It's not you, and it's *you* I care about. And aren't you the lucky bastard, living steps from the beach. I can't imagine."

Ben's response to my question sounded genuine, and I felt relieved by what he'd just said. Back in high school, I'd known kids from rich families, like the guy who drove the GTO. Mostly they hung out with one another and ignored the middle and working-class kids, like we were sub-humans. But Ben wasn't like that at all, it seemed, and now I felt a little guilty for assuming he'd be shallow enough to think less of me because of my modest home.

I flicked on the radio, an AM/FM model with stereo speakers in both the GTO's doors. I tuned it to our local FM rock station. Right after a commercial for a Tampa amusement park concluded, the DJ cued up "Whole Lotta Love" by Led Zeppelin, a song that was simply a musical description of male/female screwing and orgasm. There was nothing subtle about it.

I found myself wondering if orgasms straight guys had with their girlfriends were as enjoyable as those Ben and I experienced. Whenever I thrust inside Ben, I'd feel that familiar tingle in my groin. My body would jerk, I'd call out Ben's name, and then I'd feel like I had entered a magical land where only Ben and I dwelled.

It was all so nice.

When we reached Sand Key, just south of Clearwater Beach, I directed Ben to a parking area with a view of Clearwater Pass. Sand Key was a privately-owned, undeveloped island with thick stands of Australian pines. At night, it was a popular place for high school kids to drink beer and suck face in the back seats of cars. But right then, only a few vehicles stood in the parking area.

After Ben switched off the GTO's engine, we sat in our bucket seats, still holding hands and watching sunlight reflect off waves in the pass.

"So," I said, looking at Ben, "it sounds like the past few days have been pretty rough for you and your parents."

He nodded. "I never thought I'd learn to hate Christmas, but now I do. I'm so glad it's over. And it sure feels good being here with you. When I woke up this morning, I wanted to hold you, but you weren't there and that wasn't pleasant. I want us to always be together."

Ben's words made my heart sing and my pulse race. How I wished I could take him in my arms—right there on

Sand Key—and give him a sloppy tongue kiss. But holding hands would have to do.

"Have you ever been in love?" Ben said.

"I think I am right now."

Ben looked at me and smiled. Then he shifted his weight in his car seat.

"Back in high school, I thought I was in love with Andy. Now I don't think so. It was more about sex than anything. But what's happening between you and me is different—I can't get you out of my mind."

I glanced here and there. No one was around, so I planted a kiss on Ben's cheek, which caused him to grin again while color bloomed on his cheeks. Then he looked at me and uttered the words no one had ever said to me before.

"I love you, Johnny Darling."

FRIDAY NIGHT, MY mom served leftovers from Christmas dinner: turkey and stuffing, gravy, sweet peas, and mashed potatoes. The food tasted even better than it had on Christmas Day. Ben and I piled our plates high. We ate like two guys who hadn't had a meal in a week.

Ben, of course, was a deft conversationalist. At the table, he got my mom talking about her job and my sister describing her extracurricular activities: dance, thespian society, mixed chorus. He also talked about his home, the groves, and the cattle ranch. And he told Mom and Tricia how well I'd done at horseback riding on Merritt Island.

"I think I can make a cowboy out of Johnny if he'll give me the chance," he said while winking at me.

My mom was careful not to ask many questions about Ben's family life, which I felt grateful for. Instead, she steered the conversation to the university and how Ben liked it up there.

"Having Johnny as my roommate has made a huge difference. He's my best friend—we do everything together—and we never quarrel. Honestly, I don't know what I'd do without him."

Mom's gaze flicked between mine and Ben's, and I wondered whether she sensed that Ben and I were not just pals, that there was more going on between us than met the eye.

Ben and I volunteered to clean up after dinner. I washed dishes, pots, and pans at the sink, while Ben dried and put things away, and as we worked, we talked about how we'd spend the rest of the evening. We decided to see a movie, *Butch Cassidy and the Sundance Kid*, starring Paul Newman and Robert Redford and showing at a drive-in theater in northwest St. Petersburg.

The evening was cool, and we bundled up in sweaters, jackets, and blue jeans. On the way to the theater, we visited a liquor store parking lot where drunks often hung out under an oak tree with spreading limbs. That night, two drunks sat on wooden crates; they passed a bottle in a paper sack back and forth, taking swigs. Their breath steamed in the chilly air, and both had their jacket collars turned up.

When I approached them, one looked up and said, "Evening, junior. Something we can do for you?"

I plucked three dollars out of my wallet. Then I pointed to the store's front door. "I need a six-pack of beer—Pabst Blue Ribbon. I'll pay you two bucks if you'll go in there and buy it for me."

"No problem," the drunk said. He seemed a little unsteady on his feet when he rose, but then he righted himself and ambled toward the store with my money in his hand.

The other drunk spit on the ground. "I'd have done that for *one* buck if you'd asked me instead of Smitty. Next time, don't offer two for starters. You'll save yourself money that way."

Three minutes later, I was back in the GTO with the six-pack.

"Have you done that before?" Ben asked.

"Several times in my high school days. It's easier than asking someone's older brother to buy it, plus the drunks can use the money."

At the drive-in, Ben parked the GTO away from the main cluster of vehicles so we'd have a little privacy. Before the movie started, we bought a large cup of buttered popcorn to share and then climbed into the GTO's back seat with our beer and snack. We watched previews with our knees, hips, and shoulders touching, and it felt so cool doing this with Ben, just like my straight friends often did with girls they dated.

The movie was pretty good, with lots of humor and gunplay. Newman and Redford were convincing in their roles and likeable. Ben and I laughed a lot. Halfway through the movie, the beer and popcorn were gone and I felt bold. I looked around to be sure no one was watching us, especially not the off-duty cop we'd seen in the concession stand earlier.

I grabbed the back of Ben's neck, pulled his mouth to mine, and we kissed, a long and slurpy interaction that made me stiff as a peg. When we separated, we looked at each other for a long moment.

A grin crept onto Ben's face while he waggled his eyebrows. "That was nice, bubba, but we'd better be careful—people here can see."

"I know," I said. "I just couldn't resist."

"I'm glad you didn't," he said before pointing his chin at the windshield. "Let's watch the movie. We'll have time for that sort of thing later tonight, right?"

"You bet we will," I replied.

Chapter Eleven

SATURDAY MORNING, I woke to find Ben's cheek resting against my shoulder. His arm draped my belly and one of his legs crossed my shins as he snored softly. I buried my nose in his fragrant hair and kissed the crown of his head.

Beyond the windows, the sun shone and a mockingbird perched on the limb of an Australian pine, tootling away. I thought about the previous night, when we'd returned home from the movie. My mom and sister were already in bed. After we used the bathroom and turned off the household lights, we went to my room and locked the door. We both undressed before climbing into bed. Then I switched off my nightstand lamp, and we enjoyed sex for almost an hour.

It felt wonderful making love with Ben in my boyhood bedroom. How many nights had I lain there in darkness, imagining how it would feel to hold another guy in my arms? I realized now that in high school, despite my wonderful group of friends, I had been a lonely guy who desperately wanted another boy's touch but didn't know how to make it happen.

Now that was all history, a part of my distant past. I had Ben—he was there and real—and right then, I could touch him whenever and however I wanted to.

Amazing.

RIGHT AFTER LUNCH on Saturday, Ben and I dressed in blue jeans, sweatshirts, and sneakers. Then we took a long walk along the shore. The sky was cloudless, the air cool. A steady breeze had the Gulf churning and sea oats in the dunes swaying. Few people appeared at the beach. We walked side by side with our hands in the front pockets of our jeans, while the breeze tossed Ben's dark bangs about.

"I can see why you like it here," Ben said. "It looks like something in a post card."

"I love this beach," I replied. "Whenever I'm upset or troubled, I come down here and it soothes me like nothing else can."

"What sort of things upset you?"

"In junior high and early high school, I got picked on a lot, mainly because of my last name, but also because I was skinny and terrible at sports. I grew up in a household with two women and no father, so I never learned how to fight back if some guy bullied me. "The crap finally stopped when I became part of a circle of friends, guys who wouldn't allow anyone to give me shit. I can't tell you how good that felt."

Ben nodded. "When Chuck and I were eleven—it was the summer after sixth grade—my dad paid a guy to give us boxing lessons twice a week. The instructor was a Latin guy named Tito Alvarez who used to box down in Miami, and I guess he was pretty good in his day. Tito taught me and Chuck how to throw punches and how to avoid them. We'd practice with Tito out in the barn."

I picked up a piece of driftwood, a limb bleached by saltwater and sun. Then I tossed it like a boomerang into the air. "Were you ever in a fight?"

"In seventh grade, yeah. An older boy picked on me at the bus stop one morning. I punched him in the face, gave him a bloody nose. After that, word got out at school that I knew how to fight. No one bothered me after that."

I found it was hard to envision Ben in a brawl, but I liked the fact he had boxing skills. They might come in handy sometime.

Ben changed the subject. "Your mom and sister are nice. Do you think they like me?"

When I chuckled, Ben looked at me and crinkled his forehead. "What?"

"Of *course* they like you. Why wouldn't they?"

Ben shrugged. "I feel like I'm intruding on your family's holidays."

"You're not. We're all glad you're here, plus I think Tricia already has a crush on you. I catch her staring at you all the time."

Ben chuckled and shook his head.

"You'd better tell her I'm already taken."

WHEN WE RETURN to the house, Mom told me, "Steve called while you were gone. He wants you to phone him back."

I used the desk phone in the living room, and after I exchanged greetings with Steve's dad—a very nice man, by the way—Steve came on the line. Right away, he asked what I was doing.

After I explained how Ben was staying with me a few days, Steve snickered. "I'll bet you guys are having fun."

I swung my gaze to Ben, who sat on the easy chair and perused a magazine.

"We are, actually."

"Look," Steve said, "Kenny's folks left town this morning. They won't be back till Monday. We're putting together a party tonight—Stewart, James, Beau, and maybe one or two others. Why don't you guys join us?"

I fingered the receiver's cord. The party sounded like fun, but did I really want to squander an entire evening on guy talk and beer drinking when I could spend it alone with Ben?

"We'll see," I told Steve.

SATURDAY NIGHT WAS another chilly one, so Ben and I wore sweaters, blue jeans, and jackets to the party at Kenny's house.

When I'd told Ben about the gathering, he seemed okay with it. "You've talked so much about your friends. I'd like to meet them."

"You're sure it's not putting too much pressure on you? If it is, we can do something else."

"I'll be fine."

On the way to the party, we stopped by the liquor store. Three drunks sat beneath the oak tree, drinking beer from cans shrouded in paper sacks. One was the guy who said he'd only charge me a dollar to buy beer, and when I reminded him of that conversation, he didn't protest. He snatched my money and took care of business.

Minutes later, we cruised Central Avenue in the GTO with the stereo blaring "White Rabbit" by the Jefferson Airplane. I loved Grace Slick's powerful vocals in that and other songs on *Surrealistic Pillow*. When we halted at a stoplight, glow from nearby streetlamps reflected off the GTO's hood and air scoop.

I gave Ben the skinny on the guys at the party. "Kenny co-captained our high school's tennis team last school year. His dad owns an insurance agency and a fancy sailing yacht he races in competitions around the Gulf Coast. You'll see it at their house.

"Beau's a big, good-looking guy. Not the best student, but a great athlete. He was second-string quarterback our junior and senior years and he's a nice guy, you'll like him.

"James is super-smart; he served in student government, made National Honor Society, sang in the choir. Like me, he's no jock but has a great sense of humor. He could do stand-up comedy if he chose to.

"Stewart's the quiet type, never says much, but when he does, you can tell he's thought a good deal about what he says. He's a working-class kid like me, a Catholic with several siblings. His dad's an electrician."

Ben nodded. "And Steve?"

I felt a prickle in my scalp. I still didn't know whether or not I should tell Ben about what had gone on between me and Steve lately. Visions of me and Steve swapping fluids in his aunt's bedroom crowded my brain and I tried to shake them off but couldn't.

"I've already told you about him. He's probably my best friend in the group you're going to meet. He's super good-looking, runs cross-country, and takes calculus. He's a good listener too. I can always tell my troubles to him."

The light changed and Ben accelerated. "I never had a friend like that in high school. Guys never talked about their feelings or troubles. Everyone tried to act tough. Fortunately, I had Chuck to talk to whenever I felt the need, and that's what I miss the most—how I could tell him anything and he'd listen."

Kenny lived in a swanky waterfront subdivision. All the homes were decorated with strands of Christmas lights, illuminated Santas, and candy canes. Christmas trees glittered behind plate-glass windows. Yards were well tended and coconut palms abounded.

At Kenny's house a half-dozen cars sat in the driveway or nudged the curb. I recognized all of them, of course. We curb-parked the GTO behind Steve's VW. Then, as we approached Kenny's front door, I heard the Beach Boys' song "Merry Christmas, Baby" playing on the stereo inside.

Kenny answered the door right after I rang the bell, looking just like the country clubber he was: good haircut, oxford cloth button-down shirt, dress slacks, and shiny penny loafers. But he was a good guy, not the least stuck up. Behind him, a crush of conversation competed with the music. I introduced Ben to Kenny, and they shook hands. In the kitchen, after I peeled two beers off our six-pack, I gave one to Ben and kept the other for myself. Then I stowed the other four cans in the fridge.

Ben and I tossed our jackets onto the bed in Kenny's bedroom. We joined the other guys in the living room, and right away, Beau approached; he grabbed me in a bear hug and lifted me off the carpet.

"Merry Christmas, Darling," Beau cried. "How's UF treating you?"

After he set me back on my feet, I introduced Beau to Ben and the two shook hands. Beau was half a head taller than Ben and me. Beau's shoulder and arm muscles bulged beneath his sweater.

When I explained how Ben came from Merritt Island, Beau told Ben, "My dad was stationed at Patrick Air Force Base for two years when I attended junior high. I know Brevard County pretty well."

I told Beau about my visit to the east coast and how Ben and I had passed by the air base on our drive down to Sebastian Inlet.

"I loved Brevard County," Beau said. "I walked the beach most every day."

Ben and I circulated through the room while I made introductions and guys traded small talk with Ben. Everyone wanted to know what it was like attending the university and living up there. They asked about girls at UF and whether the classes there were tough, and I was again reminded that these guys—who I adored and always would—still dwelled in a world I had left behind.

Steve talked with Ben about surfing in Brevard County. Steve's brother, Nash, owned a board, and Nash had visited Cocoa Beach multiple times to ride waves.

I told Steve about watching the surfers at the pier over there, and then I described the visit Ben and I had made to Ron Jon's surf shop. When I made eye contact with Steve and gazed into his aquamarine eyes, I felt a shiver run through me when I recalled the first time we'd had butt sex in my bedroom.

The doorbell rang, yanking me from my reverie, and moments later, James entered the room. Tall and slender, he sported wavy auburn hair and chiseled features. Copper-colored freckles danced across his nose and cheeks like confetti.

"Whose GTO?" he hollered above the music and conversation. "Did somebody marry a rich girl?"

Everyone piled out of the house and onto the street to inspect Ben's car. Guys climbed into the front and back seats. The hood was popped and the GTO's massive eight-cylinder engine examined. In the driver's seat, James used his falsetto voice to sing the tune "GTO" by Ronny and the Daytonas. He kept the beat by tapping his fingers on the steering wheel. "This is really yours?" Stewart asked Ben.

Ben nodded. "It's a Christmas gift."

Stewart pursed his lips and shook his head. "Must be nice. I got three pairs of socks and a shaving cream warmer."

Back inside, Kenny flipped the album and the Beach Boys sang "We Three Kings of Orient Are." Kenny's family Christmas tree blazed with lights and assorted ornaments. The fireplace mantel was decorated with an illuminated Dickens Christmas set that glistened with fake snow.

After Ben and I cracked open two new beers, I asked Kenny if I could show Ben the sailboat out back.

"Sure," Kenny said. "Let me flick on the dock light. The hatch isn't locked if you want to go below decks and look around."

Kenny's house sat on the Intracoastal Waterway, and during daytime, the view it enjoyed was nothing short of amazing. But right then, all I could see was moonlight reflecting off the dark water.

The sailboat was a forty-foot Morgan with a mast that had to be fifty feet tall. The hull shone like a freshly scrubbed tooth. The teak decks shone and the brightworks gleamed. Ben and I climbed aboard, and I lifted the hatch accessing the main cabin below. We descended a ladder, and after I fumbled around for a minute, I found a light switch to illuminate the cabin.

Ben whistled while he studied the cabin. Most all the ship's furnishings were lacquered teak. The upholstery was navy-blue canvas with white piping, and the drapes sported a nautical motif. The galley kitchen was equipped with a sink, stove, and mini-fridge. A bath offered a sink, toilet, and shower. One sleeping cabin was in the bow with a V-shaped bed. The other—the master cabin—was astern, and when we inspected it, Ben put a hand on my shoulder.

I looked at him and raised my eyebrows. "What?"

He pointed at the bed. "I need a kiss."

We sat on the mattress. The ports were curtained so we had privacy. Our mouths conjoined, our tongues rubbed, and Ben's breath steamed my upper lip. The only sounds were water mumbling against the boat's hull and our slurping. After I placed a hand on Ben's sternum, I pushed his upper body to the mattress. Then I lay on top of him. We went at it for maybe five minutes before footfalls sounded on the deck.

"Johnny, are you down there?"

The voice was Steve's.

"Yeah," I hollered. Then I rolled off Ben and wiped my lips with my sweater sleeve. After Ben and I rose, we straightened our clothing.

Meanwhile, Steve spoke to us through the hatch opening. "The guys are going to McDonald's for burgers. Why don't you and Ben come with us?"

When I looked at Ben, he shrugged.

The McDonald's restaurant Steve spoke of had been a major hangout for kids from our high school when I attended there. We went to McDonald's after football and basketball games. The parking lot was always jammed with cars full of students, and much socializing took place. McDonald's was the place to see and be seen. But now the idea of going to a burger joint populated with pimply kids who had just earned their driver's licenses seemed a bit silly.

"We'll be right up," I told Steve, and then we went about extinguishing the lights below deck.

Before we left the boat, I told Ben, "Let's skip McDonald's. I'm not up for it unless you are."

"It's fine," Ben said.

Back at the house, guys slipped into their jackets and jingled car keys. After I fetched our remaining two beers from the fridge, I thanked Kenny for having us over.

"You guys aren't coming with us?" Kenny asked.

I glanced at Steve, who was staring at me, and then I swung my gaze back to Kenny. "It was great seeing you all, but we got up early and we're both pretty tired."

"You sound like a grandpa," Steve said. "It's only nine thirty."

"Sorry," I told Steve. "I'll see you guys in a day or two."

Goodbyes and handshakes were exchanged. Then Ben and I cruised toward the beach in the GTO while the radio played "Street Fighting Man" by the Rolling Stones. When we halted at a stoplight, Ben turned to me with a puzzled expression on his face.

"Why didn't you want to go to McDonald's? I thought those guys were your best friends."

"They are, but we're not in high school anymore. Hanging out at a burger joint just doesn't appeal to me like it used to."

Ben nodded. "I get that."

Before we returned to my house, we took a detour to visit a waterfront development where several homes were under construction. We parked the GTO in the driveway of a cinder-block house that didn't even have a roof yet. Then we sat on the seawall out back, sipping from our beers and staring into the Intracoastal Waterway's blackness. In the distance, an outboard engine hummed.

"I like your friends," Ben said. "They all seem nice."

I nodded. "They made a huge difference in my life the last two years of high school, became a second family to me. We did everything together: parties, water-skiing, going to the beach, and camping. I was never lonely after I became part of the group."

"I can see why you like Steve," Ben said. "He's good-looking—he has a killer smile—but he's also easygoing and I can tell he likes you."

My scalp prickled. "How?"

"By the way he looks at you when you talk. It's like he thinks everything you say is important."

Right then, sitting there on the seawall, I realized there was a second reason I hadn't wanted to go for burgers with the guys. That reason was Steve. I didn't feel comfortable being in the same place with him and Ben, I guess because I felt guilty about my sexual escapades with Steve. Even though I had enjoyed the sex immensely, I felt bad about the encounters, like I'd been disloyal to Ben in a major way.

Go on: tell him.

I drew a deep breath and let it out. Then I said, "I need to admit to something I've done and you're not going to like it."

Ben put down his beer. He looked at me and crinkled his forehead. "What?"

My stomach did flip-flops, and my voice wavered while I described my encounters with Steve, in detail. I didn't just talk about what we had done, but where, and how it had felt to touch Steve.

Ben's face remained expressionless while I yammered.

"I know I probably shouldn't have let myself get involved with Steve. The first time, it just sort of happened and wasn't planned. But the sex felt so good I couldn't say no when Steve wanted more."

Ben shifted his weight on the seawall cap. He licked his lips and looked into my eyes. "Did you enjoy it more with him than you do with me?"

"Shit no, it wasn't anything like that. Steve's a friend and that's all. I'm not in love with him like I am with you, and that's the God's honest truth."

Ben rubbed the tops of his thighs with the palms of his hands. "I leave for Merritt Island Monday morning. You'll be here another five days before you return to Gainesville, right?"

I nodded.

"Do you think you'll have sex with Steve again?"

How should I answer Ben's question? I felt nervous as hell. "Not if you don't want me to. I'll keep my hands off him, I swear I will."

A car approached on the street out front, and the glow from the headlights swept the house behind us. It was a cop car with emergency flashers on the roof and one officer inside. When he pulled into the driveway behind Ben's car, we tossed our beer cans into the Intracoastal.

The cop got out of his vehicle, switched on his flashlight, and approached. We both squinted at the flashlight's brightness. The cop's shoes crunched against bits of construction debris that littered the property.

"Evening," he said in a gruff baritone. "What're you boys up to?"

"We're just talking about girls," I said with a phony smile on my face. "It's a good place to do that."

The cop shifted his weight from one leg to his other. "It's also private property *and* an active construction site. You're trespassing."

"Sorry," Ben said. "We didn't think we were harming anything by sitting here and chatting."

"You boys need to clear out, understand?"

"Yes, sir," Ben and I said in chorus. We rose and dusted off the seats of our pants.

Moments later, the cop was gone and Ben started the GTO's engine. He shifted into reverse and backed into the street. Then he changed gears and we cruised toward Gulf Boulevard while the GTO's muffler rumbled.

"Look," I said, "maybe I shouldn't have told you about Steve, but I don't want to hide things like that from you. I hope you're not mad at me for what I did."

Ben puckered one side of his face while he stared out the windshield. "More like disappointed, Johnny. I thought sex was something special you only shared with me, but not anymore, I guess."

Shit.

"I meant what I said. If you don't want me touching Steve, then I won't. That's a promise."

Ben didn't say anything for thirty seconds or so. He only worked his jaw from side to side until we reached a stop sign at the intersection with Gulf Boulevard. Then he looked at me.

"As far as Steve is concerned, I'm not going to tell you what to do or *not* to do with him. That's a choice you'll have to make. But I don't think you having sex with other people is good for us, any more than me pledging ATO would have been."

I thought back to the moment Ben had tossed the ATO pledge pin into his trash can. He chose me over the fraternity, which spoke legions about his feelings for me. He put me first back then, and now I felt like an asshole for what I'd done with Steve.

We cruised in silence the rest of the way home.

Chapter Twelve

MONDAY MORNING ARRIVED far too quickly. It seemed like Ben's visit to St. Petersburg Beach had lasted only hours instead of days. I sat on my bed, feeling miserable as I watched Ben pack things into his suitcase: his toiletries bag, sandals, and so forth.

I thought back to Sunday, when Ben and I had slept until ten. By the time we woke, my mom and sister had already left for church and the house was ours. After we used the bathroom, we crawled back into bed and devoted a good half hour to sex. Then we showered together while talking about what we would do with our day.

We ended up fishing at the Merry Pier on Pass-a-Grille, using greenbacks for bait. I caught a redfish, Ben a speckled trout, and Sunday evening Mom prepared a seafood dinner. She battered and fried our fillets and served them with french fries, coleslaw, and tartar sauce. Ben couldn't stop praising the food, nor could I, and as the four of us sat around our dining table, I had felt like Ben could easily fit into my family's everyday life.

And how great would that be?

After dinner and kitchen cleanup, Ben and I spent the rest of Sunday night walking along the shore. We listened to waves collapse against the sand. Moonlight made phosphorus in the Gulf water glow like molten silver. I so badly wanted to hold Ben's hand, but of course, I couldn't. Someone might have seen us. So I had to content myself to walk alongside him and listen to the rise and fall of his voice as we talked about returning to school after New Year's Day and which classes we would take next quarter.

Now, in my room, Ben closed his suitcase and fastened the hasps. He stood the suitcase on end and looked at me.

"It's time I got going. I have a long drive ahead of me."

I felt like I'd jumped out of a plane and now I was free-falling without a parachute.

My bedroom door was closed, so I rose from the bed and took Ben into my arms. Already my eyes fogged and my windpipe flexed. I kissed Ben on the mouth; then I rested my cheek on his shoulder. We swayed like a couple of kids slow dancing at the prom. The cries of seagulls at the shore entered the room through the western windows, but I put them out of my mind. I only wanted to hear Ben breathe.

"Can't you stay another day or two?"

"I wish I could, but my dad needs my help with things. This is a busy time in the groves, and with Chuck not there to help, I'll work twelve-hour days until I leave for Gainesville."

I sniffled a time or two. Then I let go of Ben, squared my shoulders, and dried my eyes with the heels of my hands.

"All right, then. I'll walk you to your car."

Ben picked up his suitcase. He thanked my mom and said goodbye to my sister. We shook hands in the sunlight, and five minutes later, he was gone, leaving me standing in our crushed-shell driveway and feeling like all the life had drained out of my body.

TUESDAY AFTERNOON, I did pushups in my bedroom while listening to Creedence Clearwater Revival's song, "Proud Mary," on my portable radio. One of my New Year's resolutions was to sculpt the muscles in my shoulders and chest by doing pushups every day. I hadn't done this sort of exercising since tenth-grade PE, and I'd forgotten how tough pushups were. I was up to fifteen and already my arms ached.

Out in the living room, the phone rang.

After my sister answered, she hollered, "Johnny, it's for you."

My caller was Steve, and when he spoke, his voice sounded seductive. "I'm watering the plants at Redington Beach again, right around three. Want to join me?"

I shifted my weight from my right leg to my left while I fingered the receiver's cord. "Those sure are thirsty plants," I said, trying to decide how I would handle this.

Steve chuckled. "The humidity's low at this time of year. They dry up fast."

"I'll join you," I said, "but..."

"What?"

"Never mind, we can talk in the car."

WIND RUSHED THROUGH Steve's VW while afternoon sunlight hammered the hood. We were dressed identically: blue jeans, sweatshirts, and sneakers. Steve also wore a nice pair of Wayfarer sunglasses, a gift from his folks. His hand worked the gearshift knob as he maneuvered through traffic on Gulf Boulevard. Now that Christmas was over, the snowbirds from up north were arriving, so a lot more cars were on the road. The going was slower than during our previous trips to Redington Beach.

At that moment, we were passing through Treasure Island and approaching the John's Pass Bridge. We talked about the gathering at Kenny's a minute or two, and then our conversation turned to Ben.

"He's good-looking," Steve said, "plus his family has money. That GTO is one sweet ride."

I cleared my throat and rearranged my limbs in my seat. What I said next would need to mean something.

"After the party on Saturday, I told him about you and me having sex."

Steve glanced at me for a moment, but I couldn't read his eyes because of the sunglasses. A vertical crease appeared between his eyebrows, and he shook his head a time or two. Then he returned his gaze to the windshield.

"What is it?"

Steve pounded the steering wheel with a fist. "Why the *fuck* did you tell him?"

"Because I don't like keeping secrets from Ben."

"What did he say?"

"He wasn't happy."

We rode in silence a minute or so while the VW's muffler growled and the gears grinded. Then Steve said, "Did he ask you to stop seeing me, I mean in that way?"

I crossed my arms at my chest. "He didn't, actually, because Ben's not the jealous type. But he thinks you and me having sex isn't good for my relationship with him, and I think he's right. I should be loyal to Ben if I'm his boyfriend."

"Does he think I'm trying to steal you?"

"I don't believe so, but I'm really not sure."

We entered Redington Beach, and Steve steered us off the boulevard. We rolled down a side street. Then Steve pulled onto his aunt's driveway and killed the VW's engine. When he engaged the parking brake, the handle made a ratcheting sound. I waited for Steve to yank his tube of jelly from underneath the driver's seat, but he didn't. Instead, he exited the car and retrieved the house key from underneath the flower pot.

We went inside.

Like always, the house was as quiet as an empty church. I took a seat on a barstool facing the kitchen counter while Steve went about filling the pitcher with water and giving each plant in the living room a drink. I felt tension crackle between us. Neither of us spoke; in fact, we didn't even look at each other much.

Steve returned to the kitchen sink to refill the pitcher, but instead of doing that, he turned and *flung* the empty pitcher at me. I tried to duck, but it was too late and the pitcher struck my shoulder before it clattered to the floor.

"You son of a bitch," Steve cried. "For the past two years, I thought we were best friends, but I guess not. First of all, you hid the fact you were gay from me, like you didn't trust me. And now that I know you're gay—and now that you know I am—things could be very good between us."

"Steve, I—"

"But now you've met this rich kid with his cattle ranch and his GTO and I'm not good enough. Is that how it is?"

What was I supposed to say?

"I didn't tell you I was gay because I was afraid it might end our friendship. You were my best friend, and I didn't want that to happen."

Steve glowered at me. "Am I still your best friend, Johnny?"

I lowered my gaze and rubbed my lips together. Then I looked at Steve again.

"You're my best friend here at home, of course. But at school, I live with Ben—we have our meals together and sleep in the same bed every night. It's almost like we're married, and you can't get mad at me because Ben makes me happy."

Steve's eyes watered while he kept his gaze locked onto mine. When he spoke, his voice quivered.

"If my family was rich like Ben's, I'll bet you'd choose me over him. But I'm only middle-class. I drive an old VW, not a GTO and—"

"This has nothing to *do* with money."

Steve hissed and shook his head.

"Why don't I believe you?"

ON TUESDAY, DECEMBER 30, with my mom's permission, I organized a New Year's Eve party at our house. We had a fire pit in our fenced-in patio, and Mom said we could gather back there.

"You and your friends can drink alcohol," Mom said, "but anyone who does has to bring a sleeping bag and spend the night. No one's driving home drunk."

I made phone calls to all the guys. I asked each to bring a food item—chips, pretzels, cookies, or whatever—along with a folding lawn chair and whatever he chose to drink. Kenny and Beau asked if they could bring girls they were dating, and I told them, "Of course."

Everybody seemed enthusiastic.

Well, everyone but Steve.

The day before, when he had driven me home from Redington Beach, we didn't say a word to each other during the entire trip. We both stared out the windshield and listened to music on the radio. At one point, the Beatles' "She's Leaving Home" played, and the lyrics of the song made me feel crappy as hell. Why did so many songs on the radio affect me that way?

When we reached my house and I opened the passenger door, all Steve said was, "I'll see you around," and then I wondered if our friendship might have been altered, and not in a good way.

Now, on the phone, when I spoke to Steve about the party, his voice sounded guarded.

"I don't know that I'll make it. Jimi Hendrix put together a new group called Band of Gypsys; they're playing in New York tomorrow night and it's live on TV. I might watch at Castleman's place."

My heart skipped a beat when Steve uttered his coach's name, and I tried to keep my voice steady when I responded. "Come by my house tomorrow night, for an hour at least. I'd like to see you."

"Really?"

"Of course. Why wouldn't I?"

Steve didn't say anything.

"Listen," I said, "as far as I'm concerned, nothing between us has changed. And I can't imagine not having you here on New Year's Eve. It won't be the same without you."

"We'll see," Steve answered.

WEDNESDAY AFTERNOON, I strung Christmas lights along the upper edge of our patio fence. The sky was overcast, the air still and cool. A stack of pine logs and kindling sat next to the fire pit. I'd set up a folding picnic table to hold the food guys were bringing and borrowed a neighbor's over-sized ice chest for my guests' beer. At my request, Kenny would bring his portable eight-track player, so we'd have decent music.

Right then, I listened to the radio. "My Cherie Amour" by Stevie Wonder played, and I thought about Ben and what he was doing at that very moment. We had talked on the phone the night before for close to a half hour, and Ben sounded tired.

"I spent all day driving a pickup truck through the groves, collecting crates full of citrus and taking them to the warehouse, where I had to unload and stack them for the sorters. There must be seventy-five people working here right now. It goes on from sunrise till dusk."

When I told Ben about the party I was having on New Year's Eve, he let out his breath.

"I wish I could be there; it sounds like fun. Guess I'll watch the Times Square ball drop on TV with my folks, maybe swipe a beer or two from the fridge to drink in my bedroom."

Now, as I snaked an extension cord from inside the house and out to the Christmas lights, I heard a familiar sound—the mutter of a Volkswagen engine. I greeted Steve at our front door and right away knew something was wrong. Dark circles appeared under his eyes. I led him to the patio out back, and we sat in a pair of Adirondack chairs. Steve was dressed like I was: sweatshirt, jeans, and sneakers. His dark hair was windblown. He leaned forward, rested his forearms on his knees, and wove his fingers together. Then he stared at the patio pavement.

"You look like hell," I said. "Is something wrong?"

He lifted his gaze to meet mine. "I didn't get any sleep last night. I just thrashed around under the covers. Then, this morning, I went out for a five-mile run but gave out of gas halfway through."

"That doesn't sound like you. Are you sick?"

He shook his head. "It's something else."

"What?"

His gaze stayed with mine. "I've fallen in love with you. I can't think about anything else but us being together. And it's not just about the sex. You're my best friend and have been for over two years, and I can't stand the fact you want Ben more than me. It hurts."

I lowered my gaze and shifted my weight in my chair. I felt like crying because now I realized I never should have told Steve I was gay and *never* should have touched him sexually. By doing those things I'd opened a floodgate I couldn't close. I had changed our friendship inalterably.

I knew most gay boys would have considered my situation enviable. After all, two attractive guys wanted me. Instead, I felt miserable because I knew I was going to hurt the guy I rejected, and that person was probably going to be Steve.

"Look," I said, "you don't know how good it feels to know that you like me that way. And if it weren't for Ben, I would gladly be your boyfriend. You and I are close and—"

Steve's eyes narrowed. "We could be closer if you'll only let it happen. Listen, I'm sorry I threw the water pitcher at you yesterday. It's just that...something exploded inside my head. That's how strong my feelings for you are right now."

"It's okay," I told Steve. "I understand."

He rearranged his limbs and moistened his lips. "I'm being unrealistic, aren't I? In a few days, you'll be back at UF and I'll be here. Plus, you live in the same room with Ben. Even if I came up there for visits, we couldn't, you know..."

"No, we couldn't."

Steve's shoulders sagged.

"Are you going to Castleman's tonight?" I asked.

He looked at me and nodded. "If I came to your party and drank a few beers, I might say or do something stupid that would embarrass both of us, and I don't want that to happen."

When I thought of Castleman in bed with Steve, my stomach went into knots, and an odd emotion boiled inside me— jealousy pure and simple. I felt Steve should spend New Year's Eve with me, not Castleman. But I knew Steve wouldn't come to my party unless I gave him a reason to attend.

I swung my gaze here and there. No one was around but me and Steve. Mom was at work and my sister at the movies.

I looked at Steve again.

Don't do it, Darling. You'll only make things worse.

If I had been an honorable guy, I would have stood my ground and not touched Steve, but right then, I felt so damned weak. Plus I had the opportunity to lift Steve out of the misery he was steeped in, at least temporarily—I could do it easily.

I leaned toward Steve and sifted my fingers through his hair. "We have the house to ourselves for a couple of hours, so why don't I lock the front door?"

Steve drew a breath and let it out. "I'd really like that, Johnny."

THE PARTY WENT full force. A dozen people were there, four of them girls I'd known in high school. The table was a jumble of junk food packages. On Kenny's eight-track player, a British band named Blind Faith performed a song I really liked: "Can't Find My Way Home."

I loved Steve Winwood's scratchy tenor voice.

Pop tops on beer cans were peeled open. Guys stuffed chips and pretzels into their mouths while the girls sipped from wine coolers. The Christmas lights on the fence twinkled. A blaze burned in the fire pit, casting a glow that illuminated the patio. The pine logs hissed and popped as they burned, and the smell of wood smoke was strong.

One girl present was Julie, a pretty blonde with a knockout smile. I had served with her on the yearbook staff my senior year. She was in Steve's class, so she was a year younger than me, but cool and collected, more like a college girl. We sat next to each other on folding chairs, and she asked endless questions about UF.

"It's where I want to go next year," she told me. "I've seen all of St. Petersburg I care to."

Steve, of course, was there. Canceling his date with Castleman had been the quid pro quo for the sex we shared earlier that day. He looked so handsome in a dark-blue V-neck sweater over a white button-down shirt. Steve's monogram was stitched into the sweater's chest in fancy script. He wore khaki slacks and penny loafers that reflected the glow from the fire pit. Right then, he was chatting with Beau and Beau's girlfriend, a cutie from my graduating class.

Steve's appearance differed from what it had been when he came to my house earlier. The dark crescents under his eyes had lightened, his posture was relaxed, and he smiled frequently. I felt amazed at how much a single round of intimacy had changed him. He was like another person, the same Steve I'd known for over two years.

That afternoon, after our sex, he had lain next to me on my bed, staring at the ceiling and speaking in that syrupy voice I knew so well.

"I really needed this. I'm going to miss you when you leave for Gainesville."

Now, at the party, I looked at Steve and knew my departure for UF was probably the best thing that could happen between us. If we didn't see each other for a few months, perhaps his feelings for me would fade and I wouldn't be tempted to have sex with him again. I could remain loyal to Ben and not feel so damned guilty like I had after Steve left my house that afternoon.

I didn't like feeling guilty.

When midnight arrived, we all wore silly conical hats and honked at each other with blowout noisemakers and kazoos. Many guys swayed on their feet, and their speech sounded a bit slurred.

I felt no pain myself as I guzzled beer number six.

I approached Steve, who sat on a lawn chair and talked with James. When Steve looked up at me and our gazes met, my knees actually quivered. I pointed at the fire pit, where the blaze had ebbed.

"We need more firewood from the garage. Give me a hand, will you?"

The garage was shadowy, and I didn't bother flicking on the ceiling fixture. The room smelled of gasoline, pinesap, and rubber. Things were very quiet; the only sounds were crickets chirping and the hum of an engine when the occasional car passed on Gulf Way.

I peeled off my party hat and tossed it aside. Then I turned to face Steve.

"I need a New Year's kiss," I said. "A sloppy one."

He smiled his beautiful smile. He took off his stupid party hat and dropped it to the concrete slab floor. I slipped my arms around his waist, and he rested his arms on my shoulders. Our hips and sternums met and our mouths came together. Our tongues dueled, and our lips smacked while Steve's erection pressed against mine.

The kiss lasted a good two minutes, and when we finally separated, we panted like a pair of greyhounds at the end of a race. Steve kept his gaze locked onto mine while he wiped spittle from his lips with the forearm of his sweater.

Even in the shadows, his eyes looked glittery. "I guess anything more than a kiss would be too risky?"

I nodded. "Too many people are here."

Steve shoved his hands into his hip pockets and rocked on his heels while we looked at each other.

"I might visit Redington Beach tomorrow afternoon. Care to come along?"

Chapter Thirteen

WINTERS IN GAINESVILLE were wet, cold, and dreary, so unlike those in St. Petersburg Beach where the sun shone most every day. When I walked to class, I often carried an umbrella under an arm and wore a jacket over a sweater to keep warm. My hands turned into blocks of ice if I didn't keep them stuffed into my pockets.

That quarter, I had entirely new professors and courses, including biological science, which was far more interesting that physical science. At the moment, we studied the various components of the human cell: nucleus, mitochondria, Golgi bodies, and so forth. The whole thing made more sense to me than concepts like mass and volume.

Ben and I were taking a PE course together: volleyball. Classes were held in the gym, on the basketball court, so we weren't out in the bad weather. Our coach was a rangy guy with a crew cut, an Alabama drawl, and dry wit. He always reminded us to handle the ball gently when we passed it or set up a spike.

"Fingertips, gentlemen—*fingertips.*"

I had never been an athlete, but volleyball came pretty easily to me. I liked the ebb and flow of the game and the fact there was no real physical contact with other players. I felt I was participating in a dance performance as the ball got passed around before it sailed over the net. I was also a pretty good server; I could place the ball where I wanted to and hit it pretty hard when I tossed it over my head and whacked it with the heel of my hand. I liked the sound the ball made when I did that.

Ben, of course, was an excellent player. He did everything well: passing, setting up, spiking, and serving. He moved fluidly on the court—all of his limbs were synchronized—plus he looked so damned sexy in his gym shorts, sweatshirt, and sneakers. The shorts showed off his fuzzy legs and the curve of his butt.

Because darkness came early, we took walks to Lake Alice before we dined in the cafeteria. We bundled up, of course, and many nights our breaths steamed in the chilly air. But it was nice having this time to talk, to enjoy the beauty of the lake and its surroundings. Aside from the pines and oaks, most of the trees surrounding the lake had turned brown or lost their leaves entirely. Even the cypress trees were rust-colored. Most nights the air was still, and the smallest of sounds—bird calls or whatever—punched across the lake.

On a Wednesday in mid-January, Ben talked about his family's groves while we stood at the lake's bank.

"Due to good weather, we're having a huge harvest this winter, and because Chuck and I aren't there to help, my dad was forced to hire an assistant to help out with things. Dad just couldn't keep up with the groves on his own, and I feel bad about it. The assistant's salary comes right out of our profits."

"You shouldn't feel guilty," I said. "You're entitled to get an education, and I'm sure your parents are glad you're here, even if it means they have to hire help."

Ben shook his head. "My dad looked so tired when I was home; he's exhausted by all the work. Sometimes, I think maybe I should quit school and move back to Merritt Island so I can help out. You don't need a college degree to manage a cattle ranch and citrus groves."

I sucked air into my lungs while my vision went fuzzy. I felt like someone had punched me in the stomach. The thought Ben might leave school appalled me. What would I do without him in my life every day? I thought back to the night Ben had gone to dinner at the ATO house and how lonely I was, and I sure didn't want to feel that way again.

"Please," I said with a quiver in my voice, "don't even *think* about leaving school. I couldn't stand it if you did."

In fading sunlight, we stood at the edge of the lake; it looked like a mirror. Ben stared into the placid water with his hands stuffed into his jacket pockets. He knitted his brow and rubbed his lips together. Then he looked at me.

"I don't know if I could stand it either. Right now, you're the most important person in the world to me. I was so unhappy over Christmas break because I couldn't see you every day, but..."

"What?"

Ben shifted his weight from one leg to the other. "Chuck wasn't planning on attending UF with me. He wanted to enroll at Brevard Community College and live at home. If he were alive today, he'd help with the groves. And since it's my fault he's dead, maybe I should atone for my fuckup by quitting school and going home."

"Don't do that," I said while my eyes teared up. "I'll lose my mind if you do."

Ben lowered his chin and didn't say anything.

IN DEFIANCE OF the university's ban on freshmen having cars at school, Ben brought his GTO to Gainesville after Christmas break. He paid five bucks a month to park it behind a gas station a few blocks from campus.

Having the GTO at our disposal gave us freedom we'd never had during fall quarter.

One weekend in early February, we drove the GTO to Cedar Key, on the Gulf coast, to spend a weekend at an ancient wood-framed hotel. We rented tackle and fished from a public pier using live shrimp as bait. Ben caught a flounder the size of a serving tray, and the hotel's dining room cleaned and cooked the fillets for our dinner Saturday night, accompanied by baked Idaho potatoes and a fresh fruit salad, a very tasty meal.

Another weekend, later in February, we drove to Merritt Island to stay with Ben's folks. The weather was wet and blustery, but labor in the groves continued nonstop. Ben and I helped as best we could. Using a pickup truck, we collected crates full of picked citrus and brought them to the warehouse where we stacked them up for the folks who sorted the best oranges and grapefruits for the Stoneciphers' retail operation. The rest of the citrus would be sold to Tropicana or Kraft for juicing.

We laundered sheets and towels for the grove workers' barracks, using commercial-size washers and dryers located in a shed in the barracks area. We made up beds and swept floors and drove to a wholesale food market in Orlando to pick up provisions for the barracks kitchen. Saturday night, Ben and I were so tired we didn't even have sex before we went to sleep.

Now, on a weekday evening in mid-March, Ben and I studied for our final exams in our dorm room when the phone rang. The caller was Steve.

"Sebring is March 21st," he told me. "Are you going to make it this year?"

Attending the Twelve Hours of Sebring auto race was a ritual for my friends from high school. The race was an international competition, and that year was even more special because film actor Steve McQueen would compete in a Porsche 908 prototype. And Mario Andretti, a legend in auto racing, would drive a Ferrari 512S, also a prototype. The racetrack was a little over five miles long, with a wicked design including a hairpin turn, a chicane, and screaming straightaways where drivers punched their gas pedals to pass slower-moving vehicles.

Fifty thousand race fans were expected to attend.

"I'll talk with Ben about it," I responded.

There was silence on the line for several seconds. Then Steve said, "I guess you guys are still together?"

"That's right," I answered.

"If you come to the race," Steve continued, "I'll have a two-man tent you can share with me. You'll only need a sleeping bag and a pillow."

I glanced over at Ben while my belly did a flip-flop.

Later that evening, when I asked Ben if he'd like to attend the Sebring race, he let out his breath and scowled. "I'd love to go but can't. I'll need to devote my spring break to working in the groves. Most of the migrants leave that week, and we'll need to close things up in the barracks. It's a lot of work, and my folks are counting on me to be there."

"Screw the race," I said. "I'll come with you to Merritt Island and help out as best I can."

Ben shook his head. "I can't let you do that. I know it's an important event for you and your friends. Just go and have a good time. The Monday after the race, if you'd like, I'll come pick you up in St. Petersburg Beach, and you can spend the rest of the break with me in Merritt Island. Sound good?"

Chapter Fourteen

STEVE PICKED ME up at my house in St. Petersburg Beach on the Friday afternoon before the race. I tossed my duffel, a pillow, and a sleeping bag into the back seat of Steve's VW, next to a Coleman ice chest.

The weather that day was chilly and overcast. I wore a beat-up pair of jeans, my gas station work boots, a sweatshirt frayed at the collar, and a zippered leather jacket that had once belonged to my grandfather. There wasn't any reason to wear decent clothing to the raceway because by the end of the weekend, I'd be filthy and stinking of auto exhaust fumes and campfire smoke.

Steve wore a hooded sweatshirt with paint speckles on it and a pair of jeans shredded at the knees. His sneakers looked like he'd mud-wrestled in them, but he was still very handsome with his aquamarine eyes and dazzling smile.

He jerked a thumb toward the back seat. "There's a case of beer in that cooler and another case is in the frunk. I brought my dad's camping cook stove and plenty of food, so we won't have to buy stuff from the thieving vendors. You can pay me for half of everything."

The term "frunk" referred to the VW's trunk, which was located in the *front* of the car while the engine compartment was situated in the rear.

We crossed the mouth of Tampa Bay via the Sunshine Skyway Bridge. The bridge's peak was 150 feet above the bay's surface. Weak sunlight reflected off lips of whitecaps below us. A freighter that looked like a floating hotel approached the bridge from the Gulf of Mexico. The VW's muffler growled as we reached the apex. We drove across a metal grating that made a sound like a swarm of bees. Then we descended into Manatee County, where mangrove thickets and Australian pines lined the road shoulders.

In Bradenton, we turned eastward onto State Road 64, then passed through palmetto and pine forests that stretched as far as I could see. We also passed by occasional citrus grove or beef cattle ranch and I was reminded of the Stoneciphers' property on Merritt Island.

When Ben had called me on the phone that morning, he sounded weary. "I worked my butt off yesterday, cleaning the barracks and doing laundry. I must have folded a hundred sheets. Then my dad and I and three other guys had to unload orange crates onto a Kraft eighteen-wheeler. It took us four hours, and now my back and shoulders are killing me."

I felt guilty when I thought of how hard Ben had worked while I did nothing but relax on Thursday. I'd spent part of my day playing half-court basketball with Beau, Stewart, and Steve, and the rest walking on the beach and watching TV. Later, I had gone to a bizarre foreign movie, *Fellini Satyricon*, with James and his girlfriend. The movie had a lot of homosexuality in it, which was actually pretty hot, but it also featured some very disgusting and violent scenes that made my stomach roil. When I visited the men's room, halfway through the film, someone had barfed into one of the sinks.

Now I was headed for the raceway to spend a weekend drinking far too much beer and most likely spending time with Steve in his tent, doing things I'd feel guilty about as well. Ten weeks had passed since I'd last seen Steve, but already I experienced those same feelings I'd had during Christmas break—a gnawing desire for Steve's body, all of it, every inch.

I cracked open two beers from the ice chest, passed one to Steve, and sipped from mine. The beer was cold and crisp. Wind rushed through the VW, ruffling Steve's bangs. I studied the dark hairs growing on the back of Steve's hand that rested on the steering wheel, and then I gazed at his long eyelashes that always gave me quivers. When Steve sipped from his beer, his Adam's apple bobbed when he swallowed and I recalled licking his neck when we'd last had sex.

We talked about my winter quarter classes at UF. Then Steve talked about how his senior year had gone. He'd placed second in the district cross-country meet in late January—that was quite an achievement—and it was possible he might earn a partial athletic scholarship to either UF or FSU in the fall.

"I'm applying for admission to both schools," he told me. "But I'm not sure which I'll choose."

I knew he was fishing for a signal from me as to whether or not I'd prefer he enroll at UF, but I didn't suggest a course of action. "They're equally good universities" was all I said.

He nodded and sipped from his beer, keeping his gaze fixed on the highway before us. "So, are things still going strong between you and Ben?"

"They are. And are you still seeing Castleman?"

He nodded. "Back in February, he and I went to the state track meet in Tallahassee, as spectators. We shared a motel room two nights."

"And how was that?"

After Steve turned his head to look at me, he raised his eyebrows and grinned. "Pretty damned amazing, especially when I let him—you know."

A vision of Castleman atop Steve entered my head, and I felt a twinge of jealousy in my gut. The thought that Steve had engaged in that sort of sex with someone other than me rubbed me the wrong way.

Say it.

"Do you mind if I tell you I think it's creepy how Castleman's using you? I mean, the guy's probably what—thirty? Why doesn't he find someone his own age?"

Steve looked at me again and knitted his eyebrows. "Why should you care what he and I do together? And he's twenty-eight, by the way."

"But you're only eighteen."

Steve shrugged.

I opened two fresh beers for us. I gave one to Steve, and we rode in silence for a bit. At a small town called Zolfo Springs, we turned onto State Road 66 and traveled in a southeasterly direction, passing through more palmetto and pine forest. The temperature was cooling as the sun descended behind us, and I rolled up my passenger window to stay warm.

We passed Highlands Hammock State Park, a huge nature preserve with towering live oaks and longleaf pines, and then we intersected with US 98, a four-lane highway that would lead us to the raceway. Traffic was thick, strictly stop-and-go as we inched along. I cracked open another round of beers and tossed our empties into a paper grocery sack on the rear seat's floorboard. Shadows had grown long as the sun descended toward the western horizon. All around us cars were crammed full of guys our age, boys with shaggy hair, dressed in flannel shirts and chugging beer. Car radios played popular hits of the day: "Evil Ways" by Santana, "Celebrate" by Three Dog Night, and "Come Together" by the Beatles.

I had a decent beer buzz going, the kind where I wasn't drunk but definitely a step or two removed from reality. Already objects around me looked fuzzy at their edges.

When we reached the admissions gate, we paid a raceway attendant ten bucks apiece as our admission fees and he gave us a tag to hang from the rearview mirror. Another attendant checked the back seat and the trunk up front to be sure we weren't smuggling other guys in. Then we entered the raceway. We rolled along the main vendor area where throngs of race fans teemed, many with six-packs of beer under an arm or hanging from their fingertips.

Men outnumbered women nine to one, and most of the guys were under the age of twenty-five. This was the ultimate Florida sausage-fest, and already I could sense testosterone percolating all around me.

To reach the racetrack's infield, where our group camped each year, we had to drive over a concrete vehicle bridge that arced above the track. When we reached the bridge's apex, it offered of an excellent view of a makeshift city that had sprung to life in the infield. Thousands upon thousands of canvas and nylon tents were pitched alongside cars and trucks. Campfires glowed and a familiar Sebring smell, a blend of wood smoke and car exhaust, hit my nose. A crowd of men and boys had gathered to watch two girls in tight jeans and halter tops dance on the roof of a U-Haul moving van.

We descended to the infield where a scrim of dust and smoke hung in the air, giving everything around us a smudged look, as though I viewed my surroundings through a dirty windowpane. The most prevalent sounds were growls and pops from motorcycle engines and rumbles from car and truck mufflers. A guy on a Harley just ahead of us wore a shiny helmet with a silver spearhead rising from the crown. He looked like a WWI German army officer.

Each year, our group camped beneath a towering long leaf pine. The pine hulked above an abandoned swimming pool that likely hadn't held water since Eisenhower was president. Shrubbery grew in the pool's deep end, providing a private place to piss, puke, and even take a shit if the lines at the Port-o-lets were too long.

It seemed Steve and I were the last of our group to arrive. I recognized Beau's Chevy Impala and James's beat-up Dodge Dart. Country clubber Kenny had towed an Apache pop-up camper there behind his family's Vista Cruiser station wagon, and the camper's tent was already raised. A campfire flamed inside a pit created from pieces of broken cinder blocks. The guys had gathered around the blaze, all of them wearing jackets or flannel shirts to ward off the chill descending over the raceway. The air was still. Smoke from the campfire rose into the pine tree's massive limbs. To the east, the sky had darkened and a few stars had made their appearance, while the hem of the western sky glowed in shades of orange and crimson.

Greetings were exchanged when we joined the group, and beer cans raised in a toast to our arrival.

Beau gave me a hug and ruffled my hair. "Welcome, Darling, I'm so glad you're here."

He didn't say it in a sarcastic way; he meant it.

"Goddamn Sebring," James hollered with his chin raised and his arms spread like Jesus on the cross. "I love this miserable place."

Steve drained his beer can and looked at me. "Why don't we set things up before it gets any darker?"

The tent was nylon with a fly and a zippered entry flap. It didn't take us ten minutes to erect it, roll out our sleeping bags, and toss in our pillows. When I looked at the bags lying side by side, I wondered what would happen when the evening came to an end, but I put those thoughts aside.

Concentrate on having fun, *Darling*.

I WAS DRUNK.

Not to the point of stumbling, but at a level where everything seemed humorous. Steve, Stewart, and I walked along the main concessions area. Rednecks in ball caps and college boys with long hair rubbed shoulders. Beneath fluorescent lights vendors in booths sold popcorn, candy apples, elephant ears, and so forth. The smell of frying food was seductive, and I couldn't help myself—I succumbed to temptation. I bought a corn dog, slathered it in mustard, and wolfed it down in less than two minutes.

We ascended a metal staircase to access the Martini & Rossi pedestrian bridge that led from the main vendor area to the pit zone on the other side of the racetrack. Even though nighttime was upon us, race drivers were still testing out their cars. They flew beneath us with their headlights cutting into the blackness and mufflers rumbling so loudly that we had to yell at each other to be heard. Sometimes, when an engine backfired, blue and yellow sparks flashed from the rear of a race car.

The bridge was covered like the ones in New England post cards, as dark as tar inside, and narrow, just enough width for two people to pass. Stewart was in the lead and I was in the middle, with Steve behind me. When we were halfway across the bridge Steve squeezed my butt cheek. Then he patted my ass a few times while a jolt of sexual tension coursed through me.

We left the enclosure to descend another flight of metal stairs. Then we reached the pit area, which was nothing more than a single-story cinder-block building the length of a football field, divided into bays where mechanics tinkered with shiny cars: Corvettes, Porsches, Alfa Romeos, Camaros, and several prototypes that reminded me of UFOs. Glow from the bays' ceiling lights reflected off car hoods and windshields.

When we came to one particular bay, I gazed into its interior, and my heart leapt into my throat. Steve McQueen was only thirty feet from us. He inspected a racing harness inside a white Porsche prototype with a roll bar and the number 48 on the hood. McQueen's wavy hair was much longer than it had been in his last film that I saw, an action movie called *Bullitt*. Now his hair grew over his ears and covered the back of his neck. He had sideburns too. He leaned on a cane, and his right foot was encased in a plaster cast that looked oddly out of place in the rough-and-tumble atmosphere of the raceway.

"Damn," Stewart said, "I wish I had a camera. The other guys will never believe this when we tell them."

By the time we returned to our campsite, the time was nearly eleven and all the guys had already turned in for the night, save for James. He sat by himself in an aluminum lawn chair, staring into the dying embers of the fire pit and cradling a can of beer between his thighs. He yawned as we approached, but when we told him about McQueen, his eyebrows jumped.

"You lucky bastards," he said while he shook his head. "I should have gone with you."

Steve and I visited the swimming pool to piss, and then we crawled inside Steve's tent, me in the lead. We kicked off our shoes and wriggled out of most our clothing, other than our briefs and T-shirts. Then we climbed into our respective sleeping bags.

It was dark inside the tent, but glow from a nearby streetlamp entered through the nylon, offering a bit of illumination, enough so I could see Steve's facial features when I turned my head to look at him. He lay on his side, facing me, and when my gaze met his, he bent an elbow and propped his head against the heel of his hand.

"Are you sleepy?" he whispered.

"Not really."

"Can I join you?"

Well.

Ever since we'd crossed the Martini & Rossi bridge, I knew this moment would come but wasn't sure how I'd respond when it did. Now, when I thought of Ben and how much I cared for him, I knew I shouldn't touch Steve.

I should say, "No, I belong to Ben."

But the alcohol I'd consumed had melted away any self-control I might otherwise have exercised.

Ah, shit...

I lifted the flap of my sleeping bag, and Steve crawled in alongside me. I felt the warmth of his body as our sternums, hips, and knees met inside the bag. Steve brought his mouth to mine; he toyed with my ear while our lips smacked and our tongues writhed.

Already I was stiff as rebar.

Let it happen, Darling.

Just...let go.

WHEN I WOKE on Saturday morning, Steve was in his own bag and snoring on his back. I watched his chest rise and fall with his breathing. I gazed at his handsome facial features, especially the lips I'd kissed when we entangled the night before, and I still felt amazed that our friendship had evolved into something deeper.

Just before he returned to his bag Friday night, Steve lay next to me and stroked my cheek with his thumb. "That was amazing, Johnny."

And it *had been*, but now that I was sober, those same feelings of guilt I always got after sex with Steve crept into my head. I knew how disappointed Ben would feel if he knew what I'd done, and then I asked myself if maybe I should keep my distance from Steve in the future.

But I couldn't imagine life without Steve. Before the previous afternoon, I had not seen him in ten weeks and I thought my feelings for him might have faded. But once we were back together again, it hadn't taken more than several hours before we were skin to skin and slobbering like sophomores.

What did that say about my character?

IT TURNED OUT McQueen and his racing partner, Peter Revson, almost won the race on Saturday night, after twelve hours of cutthroat competition with Andretti's team. McQueen and Revson were narrowly edged out by Andretti in the race's final lap. Afterward, a huge crowd flooded into the pit area to catch glimpses of McQueen atop his Porsche, holding his racing helmet above his head like a trophy and acknowledging their cheers.

I clapped my hands and whistled through my teeth in the chilly night air. All my friends were there and most of us were unsteady on our feet. It had been a long day of drinking and walking around the racetrack's 5.2-mile course. My feet were sore, my lower back ached, and my nose was sunburned. My cheeks were grimy, as were my hands and fingernails. My voice was hoarse from yelling at my friends all day so they could hear me over the roar of the race cars, and my legs were so wobbly I wondered if I'd make it back to the campsite.

When we finally returned there, I visited the swimming pool to piss. Then I crawled inside Steve's tent unnoticed. I shucked off my shoes and most of my clothing, then got inside my bag and zipped the flap closed.

I fell asleep as soon as my head hit the pillow.

MIDMORNING SUNDAY, A light rain fell when Steve drove us westward on State Road 64. The VW's windshield wipers clacked as we passed through a palmetto and pine forest. The overcast sky gave everything around us a washed-out look, and the dampness made Steve's car smell like the inside of an old shoe.

My head pounded from a major hangover while my hips and shoulder blades ached from sleeping on the ground the past two nights.

A half hour before, when we'd stopped at a convenience store to buy Styrofoam cups of coffee, I used the restroom, and when I looked into the mirror over the sink, I barely recognized myself. My face was shiny and smudged with dirt, and my nose was as red as a strawberry. Stubble grew on my chin, my eyes were bloodshot, and my greasy hair stood up on the crown of my head. I looked so bad I didn't even try to clean myself up.

Why bother?

Now, as I sipped from my coffee cup, I gazed at Steve. He looked as nasty as I did: chin stubble, oily hair, filthy face and hands. His clothing was dirty and food-stained.

"You should see yourself," I told him.

"What?"

"You look like a hobo."

He looked at me and snickered while he shook his head. "You aren't exactly prom king material yourself. Were you rolling in the dirt yesterday?"

I looked down at my grimy clothing. "Actually, I was. I tripped and fell into one of those pits where people toss their empty beer cans. I think I may have been drunk at the time."

Steve lifted his chin; he gazed at the headliner and cackled.

We rode in silence for a few minutes, sipping from our coffees. Then Steve asked what I was doing for the remainder of my spring break.

When I explained how Ben would pick me up the next day and how I'd spend the week at Merritt Island, Steve looked at me and scowled.

"What is it?" I said.

He shook his head before returning his gaze to the windshield.

"Tell me what's wrong."

His fingers flexed against the VW's steering wheel when he spoke. "This is the first time I've seen you since Christmas break. Can't you at least spend a few days with me before you leave for Ben's?"

I rubbed a knuckle against my stubbly chin. "You don't understand; he needs my help over there."

Steve looked at me and narrowed his eyes. "I could use your help too. Have you thought about that, or do I even *matter* to you these days?"

I made a face. "Of course you matter—don't be ridiculous—but what kind of help are you talking about?"

Steve swung his gaze to the road while he moistened his lips.

"The way I felt Friday night, when we were together in the tent, is how I want to feel a lot more often. You need to give me what you give Ben whenever possible."

Aye-yi-yi...

"Look," I said, gesturing with my hands, "you know how much I care for you as a friend—I'll do most anything you ask of me—but Ben is my lover. He counts on me and needs me right now. I can't just call him and say I'm not coming—I made a commitment."

Steve shook his head. "I guess what we did in the tent Friday wasn't important, not to you anyway. I was only a convenience because Ben wasn't there. And by the way, I sure don't appreciate how you went off to sleep Saturday without even saying good night. Later, when I came inside the tent, I tried to wake you up so I could get in your bag, but..."

"What?"

"You were so drunk I knew I was wasting my time. I got into *my* bag instead and jerked off—what a great way to end the evening." Steve let out his breath and shook his head again. "Thanks a lot, Johnny."

I scrunched one side of my face and stared out my rain-speckled passenger window. On a personal level I had fucked up everything that weekend. My behavior had left Steve wanting and would certainly disappoint Ben if he learned of it.

Great, Darling—just great. You're a goddamned asshole.

Chapter Fifteen

AT THE STONECIPHERS', I helped Ben clean a groves barrack. I swept the concrete-slab floor with a push broom while Ben scrubbed bathroom sinks with powdered cleanser and a brush. Morning sunlight poured through the windows, and somewhere close by a mockingbird tootled. Earlier, we had stripped mattresses and pillows off all the beds, and now the linens—sheets, pillowcases, and towels—were stuffed into a pair of canvas laundry bags.

A portable radio was plugged into a wall socket and tuned to an Orlando station that played top-forty hits, and right now, the song "ABC" by the Jackson 5 had me twitching my hips while I pushed my broom and dust motes glistened in the air around me.

I thought back to the previous day when Ben had picked me up at St. Petersburg Beach. We cruised over to Tampa in the GTO with the windows rolled down, and when we crossed the Howard Frankland Bridge, the bay was so calm it looked like a mirror. Ben steered with his left hand and held my hand in his other. I chattered away about the Sebring race and Steve McQueen, and then I felt guilty when Ben described his twelve-hour workdays and the menial tasks he'd performed since I last saw him. For the twentieth time, I asked myself if I should have forgone the race and spent the past weekend helping Ben and his folks, but when I said something about it to Ben, he only shook his head.

"I'm glad you went to the race with your friends. That's how a guy *should* spend his spring break instead of toiling in the groves."

The night before at the Stoneciphers' dinner table, Will had insisted he pay me for my help that week, whether I liked it or not, and I knew it would have been futile to argue about it, so I was doing the best job I could while I was there.

Will looked haggard. He had bags under his eyes and had lost weight since I was last there. When I asked Ben about Will's appearance, Ben grimaced and shook his head.

"Dad's wearing himself out and I'm worried about it—Mom is too. Even with the new assistant he hired, there aren't enough hours in Dad's day to get everything done."

Once I finished sweeping, I helped Ben clean shower stalls with an ammonia solution and scrub brushes. We used mildew-cide in spray bottles to get rid of dark spots in the grout. The work was tedious, but at least the air was cool and dry so we weren't sweating like we would have been in May or June.

And I actually *liked* working alongside Ben. We were a team, plus I could sneak a kiss or pat Ben on the butt whenever I felt like it. He looked so sexy in his flannel shirt, jeans, and steel-toed work boots that I wanted to grab him and drag him into a dark corner for something more than a kiss.

The migrants were all gone now, and when Ben and I had taken a walk through the groves the previous night, the place seemed eerily quiet. The only sounds were crickets chirping and a whippoorwill's call.

Woo-hoo-hoo. Woo-hoo-hoo.

Now, over in the barracks kitchen, the cook packed things away. Pots and pans clanged and cabinet doors squeaked.

I asked Ben, "Will things slow down, now that the citrus is harvested?"

He shook his head. "On our ranch, we breed the cattle in July, so the cows will give birth in April. Calving is a lot of work because certain cows will need assistance with delivery. Most of the time, we do that ourselves, but sometimes, we'll call a vet to assist if the calf's not presenting well."

"Presenting?"

"A calf should emerge from the birth canal headfirst, but sometimes, it does the opposite. That's when the trouble starts. Then there are certain cows whose water sacs don't break properly. It's complicated, and sometimes, we're up in the middle of the night, helping with the birthing process."

We toted the sacks full of dirty linens to the laundry shed, where we loaded the linens into a pair of commercial-size washers. Ben tossed powdered soap in and switched them on. The washers made a rumbling sound as they filled with water.

We returned to the barrack to clean toilets in metal stalls, not the most appealing of tasks, but necessary. Again, we used an ammonia solution to sanitize each toilet. We knelt at the bowls and scrubbed away. Then we cleaned the seats with rags. The solution's acrid scent made my nose crinkle and my eyes sting.

When I'd first met Ben in Gainesville, I never would have believed he'd perform menial jobs like the ones we engaged in that day. But the work didn't seem to bother him. He accepted it as part of his obligation to his family, and I respected that. And I didn't mind the work either, really. It sure beat burning my hands on car hoods like I had during the summers I worked at the gas station in St. Petersburg Beach. It was better than changing flat tires and cleaning windshields while my coveralls stuck to the small of my back.

"There's a drive-in theater in Melbourne," Ben said while scrubbing in the stall next to mine. "I checked the *Sentinel* this morning. A movie called *Midnight Cowboy* is playing there. My parents saw it last fall and didn't care for it, but it won Best Picture at the Academy Awards. Want to go?"

I stopped my scrubbing. "Only if you promise to buy us popcorn and beer."

Ben snickered.

"Sure, boyfriend. I'll bring a blanket too."

MIDNIGHT COWBOY TURNED out to be the weirdest film I'd ever seen, even stranger than *Fellini Satyricon*. Jon Voight, a good-looking guy, portrayed Joe Buck, a dishwasher from Texas who comes to New York City in search of a wealthy woman to exploit. He joins forces with a two-bit con man named Ratso Rizzo, portrayed by Dustin Hoffman. Rizzo suffers from poor health and a limp. Things go from bad to worse as the story progresses, and Joe eventually turns to hustling gay men for cash.

The movie was rated X.

Because it was a Tuesday night, hardly any cars were present at the theater, maybe a dozen at most. Ben parked the GTO about thirty yards from the nearest vehicle. We had a six-pack Ben had bought at a sketchy convenience store where they didn't check IDs, and we'd purchased a box of popcorn at the theater's concession stand. In the GTO's back seat, we snuggled under the blanket Ben had brought. Ben rested his arm on my shoulders and occasionally he'd nuzzle my ear or kiss me on the cheek.

The movie, while somewhat depressing, was made special by the performances of Hoffman and Voight. They didn't even seem like they were acting. Their characters came across as genuine people caught up in a world they were unprepared to deal with, a pair of losers who failed at everything they tried to accomplish during the film.

Halfway through the movie, the popcorn was gone, and I felt a little woozy from the beer I'd drunk. I slipped my hand under the blanket and placed it between Ben's thighs. Right away, I felt him stiffen. Emboldened by the tawdry story unfolding on the movie screen, I popped the button on Ben's jeans and lowered his zipper. Then I worked my fingers inside his briefs.

Ben looked at the headliner and clenched his jaw while I stroked him, and it didn't take long before his hips bucked. He groaned deeply in his throat, and suddenly my hand was wet and sticky. I wiped it clean on the blanket while Ben's breathing slowed.

Ben looked at me and winked while his lips parted into a grin. "Want me to return the favor?"

Moments later, my pants were open and Ben's face was burrowed in my lap. He slurped away as I stared at the movie screen, feeling so damned good I wanted to shout.

But then something weird happened: a beam of light from outside the car shone into the back seat and I jerked in reaction. Ben bolted into a sitting position while I covered myself with the blanket and squinted at the brightness.

A baritone voice with a Florida drawl spoke. "Out of the car, boys—now."

The voice belonged to a cop with a badge, a hat, a nightstick, and a gun.

I zipped up my jeans and buttoned them as quickly as I could. Then Ben and I scrambled from the back seat and stood side by side next to the GTO with our hands at our hips. Our breaths steamed in the chilly night air.

The cop was a tall guy with broad shoulders and big hands. He tapped the GTO's passenger window with his flashlight. "Whose car?"

Ben's voice broke like he was thirteen years old. "It's mine."

"Let me see your driver's license."

Ben pulled out his wallet and handed the license to the cop.

The cop focused his flashlight on the license while he chewed his lips. Then he shone the light in Ben's face. "Benjamin, you ought to know better than to do that sort of thing in a public place like this. It's illegal and I'm sure you know that."

Ben swallowed. "Yes, sir, I do."

The cop swung his light to my face and I squinted.

"Son, if you have a driver's license, let me see it now."

After I gave the cop my license, he studied it. Then he shone the light in *my* face again. "John, maybe that sort of behavior's okay in Pinellas County, but it's not tolerated in Brevard. I'm placing both you boys under arrest for lewd and lascivious conduct."

My knees wobbled and my vision blurred.

We're going to jail?

The cop swung his light back to Ben. "Lock up your car."

The ride to Titusville in the back of the cop's cruiser seemed to last forever. Both Ben and I sniffled while tears streamed down our faces, and our lips trembled. A police dispatcher's voice barked on the cruiser's radio, and I kept asking myself what would happen to me and Ben. I was sure we'd have to contact Ben's parents to bail us out of jail, and how would they react to the circumstances of our arrest?

What would my mom and sister think when they found out? And would the university be notified? If so, would we get kicked out of school?

This whole thing was a nightmare. How could we have been so careless and stupid?

At the county jail in Titusville our mug shots were taken, and we got fingerprinted by a sheriff's deputy as big as Frankenstein. Ben was permitted to phone his parents.

We surrendered possession of our wallets, belts, wristwatches, and Ben's car keys before they placed us in a holding cell that stank of cigarette smoke and disinfectant. Overhead, a fluorescent ceiling fixture hummed and flickered. The cell's only furnishings were wooden benches and a toilet with no seat.

Three other prisoners were present. Two were guys who'd brawled in a local bar. One guy had a shiner, the other a cut lip. The third prisoner was a man in rags with the DTs. He shook and whimpered while rolling around on the concrete floor.

Ben and I didn't say a word to each other or anyone else. We sat on a bench with our forearms resting on our knees and our chins lowered. I had a raging headache that caused a ringing in my ears.

Ninety minutes passed before a deputy came for us and told us Ben's parents had posted our bail. They'd come to take us home, he said.

After our possessions got returned to us, the deputy released us into the jail's lobby where Will and Sarah Stonecipher waited. They sat on a wooden bench, and both of them looked stricken, especially Sarah, whose eyes were puffy and red. Will's shoulders sagged when he rose from the bench. His mouth was a thin line when he looked at Ben.

"Where is your car?" he asked.

After Ben explained, Will said, "You can go get it tomorrow. I'm sure the drive-in's closed by now."

In the jail's shadowy parking lot, Ben and I climbed into the cavernous back seat of Will's Cadillac while Sarah sat in front and Will drove.

"Dad," Ben said once we were underway, "I want to explain—"

"We'll talk when we get home," Will responded. "Stay quiet for now."

A half hour later, we all sat in the Stoneciphers' living room, me and Ben on the sofa, Will and Sarah in wingback chairs facing us. Two table lamps were lit, and their warm glow was such a contrast to the spooky lighting in the holding cell. Over on the fireplace mantel, an antique clock ticked. The aspirin tablets Sarah had given me slowly dulled my headache, but the time was close to 1:00 a.m. and I felt exhausted by the events of our evening.

"Tell us what happened," Will said to Ben.

Ben's voice had a quiver when he said, "Are you sure you want to know?"

Will nodded. "We'll find out sooner or later, so you might as well tell us now."

Ben rested his forearms on his knees. He moistened his lips and cleared his throat. "Johnny and I are gay—he's been my boyfriend since October. At the drive-in, we were fooling around in the back seat of my car when an off-duty cop caught us in the act."

Sarah bit her knuckles while her eyes glistened with tears. Her gaze flitted back and forth between me and Ben.

"When you say fooling around," Will said to Ben, "exactly what were you and Johnny doing?"

Ben lowered his gaze and worked his jaw from side to side. Then he looked up at Will. "I had Johnny's penis in my mouth, Dad. It's what gay men do."

"Oh, Ben," Sarah cried. "How could you?"

"I'm sorry, Mom—not for being gay but for being stupid. We had no business doing that sort of thing in a public place."

"News of your arrests may appear in the local newspaper," Will said, "and Lord help us if it does. We'll be disgraced before all of Merritt Island."

"Is this Johnny's doing?" Sarah asked Ben. She looked at me briefly before returning her gaze to Ben. "Did he lead you down this path?"

"Absolutely not," Ben said, straightening his spine. "Don't think that for a minute. You should both know that Johnny's not my first boyfriend. There was another, back in high school."

"Who?" Sarah asked.

"I'm not going to tell you," Ben said to Sarah, "because what I did then is my private business. But Chuck knew about it and he never judged me for being gay—he accepted me for who I am. I hope you and Dad can do the same."

"It's late," Will said as he rose to his feet, "and we're all tired. In the morning, I'll call Bob Tate for a referral to a criminal lawyer. This sort of thing can ruin a young man's life, but maybe we can keep that from happening. There has to be a way."

Speak up.

"Will and Sarah, I feel terrible about this. It's as much my fault as Ben's. We both acted stupidly and we know it. But please understand that I love Ben more than anyone else in the world. That may sound strange to you, but it's true. And whatever happens in the days ahead, I'll still love him."

Will and Sarah lowered their gazes. They didn't say anything in response to my statement; they just told us good night and left the room.

In Ben's bedroom, we undressed and showered together. I felt like I was washing away the stink of the jail and the stigma of my arrest as I scrubbed my skin with soap and a washcloth. The warm water pounding my shoulders relaxed some of the tension inside me.

While Ben washed my back, he said, "Thanks for saying what you did to my parents. It meant a lot to me to hear those words come from you, especially at a time like this. We'll get through this together somehow, Johnny. I'm not letting anything come between us."

"Do you think your parents hate me now?"

"Not really. But look—we just dumped a bombshell on them, and right now, they're probably in shock. I'm sure they don't know *what* to think about what happened tonight, much less about you and me being a couple. We'll have to give them time to absorb it all."

"Should I go back to St. Petersburg Beach tomorrow?"

Ben stopped scrubbing my back, took me by my shoulders, and turned me around so I faced him. "I'm not *letting* you leave. If you did, it would look like we're ashamed of loving each other."

I lowered my gaze and listened to water gurgle in the shower drain.

"Look at me, Johnny."

I gazed into Ben's beautiful eyes.

"Are you ashamed of loving me?" he asked.

I shook my head.

"Then you're staying right here till it's time to go back to school. Agreed?"

"Okay, all right."

And so it was decided. We would stand our ground together and deal with whatever shit life might throw at us.

Chapter Sixteen

IN THE DAYS following our arrest, I learned a lot about Florida law that I hadn't known before.

Will, Ben, and I met with a Titusville criminal lawyer named Jeff Sawyer, a guy in his midthirties with a swanky office in a bank building, a slick haircut, and a tailored suit. He was a former prosecutor.

"In the eyes of Florida criminal law," he told us, "Ben and Johnny are still minors, so their cases will process through the juvenile justice system, and that's good. Our area newspapers have a policy of not printing names of juveniles charged with crimes. Also, court records of an individual's juvenile offenses are sealed when he reaches the age of twenty-one, so they don't become part of his permanent record."

Ben and I glanced at each other while Sawyer continued.

"Our juvenile court judge in Brevard County is Robert Tilly. I've had multiple cases before him, both as a prosecutor and a defense lawyer. He's a conservative guy— the boys' conduct at the drive-in theater won't sit well with him. But since this is a first offense for both of them and a misdemeanor, the judge will likely put Ben and Johnny on probation for six months. If they stay out of trouble during that time, the court will dismiss the charges. That way they won't even have a conviction on their juvenile records."

Ben and I looked at each other again while we both let out our breaths.

Will rearranged his limbs in the chair he sat on. "Will the university be notified of the charges against Ben and Johnny?"

Sawyer rubbed his chin with a knuckle. "To my knowledge, the state attorney's office won't tell the school nor will the court. The student code of conduct may require Ben and Johnny to inform the university of their arrests, but if they don't, who's the wiser?"

ON SATURDAY MORNING at the end of spring break, Ben and I drove to St. Petersburg Beach in the GTO, and now Ben, my mom, and I occupied the living room at my family home. Ben and I sat next to each other on the love seat while Mom rested in her easy chair.

The day before, when I had called Mom and told her Ben and I would come over Saturday, she sounded surprised.

"I thought you were staying in Merritt Island until school starts."

"That was the plan," I said, "but there's been some trouble over here. Ben and I need to talk with you about it, and I don't want Tricia there when we do. Tomorrow, Ben and I should get to St. Petersburg Beach around noon. Maybe we can talk after lunch."

Now, in the living room, my heart slammed against my rib cage when I looked into Mom's eyes. She wore wool slacks and a pullover sweater, and her hair, like always, was neatly combed. She had crossed one knee over her other one, and her hands rested in her lap. I took a deep breath and heard myself talk in a voice that didn't sound exactly like mine.

"What I'm about to say is going to disappoint you, I know, but I'd rather you heard it from me instead of someone else."

"All right," Mom said.

The room seemed to shrink as I continued. "I'm gay and so is Ben. We've been boyfriends for nearly five months—we're in love. I know that may sound strange, but it's how things are and I've never felt so happy in my life."

Mom closed her eyes and nodded. She looked at me and said, "When Ben visited here at Christmastime, I suspected something was going on between you two."

"Why?"

"Because of the way you look at each other when you're together."

Ben and I exchanged glances before I swung my gaze back to Mom. "Are we that obvious?"

She nodded. "At least to me, but then I'm your mother, so of course I'd notice."

"Are you ashamed of me?"

"Of course not. If Ben makes you happy, it's all that's important. He seems like a fine young man from a good family. Have you told Ben's parents?"

I lowered my chin and cleared my throat. Then I brought my gaze to Mom's.

"They sort of found out...the hard way."

Mom arched her eyebrows.

Go on...

The story of our arrests in Melbourne spilled from my lips as if I couldn't get the words out of my mouth quickly enough. I told Mom everything, all the details while she listened impassively. I told her about the meeting with Sawyer and what he'd said to us.

At the end, all I could think to say was, "I know we acted stupidly at the drive-in, and I hope you'll forgive us for it. Nothing like that will happen again, I promise."

Mom shifted her weight in the easy chair. "Listen," she said while her gaze traveled from Ben to me, "we all do things at your age we regret. That's how young people learn. But it sounds like no permanent damage was done."

Mom asked about Sawyer's fee for representing me.

"Mr. Stonecipher is taking care of it," I told her. "This summer, I'll repay him by working in Merritt Island with Ben."

That arrangement was one I'd proposed to Will right after he wrote a $250 check to Sawyer on my behalf, at the conclusion of our meeting with Sawyer. Will, Ben, and I were riding back to Merritt Island in the Cadillac when I made my pitch.

"I'll work for a dollar an hour. I'll do any task you assign me, no matter how lowly or nasty it is, and I'll pay back every cent I owe you. If you'll let me live in your house this summer, I'll pay you for my room and board as well, whatever you think is reasonable."

The four of us—Will, Sarah, Ben, and I— discussed the arrangement over dinner that same day. By then, I had already noticed a lessening of tension between Ben's parents and me, and I sensed they'd resigned themselves to the fact I would be part of Ben's life whether they liked it or not.

"Will and I talked at length earlier," Sarah told me. "You needn't pay room and board, just help with the household chores. But we'll expect you to occupy Chuck's room. No more sleeping in Ben's, is that clear?"

Ben and I looked at each other and he shrugged as if to say, "What choice do we have?"

"All right," I said. "I understand."

Now, in our living room, Mom uncrossed her legs and wove her fingers together at a knee. "So you'll spend this summer at the Stoneciphers' property?"

I nodded. "Mr. Sawyer's fee is my responsibility, and I intend to pay it."

"It's fine with me," Mom said, "if that's how you want to handle things."

Mom looked at Ben. "I know your family's endured a terrible tragedy with the loss of your brother. And I'm sure your arrest has been hard on everyone as well. Sometimes, it seems as if life is testing us to see if we'll break under the pressure."

Ben lowered his chin and nodded while Mom continued.

"I hope having Johnny in your life will help you get through it all. And I want you to know that I don't disapprove of your relationship with him in the least. I know you love Johnny and he loves you, so now you're part of our family. You are always welcome here, Ben."

"Thanks, Mrs. Darling," Ben said, looking up.

I love my mom.

Chapter Seventeen

BACK IN GAINESVILLE, the weather had changed from chilly and wet to sunny and cool. The dogwood trees on campus were in bloom, looking like cream-colored clouds tossed against the backdrop of the university's redbrick buildings. When I walked to my morning classes, the air smelled fresh and fragrant. Dew glistened in the grass and songbirds tootled.

Instead of a science class, that quarter I was taking a course in logic, a subject far more interesting than the islets of Langerhans. I was learning a whole new language of sorts. My favorite term was *non sequitur* because, in a sense, my entire life had become a *non sequitur*. The person I was then had no logical connection to who I had been before I came to Gainesville. I was more independent. I could take care of myself, and was learning the art of critical thinking. Most importantly, I was Ben's lover and confidant.

Through the mail, we learned that Jeff Sawyer had entered not-guilty pleas to the charges against us. A pretrial hearing was set for a Tuesday at the end of April, and Sawyer said our attendance was mandatory so we'd have to skip classes that day. The following week, Sawyer would meet with an assistant state attorney assigned to our cases and attempt to negotiate a plea deal.

ON A TUESDAY evening in mid-April, Steve phoned me. I hadn't spoken to him since the morning after the Sebring race, and like always, the sound of his syrupy voice made my pulse quicken. I stood next to our wall-mounted phone, fingering the receiver and twisting the spirally phone cord around my finger while Steve talked.

"I'm coming up to Gainesville next Friday. A track team member will give me a tour of campus, and I'll stay in a motel on Thirteenth Street Friday night. I was hoping you and I could, you know..."

Ben was down the hall, taking his evening shower, so I could speak freely.

"Listen, I tried to explain this to you on the drive home from the raceway. Ben and I are a couple—we belong to each other—and I can't just spend the night with you next Friday. It would hurt Ben's feelings and I'd feel lousy about it too."

"What about *my* feelings," Steve asked, "and what about our friendship? Don't they count for anything?"

"Of course they do, it's just..."

Steve's voice had an edge to it now.

"Forget it, Johnny—forget I even called."

Steve hung up before I could say anything more, and I was left standing there and feeling like an idiot. Had I done the right thing in declining Steve's invitation? Had I irreparably damaged what was once my closest friendship?

I stared into space while the dial tone hummed in my ear.

THE WEDNESDAY BEFORE Steve's campus visit, Ben and I took a pre-dinner walk to Lake Alice. The days had grown longer now, and at 5:30, there was still plenty of daylight. All around us, banks of azaleas were in bloom; they looked like parade floats with their showy blossoms of red, purple, pink, and white. The air was fragrant from all the new growth on trees and shrubs. In the woods surrounding the lake, violet blossoms on wisteria vines reminded me of bunches of grapes, and the sound of a woodpecker's knocking echoed through the trees.

As we walked, I told Ben about the call I'd received from Steve last week.

"I know I shouldn't feel guilty about telling him no, but I do. We've been the closest of friends for a long time, and I don't want to lose that."

"Of course you don't," Ben said, "but he shouldn't insist on sex as a condition of his friendship. If he's truly your friend—and I believe he is—he should understand that you're already spoken for and he needs to back off."

"You're right," I said while I gazed at the lake's placid surface.

"Why don't you call him later today?" Ben suggested. "Ask him to have dinner with you Friday. There's that pizza place on University Avenue where the prices aren't too high."

Later, when I phoned Steve, his voice sounded guarded.

"If I meet you for dinner, will you visit my motel room afterward?"

I fingered the receiver while I tried to think of what to say.

"I can't do that, and we should talk about *why* I can't when we meet. Your friendship's important to me, and I don't want any misunderstandings between us."

There was silence on the line for a few moments. Then Steve said, "I'll see you at the restaurant Friday. Is seven o'clock good for you?"

IT RAINED LIKE hell Friday night, and I used an umbrella to shield myself when I walked across campus to reach the restaurant. I sloshed through puddles while listening to rain clatter against the sodden ground. I passed by the Murphree Area dormitory where desk lamps in many rooms glowed and guys studied, even though the weekend had arrived.

I crossed University Avenue in the middle of the block, pausing in the median to wait for a break in the traffic. Headlights shone in my face and made me squint. Windshield wipers clacked, and cars spewed plumes of rainwater when they passed me. Already the lower halves of my pant legs were soaked.

The pizza place was crowded with students, the crush of voices in the room deafening. Male chuckles mixed with co-ed giggles. The place smelled of pepperoni and damp clothing. A juke box played "Come and Get It" by Badfinger.

I found Steve seated at a table with four chairs, and right away, I noticed something strange. A man's zippered jacket hung from the back of a chair opposite Steve, and a half-full glass of beer sat on the table in front of the chair with the jacket. Steve sipped from a glass of cola and ice while he studied a menu.

When I approached and Steve saw me, a grin crossed his face as he rose to shake my hand. He looked princely in a crew-neck sweater and blue jeans. Glow from the restaurant's ceiling fixtures made his aquamarine eyes sparkle.

"You look like you fell into a mud puddle," he told me while his gaze traveled from my forehead to my feet.

I pointed to the beer on the table. "Whose is that?"

"Castleman's."

"What the hell is *he* doing here?"

Steve shrugged. "I asked him to come up with me. It's not often I have a motel room, and I figured since you and I aren't going to put it to use, at least Castleman and I can."

I could almost feel steam coming out of my ears.

"Look, I don't understand this. I thought you and I were having dinner tonight so we could talk about personal things, but with Castleman here, we can't do that."

Steve shrugged again. "I guess that talk will have to wait for some other time."

Castleman approached. He looked much the same as when he'd taught my driver's ed class: tall and rangy with dark hair and eyes. His cheekbones were craggy, his nose came to a point, and a five-o'clock shadow blued his face.

Most people would have said he was good-looking.

When he and I shook hands, his grip was firm and warm, and he smiled when his gaze met mine.

"Hi, Coach Castleman. How are you?"

"Johnny," he said in his rich baritone, "at this point, I think you're old enough to call me Pete. Will you do that from now on?"

We all took seats, and moments later, when the waitress came to our table, I ordered a cola with ice. Castleman drained his beer and asked for another.

Already I felt uncomfortable for more reasons than one.

First of all, I felt ambushed. Steve should have let me know about Castleman before my arrival, but I suspected he'd intentionally created a situation I wasn't prepared for, perhaps as revenge for my refusal to come to his motel room that night. Or maybe he was trying to make me jealous, and if so, he had accomplished just that. I was angry that Castleman was coming between me and Steve.

And then there was something else.

I didn't know whether Steve had told Castleman I was aware of their sexual relationship, nor did I know if Steve had told Castleman that I'd had sex with Steve more than once. Was I supposed to assume that everyone at the table was fully informed on these matters? Or should I behave as though we were all just friends and nothing more?

Castleman said, "Dinner's on me tonight, guys."

When the waitress returned with my cola and Castleman's beer, the three of us ordered a large pizza to share. Then we talked.

I asked Steve about his campus tour, and he spent several minutes describing all that he had seen that day, including the track team's training facility. "It's pretty damned impressive, with a first-class locker room and all."

It seemed Castleman had taken the tour along with Steve—in his capacity as Steve's cross-country coach, of course—and I wondered what Steve's parents would think if they knew what Steve and Castleman would be up to later that night.

I pointed to Castleman's college class ring from Drake University. "Did you run track there?"

He nodded. "I was a miler; my best time was four minutes, eighteen seconds."

Steve whistled. "That's amazing," he said.

I felt rankled by Steve's fawning over Castleman. Sure, Castleman was good-looking, but he had ten years on Steve and god knew what would happen if details of their ongoing affair reached the wrong ears. This was 1970, a conservative era in Florida, and Castleman would likely lose his job if the school board found out he was gay.

Once our pizza was brought to the table, we all took slices. The pizza smelled delicious, but at that point, I wasn't even hungry. The whole situation made me nervous, and all I wanted to do was leave. When Castleman asked me about

UF and whether I liked it there, I felt so distracted I had to take a few seconds to collect my thoughts before I answered.

"It was hard at first," I told him, "adjusting to living away from my family and not seeing my friends from home."

Castleman nodded. "That's what I told Steve on the drive up. Going away to school isn't for everyone. And besides, St. Pete Junior College is an excellent school—he could save a lot of money by attending there."

I only ate one slice of pizza before Castleman called for the check, and I felt relieved when the time came for me to say goodbye. Handshakes were exchanged, and I told Steve I'd see him down south when spring quarter ended, but I didn't mention that I'd spend my summer on Merritt Island because I knew he'd be unhappy when he learned that I would.

The rain had let up when I left the restaurant, and I made my way back across campus. A fine mist swirled in the air. All around me water dripped from the limbs of live oaks, and not many people were about. I swung my rolled-up umbrella as I walked along, and all I could think about was Steve and Castleman and what they would do once they arrived at the motel.

Okay, I knew I shouldn't care about their private life. After all, it was their business, not mine. But I *did* care, and far too much. Just thinking of Castleman mounting Steve got my breath whistling in my nose. And then it occurred to me that Steve might have similar feelings about my relationship with Ben. After all, on the way home from the Sebring race, he'd made it clear that he wanted me as his lover, and that the next school year, he'd like to live with me at UF.

But that wasn't what I wanted.

Or was it?

Shit.

Chapter Eighteen

"YOU YOUNG GENTLEMEN ought to know that engaging in this sort of behavior at a drive-in theater is not only unacceptable, but it's illegal."

Ben and I stood side by side in a windowless courtroom in the Brevard County Courthouse in Titusville, facing Circuit Judge Tilly, a white-haired guy who was stoop-shouldered and walked with the help of a cane. Tilly sat behind an elevated bench, wearing a black robe. His bushy eyebrows twitched as he spoke.

Jeff Sawyer also stood with us before the judge, while Ben's parents and my mom sat out in the gallery. Thank god a court stenographer and a bailiff were the only other persons present.

I wore my sports jacket, dress slacks, a white shirt, and a necktie, and I did my best to keep my knees from shaking. Ben wore a dark suit and tie, and he kept licking his lips.

The judge swiveled in his chair toward an assistant state attorney who didn't look much older than me and Ben. "I understand the State and defense counsel have a joint recommendation to the court regarding disposition of the charges against these boys?"

"We do, Your Honor," the assistant state attorney said.

"And?"

"The State's agreeable to the defendants changing their pleas to no contest and the court's withholding adjudication of guilt. The defendants would be put on probation for a period of six months. If they serve their probation without incident, the court will dismiss the charges against them and the records of their arrests will be sealed."

Tilly looked at Jeff Sawyer. "Is that correct, Counsel?"

"Yes, Your Honor."

The judge looked at me. "Mr. Darling, are you agreeable to the terms recited by the assistant state attorney?"

I nodded. "Yes, sir."

The judge turned to Ben. "Mr. Stonecipher, how about you?"

Ben's voice cracked when he answered. "Yes, Your Honor."

The judge pointed fingers at me and Ben. "Boys, I'm sure this entire incident has been an embarrassment, not only to you but also to your families. Your behavior at the theater was unbecoming of university students, and I want you to know that if you get into any more trouble while you're on probation, I won't be so lenient when we see each other again. Understood?"

Ben and I both replied, "Yes, sir."

"The plea agreement's acceptable to the court," Tilly said. Then he looked at Sawyer. "Counsel, furnish me with a written order to sign, stating the terms of the agreement and approving it. Court's adjourned."

We all rose as Tilly hobbled off the bench and walked through a swinging door.

In a hallway outside the courtroom, everyone but the assistant state attorney gathered around Jeff Sawyer.

Sawyer told us, "Johnny and Ben are lucky this case was disposed of as it was. In certain other counties, it would have been far worse; they could have been sentenced to jail for a spell."

A shiver ran through me when Sawyer mentioned jail.

"Needless to say," Sawyer told us, "both boys need to be on their best behavior between now and the end of November. Any questions?"

Nobody said a word, and hopefully, our nightmare was over.

ON A SATURDAY midmorning in early May, the sun shone, and a light breeze tickled my cheeks while Ben and I strolled along the shore in Pass-a-Grille Beach. We both wore swim trunks and shuffled our bare feet in the sugar-like sand. A flock of brown pelicans flew overhead in a vee formation, looking like a squadron of warplanes. Gentle waves lapped at the sand; their remnants swirled around our ankles. The temperature was in the low eighties, perfect for beach going.

The previous afternoon, we'd made the two-hour drive down from Gainesville in the GTO, both of us feeling excited about spending the weekend at the coast. Mom made my favorite meal for Friday's dinner: fresh Gulf shrimp battered and fried, homemade tartar sauce, french fries, and a garden salad with Italian dressing.

Just before dinner Mom took me aside while Ben talked with his folks on the phone in our living room. We spoke in whispers while Mom sliced a Ruskin tomato as big as my fist and as red as a stop sign.

"I know you and Ben will share your bed tonight," Mom said, "and that's fine. But I felt your sister should know what's going on between you two, so last night, I told her Ben is your boyfriend. I didn't want her to find out by accident."

"What did Tricia say?"

"She was shocked, of course. I had to explain a few things to her."

"Like what?"

"She wanted to know what two boys do with each other when they're in the bedroom."

The tops of my ears burned, but I also felt a sense of relief. Now everyone in our household, and at the Stoneciphers', knew the truth about me and Ben. No more secrets or sneaking around.

At the dinner table Tricia fidgeted while her gaze traveled between me and Ben, and I felt pretty sure she was trying to imagine us pawing each other between the sheets in my bedroom. But after Ben asked her a few questions about her recent school activities, she seemed to calm down as she responded, and I sensed she'd accept my relationship with Ben pretty quickly.

When Ben and I went to bed on Friday night we were both tired and decided to postpone sex until the next evening. We fell asleep spoon-style wearing only our briefs, and I slept like I'd been drugged.

Now, on Saturday, as Ben and I walked the shore, we passed by groups of high school and college-age kids. Bikini-clad girls lay on blankets, sunning themselves, while guys in swim trunks tossed footballs and Frisbees. A cop driving a Jeep passed by us, looking out of place in his uniform. The Jeep's wheels kicked up sand.

We'd already planned out our day. After lunch, we would buy bait at the Merry Pier, just down the street from my house, and then we'd fish from the seawall on the Intracoastal Waterway. That night, we'd attend a concert at Jack Russell Stadium in Clearwater where three rock bands would play outdoors. A Tampa radio station was sponsoring the show.

When we talked about going to the concert, Ben asked if we should invite Steve or some of my other friends to join us.

Right away, I shook my head. "I'm still sore at Steve for showing up in Gainesville with Castleman. He did it to embarrass me and make me feel jealous, and now it's going to be a while before I feel like seeing him again. Honestly, I don't even want him to know we're in town."

Ben shrugged. "It's your call. I only thought—"

"Let's just go by ourselves, okay?"

THE CONCERT SATURDAY night turned out to be a disaster. The stadium was packed with people in their midteens to early twenties. Many wore bell-bottom jeans and were barefooted. A lot of guys had long hair, and the odor of burning marijuana scented the air.

The members of the first band looked like they were still in high school. Their attempt at playing songs by the Rolling Stones failed miserably, and their lead singer couldn't dance or sing like Mick Jagger at all. The crowd booed them off the stage after a half-dozen numbers. When they departed, the band's lead singer dropped his pants and mooned the crowd.

The second group was much better, but their equipment had a glitch that caused the sound to die after they played three songs. Technicians were called in and the crowd grew restless. Several guys in the audience hollered, "I want my money back." By the time the glitch was fixed, the band had time to play two more songs by Creedence Clearwater Revival before they had to leave the stage to make way for the headliner act.

An announcer explained that under the city's sound ordinance, the concert must end by 10:00 p.m. and the time was already 9:15.

Again, the crowd booed.

The Impacs, a group I had seen perform when I was in high school, was the third band and they were pretty good, but twenty minutes into their set, lightning crackled to the west and thunder rumbled as a storm rolled ashore from the Gulf. Minutes later, the wind picked up and rain fell in buckets. Everyone ran for the exits which were, of course, bottlenecked. By the time Ben and I reached his car, our clothes stuck to us like second skins and our hair was plastered to our skulls.

We sat in the GTO's front seats, listening to rain pound the hood and windshield.

Ben turned to me and said, "I guess this wasn't such a good idea, was it?"

We both laughed like fools while we peeled off our shirts and used them to mop our faces. Ben started the GTO's engine, and we cruised down Gulf-to-Bay Boulevard, toward US 19. Both of us kept our windows rolled up so we could stay somewhat warm. Ben flicked on the radio, to the station that had sponsored the concert, and we listened to a DJ talk over the phone with a disgruntled attendee.

"The whole thing was a screw-up," the attendee said. "You should refund people's money."

"Hey, man," the DJ said, "we can't control the weather."

By the time we returned to my house, the time was 10:30 and my mom and sister watched *Mannix*, a popular detective TV show. Both Tricia and Mom wore nightgowns. When we walked in the door shirtless and damp, they looked at us with puzzled expressions.

After I explained what had happened at the concert, I grabbed two towels from our linen closet. Ben and I visited my bedroom and closed the door. We got out of our wet clothes—all of them—and when my gaze traveled over Ben's naked flesh, I felt the urge to grab him and pull him onto my bed. But I didn't because Mom had been very understanding about Ben sharing my room with me that weekend, and I didn't want to make a bunch of noise and make her think I was taking advantage of the situation.

Sex could wait until after everyone's lights were switched off.

Ben yawned while he stepped into a pair of dry briefs.

"Are you tired?" I asked.

He nodded. "How about you?"

"I could use a little something to eat before we go to bed."

After we dressed in dry clothes, we raided the cupboards and fridge. Seated at the kitchen table, we munched on cookies and chased them with cold milk while out in the living room, the TV droned.

"I'm sorry our evening didn't work out," I told Ben. "What a mess."

He shrugged. "As far as I'm concerned, the best part's still to come."

I reached beneath the table and squeezed Ben's knee while our gazes met and Ben waggled his eyebrows. Already I was stiff inside my shorts because I knew what we'd do in my bedroom once Mom and Tricia were asleep in theirs.

After the *Mannix* episode concluded, Mom switched off the TV and entered the kitchen. "Good night, honey," she said to me before kissing my cheek. Then she said good night to Ben and kissed his cheek as well, and the sight of her doing so made me feel all warm inside, like I'd swallowed a shot of Southern Comfort. By kissing Ben, Mom was letting both of us know she accepted our relationship.

What more could a faggot ask of his mother?

Minutes later, the household lights were off. Silvery moonlight stole into my room through the venetian blinds while Ben and I undressed. Once naked, we slipped between the sheets and our bodies entwined. I brought my mouth to Ben's. Our tongues dueled while we caressed each other.

When we reached orgasm, Ben let out a wail. "Johnny Darling," he cried, and my once-detested name had never sounded so beautiful.

After we cleaned ourselves up, we snuggled between the sheets with Ben's cheek resting on my sternum.

"I can hear your heartbeat," Ben said. He yawned and very quickly fell asleep.

I stared at the tongue-in-groove ceiling, listening to Ben's soft snoring. I kissed the crown of his head and buried the tip of my nose in his hair that smelled like freshly mown grass. I thought about all the difficulties Ben had faced during the past year: Chuck's death, Ben's mental illness, our arrests, the pressures at school, and the ones at Merritt Island, and I marveled at the way Ben had endured these challenges with such grace. Then I wondered if having me in his life had truly helped him get through it all.

Did I count that much?

It had been six months since our Cuba Libre Night. How quickly those months had passed, and it occurred to me that in all those months, Ben and I had never quarreled. A lot of couples, I knew from experience, squabbled constantly. How come Ben and I didn't? Was it because we weren't selfish people?

Then I thought of Steve and the sex I'd had with him and I knew it was selfish of me to get intimate with Steve when Ben and I were a couple. The last time I'd made love with Steve had been in his tent at Sebring six weeks ago, and I still hadn't told Ben about it. Should I? Or was it best to try and forget what happened?

When I thought of Steve that night at the pizza place in Gainesville, I worked my jaw from side to side while anger boiled in my chest. That entire evening had been designed to punish me for refusing to spend a night in Steve's motel room, and knowing that Steve had deliberately hurt my feelings was disappointing.

Steve's friendship had meant so much to me when we were only friends, but now the sex we'd shared had fucked up our friendship in a serious way. Steve wanted *more* than friendship from me, and while he was a beautiful, bright, and personable guy, he still wasn't Ben.

Go to sleep, Darling. You're thinking too much.

I closed my eyes and listened to Ben snore.

Chapter Nineteen

SPRING QUARTER HAD ended, and like always, I felt exhausted when Mom arrived at UF on a Saturday to pick up me and my belongings. My final exams had been brutal, but I thought I'd done pretty well. I just didn't have any energy left, and it took all my strength to carry things down the stairs to Mom's car.

The weather had turned warm and humid in Gainesville, and I sweated through my T-shirt as I stacked boxes in the trunk and rear seat of Mom's car. I had so much stuff I wouldn't even be able to lie down and sleep during the trip home.

Ben was already gone. His folks had picked him up the day before, and it killed me to see him go, knowing that I wouldn't see him for ten days. Our dorm room, our little love sanctum, looked forlorn now that it was stripped of our personal possessions.

Our plan—Ben's and mine—was simple. I'd spend a week or so in St. Petersburg Beach, where I'd stow my things and spend a little time with my mom and sister. On June 15, Ben would pick me up, along with whatever clothing I'd need in Merritt Island, and then we would head for the east coast.

It would take me till mid-July before I earned enough money to reimburse Ben's dad for the legal fees he had paid Jeff Sawyer. Beyond that, who knew? I might remain in Merritt Island until school started, or I might spend a few weeks at home before returning to Gainesville for fall quarter. I would play that by ear and see how things went between me and Ben's folks while I was living with them.

When they had picked up Ben yesterday, both Will and Sarah were friendly enough, but I hadn't gotten a hug or a kiss on the cheek from Sarah like I thought I might.

Maybe that was expecting too much.

The drive to St. Petersburg Beach seemed to last forever. Mom's car was not air-conditioned. Hot air rushed through the interior as we cruised down I-75, and heat shimmered over the asphalt roadbed. My T-shirt dampened in the armpits. Mom and I had to practically shout at each other to be heard over the engine's roar and the wind coming in the windows. We talked about my exams and what courses I'd take in the fall, and we spoke of the work I'd do in Merritt Island that summer.

Then our conversation turned to Ben.

"How do his parents feel about you two being a couple?" Mom asked.

I rearranged my limbs in the car seat before I answered.

"It's hard to tell. I mean, I'm sure they're not happy about it. Ben's their golden boy, the heir to the throne so to speak. I think they expected him to get married and have kids, and I don't fit into that equation. But they'll tolerate me, I suppose."

"Give them a chance," Mom said. "You're a nice person, and when they get to know you better, they'll probably warm up to you. These things take time."

Once we pulled into our driveway in St. Petersburg Beach, I deferred unloading my things from the car. Instead, I stumbled to my bedroom and collapsed onto my bed. I kicked off my shoes but didn't even bother to wriggle out of my clothing, and in moments, I was in dreamland.

By the time I woke, the sky was nearly dark. I sat up and yawned a time or two while I rubbed my eyes with my knuckles. In the kitchen, Mom banged pots and pans. Scents of cooking garlic, tomato sauce, and oregano filled the house, and I knew what she was preparing—lasagna, one of her best dishes. My stomach growled, and then I realized I'd never eaten lunch.

I rose and looked at myself in the bureau mirror. My hair was in tangles, my T-shirt was rumpled, and stubble grew on my chin. My mouth tasted like it was full of pennies. I shuffled into the kitchen in my stocking feet and kissed Mom on the cheek while she stirred curly-edged noodles in a pot of boiling water.

"Hello, Rip Van Winkle," she said. "I thought you'd never wake up."

I yawned again and stretched my arms like a housecat. "Those all-nighters I pulled caught up with me, I guess. Do I have time for a shower before dinner?"

Mom nodded, and moments later, I stood under the nozzle, feeling warm water sluice over my limbs. I soaped my body and washed my hair while I whistled the tune to a Simon & Garfunkel song, "Cecilia." And then I wondered what I'd do with my evening. Now that I'd gotten some sleep I wouldn't want to go to bed until late.

I thought about Steve. It had been a month since I'd seen him in Gainesville, and we hadn't spoken since. Should I call him and suggest we get together?

Go ahead. Try to forget about Castleman and the pizza place. Steve's still your friend. You know he is.

After I put on fresh clothes, I called Steve from the extension phone in Mom's bedroom. Like always, his dad answered my call, and we talked for a least five minutes before Steve came on the line.

"Hey," he said. "Where are you?"

After I explained, I asked Steve what he was doing that night.

"I *was* going to the movies with Stewart, but his allergies are kicking up and he backed out. What are you up to?"

"Nothing," I said.

"Want to hang out, maybe go for a drive?"

I chewed my lips while wondering whether or not I should.

"Johnny?"

"Yeah?"

"Do you want to get together or not?"

WE SAT PARKED in a shadow cast by our high school's auditorium, a hulking cinder-block building I'd walked past a dozen times each day when I attended there. Moonlight illuminated Steve's facial expressions.

"I shouldn't have brought Castleman to Gainesville. It was wrong and I knew it, but I felt so damned angry that you wouldn't stay with me at the motel, and I guess I figured I'd get my revenge by making you jealous."

I thought back to that night when I'd walked back to the dorm and rain dripped from the live oaks on campus. I remembered how crappy I felt and how angry I was with Steve.

"I never thought you would hurt me intentionally," I said now, "but you sure did that night. It's why I haven't called you since."

Steve nodded. "I thought about calling *you*—many times—but I was afraid you'd hang up on me and I wouldn't have blamed you for it. I behaved like an asshole in Gainesville and I'm sorry for that. Will you forgive me?"

My brain churned while I worked my jaw. What should I say? In the nearly three years I had known Steve, he had never asked my forgiveness for anything he'd done, so this was a rare moment between us and I was pretty sure his apology was sincere.

He's your friend. Do the right thing.

I gazed out the windshield, into the darkness. In the distance, someone gunned his car engine and a muffler growled and popped.

Go on.

I looked at Steve. "Apology accepted."

He lifted his chin to stare at the VW's headliner, and a tear rolled from the corner of his eye before it slid down his cheek. He blinked and sniffled, then spoke in a shaky voice. "Thank you, Johnny. I couldn't stand it if I lost your friendship."

I felt like crying myself as the tension between me and Steve melted. I placed my hand on the back of his neck and gave him a squeeze. Then I left my hand where it was. The warmth of his skin felt good. This was the first time I'd touched him since the Sebring race.

"I'm not seeing Castleman anymore."

"Why? What happened?"

Steve sniffled again. He wiped his upper lip with the back of his wrist. Then he shrugged. "Things got too serious. Right after our trip to Gainesville, we had a long conversation. He told me he doesn't want me to go out of town for school. He prefers I stay here and attend community college. And he wants me to move in with him— not in the fall but right now."

I pulled my hand from Steve's neck and straightened my spine. "He said that?"

Steve nodded. "Now that I've graduated, it wouldn't break any rules if I did. But how could I explain the situation to my folks? And I don't want to stay here for school anyway—I want to go away like you did."

"Did you tell Castleman that?"

Steve nodded again. "He got upset when I did. I mean...he was in tears. He told me he's in love with me, that he wants us to spend our lives together, maybe move to someplace in Southern California where no one knows us and we can live as we please."

"Jesus..."

Steve blew air out his nose and shook his head. "What a mess. Huh?"

"Have you talked with him since?"

Steve shook his head again. "I think it's best I don't."

We sat in silence for a few minutes, listening to traffic pass on the nearby street. Then, for some reason I couldn't really understand, I felt famished.

"I need something to eat. Let's get a burger."

Steve nodded. He turned the key in the VW's ignition, and the engine sputtered to life. He flicked on the headlights and shifted into first gear. We left the school's parking lot and cruised down a well-lit avenue, passing darkened storefronts, gas stations, and churches with illuminated steeples. The time was around 9:30 when we reached the A&W drive-in on Treasure Island, where a girl came to our car and took our order: two burgers, one sack of fries to share, and two root beer slushees. All around us, high school kids on dates occupied cars. Guys wolfed down burgers while girls sipped from paper cups through straws.

A loud speaker played "American Woman" by the Guess Who, a song with a good beat. I liked the lead singer's raspy vocals, but I found it hard to feel cheerful after the discussion Steve and I had shared at the high school. I tried to imagine Castleman pleading his case to Steve but couldn't get the picture inside my head. Castleman had always seemed like such a composed and confident guy, but he clearly was not, at least when it came to Steve.

"So," Steve said, "we've talked enough about me for one night. What's going on with you and Ben?"

I shifted my butt in my seat. Then I explained how I'd spend most of the summer at the Stoneciphers', working in the groves and also at the cattle ranch. After the girl brought our food, I told Steve about Ben and me getting arrested in Brevard County and how I owed Ben's dad $250 for my legal fees.

Steve looked at me and knitted his eyebrows. "Does your mom know about this?"

"She knows everything."

Steve shook his head while reaching for the french fries. "Damn, Johnny, and I thought my life was crazy. What was jail like?"

"Awful, the most disgusting place I've ever been, and going to court was so embarrassing. My mom and Ben's parents were there, and the judge chewed us out right in front of them. I hope nothing like that ever happens to me again."

"When do you go to Merritt Island?"

"On the fifteenth," I said before sipping from my slushee, a sweet and creamy mix so cold it numbed the back of my throat.

"So you're here for about a week?"

I nodded and licked my lips.

Steve rubbed his chin with a knuckle. "Before you go, we should have a serious talk, the one we were *going* to share in Gainesville before my stupidity got in the way."

I nodded again. "My mom and sister will go to church tomorrow morning around ten—they won't be back till noon at the earliest. Why don't you come to my place around 10:30?"

RAIN FELL SUNDAY morning when Steve pulled to the curb in front of my house. Thunder rumbled and lightning flashed and the air smelled metallic. Steve made a dash from his VW to my front door, but his shoulders and the top of his head were soaked by the time he got inside. I loaned him a towel, and after he dried himself off, he borrowed my brush to put his hair in order. Like always, I was struck by his beauty.

I flicked on a floor lamp and we sat on the love seat, both of us hanging our hands between our knees. Outside, thunder rumbled anew while raindrops clattered in puddles.

Steve stared at his sandals and rubbed his lips together. "There are things I want to say to you—stuff I've thought about over and over—ever since the Sebring race."

"Go ahead."

Steve pointed to the open door of my bedroom. "Do you remember when you..."

"What?"

"You know, it was Thanksgiving weekend."

I lowered my gaze and bobbed my chin. "I'll never forget it."

"And I won't either. When I felt you inside me, I told myself, 'This is all I need to be happy.' It was a damned *epiphany*, Johnny. And when I think back to all those nights in high school when I slept over here, it seems like such a waste how we didn't touch each other."

I nodded my assent.

"Now it seems we're wasting more opportunities. You're my closest friend. Hell, you're even more than that— you're the guy I want to spend my life with. It's been okay with Castleman, but he's not you."

I shifted my weight on the love seat's cushion while I tried to decide what I should say. I drew a breath and let it out before gazing into Steve's eyes.

"If I didn't already have Ben, I would jump at the chance to be your boyfriend. Believe me I would."

Steve crinkled his forehead. "Does he really mean more to you than I do?"

"I'm sorry, but yes."

"How can that be?"

"It's hard to explain. Even before I had sex with Ben, he'd become a huge part of my life, someone I relied on for companionship. When we became lovers, Ben grew even more important to me. It's like we're one person; that's the only way I can describe how I feel about him."

Steve rose and paced the living room floor. "It could be the same with you and me if you'd only give me a chance, and you could do that before you leave for Merritt Island."

"How?"

Steve stopped pacing and rested his hands on his hips. "Spend a few nights with me at the Withlacoochee River. It'll be just the two of us with no interruptions. We can leave tomorrow and come back Thursday."

Steve referred to his family's fishing camp, situated sixty miles north of Tampa, a comfortable cabin with a dock and motorboat. The cabin sat on a very private wooded lot. I'd been there several times, but always with Steve's family or with a group of guys, never just with Steve.

I rubbed the back of my neck while I gazed at Steve. "What do you plan on doing while we're up there?"

Steve paced anew. "We have never spent that much time together, not when it's only the two of us. I want to see how it feels to live with you—even briefly. Is that asking too much?"

I lowered my gaze and rubbed the tops of my thighs with the palms of my hands. I didn't want to get Steve's hopes up by visiting the camp with him. If I went up there, things might only worsen between us. But Steve was right; he wasn't asking a lot, just a few days alone with me.

Go on, Darling.

"What time do you want to leave tomorrow?"

Chapter Twenty

THE WITHLACOOCHEE RIVER water was coffee-colored, stained by tannin in fallen leaves of live oaks that grew along its banks. Steve's cabin had a pitched roof, asbestos-shingle siding, a one-car garage, and a screened porch overlooking the river. There were two bedrooms, a full bath, a living room, a kitchen, and a dining area. The furnishings were out-of-date and beat up, but serviceable. A studio portrait of Steve and his brother, Nash, probably taken eight years ago, hung over the fireplace. The place smelled a bit musty, but it was clean and plenty of double-hung windows admitted sunlight into each room.

"We'll sleep in here," Steve told me, leading me into the larger bedroom, furnished with a queen-size bed with a chenille spread and four pillows, a double bureau with a mirror, a nightstand with a lamp, and a ladderback chair that I rested my overnight bag on. Venetian blinds hung at the windows.

After Steve tossed his bag onto the bed, we returned to his VW to unload groceries from the back seat and place them in the kitchen. We'd brought two cases of beer and we stashed a dozen cans in the fridge. Then Steve grabbed a key chain from a hook on the kitchen wall.

I followed him out to the dock.

The day was sunny and warm, and we both wore shorts and t-shirts. We passed beneath the limbs of massive live oaks that shaded the Bahia grass yard. Cicadas hummed, and overhead a bushy-tailed squirrel barked while it jumped from branch to branch. Houses on either side of us were barely visible because of dense foliage surrounding Steve's cabin.

The land on the other side of the river was undeveloped and forested.

Steve's family boat, a twenty-foot fiberglass center console model with a 50 HP Evinrude outboard, floated in a covered slip with a corrugated tin roof. Most of the dock was shaded by a live oak that towered over the river bank.

"I'm not sure whether it'll start right now," Steve said, pointing to the boat. "But I'll see if she cranks."

Steve climbed aboard, and the boat rocked from side to side in the placid water. He flipped a lever and manually lowered the outboard engine's stem into the water. He pumped a rubber ball attached to the engine's fuel line, to get gasoline flowing to the carburetor, then inserted the key into the boat's ignition and rotated his wrist.

All I heard was a clicking sound.

Steve puckered one side of his face and shook his head. "No one's been up here for a couple of months. I'll have to hook up the battery charger before we can fish."

We visited the garage, a dingy room that smelled of gasoline and rubber. Metal shelving was stacked with oil and paint cans and bags of fertilizer. Tools hung on a pegboard over a workbench. Steve found the battery charger, a device the size of a bread toaster with black and red cables and copper clips. Then we returned to the dock, where Steve plugged the charger into a pole outlet before he attached the clips to the battery posts. The charger made a little humming sound.

Beyond the dock, the river flowed at a lazy pace, with little eddies appearing here and there. I stood at the edge of the dock, next to Steve. He placed a hand on my shoulder. Then, after looking here and there, he kissed my temple.

"I'm so glad you're here," he said.

I looked into Steve's eyes and nodded before returning my gaze to the river.

Steve kept his hand on my shoulder.

"It'll take an hour for the battery to charge. Let's go back inside."

He led the way, and I liked the way his butt twitched in the seat of his shorts. His dark leg fuzz looked enticing.

We passed through the screened porch and entered the house, where Steve led me into the bedroom. He seized a tube of jelly from his bag and plucked two hand towels from the linen closet in the hallway. Then he peeled off his T-shirt and tossed it onto the bureau.

I stood at the foot of the bed with my gaze lowered. My hands hung at my hips, and I rubbed my thumbs against the pads of my index fingers.

"What is it?" Steve said.

"I'm not sure we should do this."

Steve let out his breath. "Come on, Johnny, it's what we're here for."

"Is it?"

When I looked up, Steve nodded.

"You're mine for three whole days. Just let it happen and see how it feels to be my boyfriend instead of Ben's."

I lowered my chin and licked my lips.

Eleven weeks had passed since the Sebring race, and since then, I had belonged exclusively to Ben. He and I went through so much together during that time: laboring at the Stoneciphers' property, getting arrested and going to court, coming out as gay to my mom and sister and to Ben's parents.

Before he'd left for Merritt Island last Friday, Ben told me, "I think my depression has lessened because right now I feel better than I have since we lost Chuck. I want you to know how much it's helped having you here every day."

Now, at the cabin, I knew I'd feel guilty as hell if I got intimate with Steve, but then I looked at Steve's carved chest and rippled belly and desire stirred within me. Steve was so beautiful and he was offering himself to me, practically begging.

How could I say no?

WE LAY SIDE by side on the bed, both of us gazing at a ceiling fan that twirled above us. The uncapped jelly tube rested on the nightstand and a pair of soiled hand towels lay on the pine floor. The room smelled of butt sex. The windows stood open, and somewhere outside a blue jay tootled. Our chests rose and fell with our breathing.

"I've never felt better than I do right now," Steve said. "It wasn't ever this good with Castleman—that was all about sex—but this is different. Right now, I feel one hundred percent *whole*, if you know what I mean."

I knew just what Steve was talking about because minutes before, when I thrust inside him and gazed into his eyes, a wave of emotion engulfed me. Memories of all the things we'd done together as friends paraded through my head, all the laughing and sorrow and the camaraderie we'd shared. There in the bedroom, I didn't weep when I reached orgasm, but I came mighty close and I remembered my first time with Ben, when I'd cried like a five-year-old and he stroked my hair.

Now, for the twentieth time, I found myself wishing I could divide myself in two so I could share life with both Ben and Steve. But of course, that wasn't possible, and again I realized that a day would come when I'd have to make a choice and stick to it. After all, I couldn't keep having these on-again-off-again episodes with Steve if he wasn't going to be my partner in life.

But now I was alone with Steve and we would have these three days to ourselves in a very private and beautiful place, so I would put Ben out of my mind and concentrate on the sheer joy of Steve's presence and the wonder of his touch.

I would cherish him like the gift he was.

STEVE ANCHORED THE boat near a group of stumps that thrust their heads from waist-deep water near a river bank. A few lily pads floated among the stumps and a squadron of dragonflies hummed above it all.

Steve and I wore swim trunks, nothing else. The time was around 2:00 p.m., and the sun warmed my shoulders and the top of my head.

Steve coated a black plastic worm with an oily liquid that smelled like grape soda. He slipped the worm onto a weedless and weighted hook tied to the line on his rod and reel, then cast the worm to a spot just this side of the stumps. The worm made a splash when it hit the surface and sank.

I followed suit, and we inched our worms along the river bottom by twitching our wrists and reeling in the line a little at a time, a common technique for catching largemouth bass. In the woods beyond the river bank, an osprey chattered from the apex of a long leaf pine while it searched the river for a hapless fish to dine on.

We'd brought an ice cooler, and I reached inside it to retrieve two beers. After handing one to Steve, I cracked open the second and took a sip. The beer was cold and crisp; it tasted delicious on my tongue. I yawned deeply, feeling so relaxed I could take a nap.

Steve reeled in and recast his worm, and I watched his back muscles move under his skin, recalling how I'd given him a massage after our sex earlier. He lay on his stomach, and I straddled him at his waist and worked his shoulders and shoulder blades before kneading his spine with my thumbs. I switched position and squeezed his compact buttocks, over and over until they relaxed. Then I worked my way down each leg. Distance running had turned Steve's thighs and calves into marble, and I guess my attentions made them feel pretty good because Steve groaned as I rubbed him down there. I even massaged the soles of his feet and worked my fingers between his toes.

When the massage was over, Steve rolled onto his back and I lay atop him. Our hips and sternums met, and I kissed Steve for the longest time, savoring the feel of his tongue rubbing against mine. I explored the corners of his mouth and the contours of his teeth. I toyed with his ears and ran my fingers through his thick hair.

God, I loved Steve.

Now, in the boat, the tip of my pole twitched. I jumped to my feet and jerked it toward my right shoulder to set the hook in the fish's mouth. Right away, my rod bent into a *J* shape and the fish ran with my lure, peeling line off the reel and making that humming sound every fisherman loves to hear.

"Looks like a big boy," Steve said. "Loosen your drag so he doesn't bust your line."

I turned the little knob on top of my reel counterclockwise so the fish could take line more easily. It did so for maybe thirty seconds, then yanked at the worm, trying to get itself free.

I pumped my rod and reeled in line. I did this repeatedly, bringing the fish closer to the boat, but then the fish made another run and took back all the line I'd just reeled in.

"Damn," Steve hollered while he reached for the dip net, "you have a fighter on the line."

The battle lasted another couple of minutes before the fish tired and I brought it to the surface, alongside the boat. Steve bent over the boat's gunwale and scooped the fish from the water, a largemouth bass nearly two feet in length, olive green and silver, with shiny scales and a spiky dorsal fin. My catch wriggled and thrashed about in the net.

"He must weight eight pounds," Steve said while he lowered the net to the deck and the bass thumped around frantically.

This was only the third time I'd fresh water fished, and this was the first bass I'd ever caught. A shiver ran through me as I studied the fish's beauty and recalled the power it had exhibited during my struggle to get it in the boat.

It deserves my respect, doesn't it? The fish deserves to live.

"Are you nuts?" Steve said when I told him to release my catch. "It's a trophy fish and the fillets will feed four adults, no problem. I have a camera at the cabin. I'll take your picture with it."

I shook my head while watching the bass's gills flex.

"He's my fish. Let him live please."

Steve puckered one side of his face and shook his head, but he did as I asked. Using pliers, he pried the hook and worm from the fish's jaw. He slipped his fingers into the gills and lifted the bass, then tossed it over the gunwale. My catch floated on its side for a few seconds. Then it regained its senses, righted itself, and swam away.

Steve stood with the pliers in one hand and his other hand on his hip.

"You know," he said, "some guys fish all their lives and never catch one like that."

TUESDAY MORNING, I woke to the sound of rain drumming the cabin roof. I lay on my back and Steve's temple rested against my shoulder. One of his legs crossed one of mine. Dim light passed through the venetian blinds. I buried my nose in Steve's hair and inhaled its grassy scent.

Last night, when we'd turned down the covers and got undressed, the whole situation seemed unreal. Yes, Steve and I had slept in the same bed many times before then, but only as friends, not sex partners and never naked. And the thought I would fall asleep holding Steve in my arms made me tremble. We positioned ourselves spoon-style with my chest touching Steve's shoulder blades, my hips pressed to his butt cheeks, and my arm draped across his chest.

Just before Steve turned onto his side, he kissed me on the mouth.

"I love you, Johnny, I truly do."

And I swear, for a few seconds, my heart stopped beating.

Holy shit.

Before I even thought logically, I said, "Steve, I love you more than you'll ever know."

Okay, maybe I shouldn't have said that if I was going to stick with Ben. But I couldn't help myself because, to be honest, I *did* love Steve. It was a different kind of love than I felt for Ben, more like the love between two brothers, only with a sexual element involved.

Now, in the dim morning light, I reached between Steve's thighs and gave him a gentle squeeze. Then I left my hand where it was. Within moments, he was as stiff as PVC pipe. His eyelids fluttered open and he looked up at me for a second before returning his cheek to my shoulder. He kissed me there and rubbed his chin stubble against my skin.

"How'd you sleep?" he asked.

"Like a guy in a coma. How about you?"

"The same—this is really nice, Johnny."

I worked Steve's erection with my fingers. His rigid flesh felt warm and smooth.

Steve brought his mouth to mine and we kissed. The only sounds in the room were the ceiling fan's whir and the smacking of our lips. Steve made a trail of gentle kisses down my neck, chest, and belly. He took me into his mouth and I groaned. I ran my fingers through his hair while his head bobbed.

After a minute or so, Steve looked up at me. He raised his eyebrows while he clutched my erection in his fist.

"What is it?" I asked.

"You know what I want, right?"

I chuckled. "Yeah, I know."

Moments later, Steve was on his back with his legs resting on my shoulders while I thrust. Our orgasms came quickly, and mine was so intense I couldn't help myself; I hollered nonsense like a madman.

Steve scattered his chest and shoulder with opals I lapped up like treasure. I stayed inside him for the longest time, listening to him breathe while rain continued to fall and somewhere to the west thunder rumbled.

"Johnny?"

"H-m-m-m?"

"That was goddamned amazing."

I kissed Steve's cheek while he shifted his weight beneath me.

"I want to do this with you every day," he said. "This fall, if we live together at UF, we can—"

"S-h-h-h," I whispered. "Let's not talk right now, okay?"

My thoughts swirled. Where were things going in my life? Why was it so hard to figure out what I wanted? And why was I such an emotional jellyfish?

Aye-yi-yi.

WEDNESDAY AFTERNOON, STEVE and I shared a glider sofa on the cabin's screened porch that overlooked the river. Both of us wore only our briefs. I was sitting up straight while Steve lay flat on his back with his head resting in my lap. I sifted my fingers through his dark hair while the sofa creaked with our rocking movements. We had eaten lunch a half hour ago—ham sandwiches and potato chips washed down with soda—and now our stomachs made little gurgling sounds as our food settled.

"I wish we could stay here forever," Steve said. "I've never felt as close to you as I do right now."

"It *is* nice, the two of us sharing this place with no interruptions from anyone."

Steve took one of my hands in both of his and toyed with my fingers. "Explain something—how come Ben means more to you than I do? You've known me much longer than him, and you like me physically, always have. If we became a couple, I think things between us would last a long time, maybe all our lives. Doesn't that mean something to you?"

I drew a breath and let it out. How could I answer Steve's questions without hurting his feelings?

"You're comparing apples to oranges. My feelings for Ben have nothing to do with my feelings for you. And I'm not with Ben because he's the better deal, financially or looks-wise or any of that. You know how much your friendship means to me, and the sex we share is amazing. But I'm deeply in love with Ben. I'm closer to him than I am to my mom or my sister or even you, and I can't walk away from him just because you're asking me to."

Steve brought my hand to his lips and kissed the back of my wrist.

"Hear me out," he said.

"Okay."

"I checked the UF student manual. I don't have to live in the dorms my freshman year if I share off-campus housing with a UF student in a higher class. You and I could rent an apartment or a small house in Gainesville. That way we'd have complete privacy like we have here. Think about it—every night, we'd fall asleep holding each other."

"It sounds like a dream."

Steve looked up at me from my lap. "It doesn't have to *be* a dream if you'll only let it happen."

"Look, I—"

"Just promise me you'll give it some thought. I don't need an answer today or tomorrow or even next week. But think about how nice it's been since we got here; then imagine having this every day when fall comes. We can make it happen, Johnny."

I lifted my gaze and stared at the river.

Chapter Twenty-One

BEN ARRIVED IN St. Petersburg Beach on June 15, a Monday, in midafternoon. The GTO's engine ticked when I greeted Ben on our driveway. Ten days had passed since we'd last seen each other, but it felt more like a month, and my knees turned to jelly when we shook hands and I heard Ben's voice. He wore a T-shirt, khaki shorts, and sandals. Sunlight reflected in his dark hair.

I wore the T-shirt Ben had bought me at Ron Jon's and a faded pair of blue jeans with holes at both knees.

Ben would spend the night. After greeting my sister in the living room, he toted his overnight bag into my room. I followed him there and closed the door behind us. Then we embraced and our lips conjoined. The warmth of Ben's body enchanted me while his breath steamed my upper lip and our tongues dueled.

Beyond the door, my sister cued up *Abbey Road* on the stereo, and the song "Come Together" began. Fuzzy guitar notes oozed through the house, and John Lennon sang the opening verse. "Here come old flat-top..."

Ben and I changed into our swim trunks. When we got naked, it took all my willpower not to tackle Ben and drive him onto my bed, but I had to satisfy myself with squeezing one of his beautiful butt cheeks and savoring its firmness before he put on his suit.

At the beach, we dropped our towels onto the sand and waded into the Gulf until we were chest-deep. We dunked ourselves in the lukewarm water and stood facing each other. Ben talked about his drive from Merritt Island while salty droplets glistened in his hair and on his shoulders.

"Ever since construction began on Walt Disney World, the traffic around Orlando and Kissimmee has been terrible. I sat in a snarl for nearly a half hour before we got moving again."

I asked how things were at the Stoneciphers' property.

"It's that time of year when we have to spray the cattle with insecticide to control horn and face flies. It's hot and nasty work that takes a lot of time to do properly. You'll see what I mean when we get to Merritt Island tomorrow. Then, come July, we'll start breeding the cows, some by pairing them with bulls, others by artificial insemination."

When Ben asked what I'd done the past week, I said, "Not much, really. I slept a lot—I think I was exhausted from final exams. I spent time with my mom and sister, and took care of yard work that needed done—trimming hedges and hoeing weeds, that sort of thing. I washed and waxed my mom's car too."

"What about the guys you went to the Sebring race with? Have you seen them?"

I lowered my gaze and rubbed my lips together. Ever since returning home from the Withlacoochee River, I'd debated whether or not I should tell Ben about the three days and nights I spent with Steve at the fishing camp.

In the end I decided it was best not to mention Steve at all.

"We all got together one night at Kenny's," I lied. "We drank beer and watched a St. Louis Cardinals game. That's about it."

When I returned my gaze to Ben, his eyes were narrowed. "That's all?"

I nodded. "Everyone seems busy with summer jobs and all."

I asked Ben how his folks were doing, to change the conversation's bent.

Ben puckered one side of his face and shook his head. "They're much the same. Dad's overworked and stressed out, and Mom hovers over me like I'm ten years old. It drives me crazy sometimes."

We left the water and toweled ourselves. Then we walked northward, along the shore, with our arms swinging and our feet scuffing the sugar-like sand. Because it was a Monday, very few people were on the beach, just a few families, likely summer vacationers. Fifty yards offshore, a pair of bottle-nosed dolphins surfaced to breathe, and their blow holes made sucking sounds as the creatures inhaled.

"Do your folks ever talk about me?" I asked.

"Not much."

"Why do you think that is?"

Ben picked up a piece of driftwood and tossed it westward. It twirled like a boomerang before hitting the water with a splash.

"It's only been a couple of months since we got arrested and they learned we were boyfriends. I don't think they've fully absorbed it all."

"Do you think they ever will?"

Bens shrugged. "We'll have to wait and see. This summer will be a test for all four of us. It's my hope they'll come to accept things after they've spent more time around you."

We walked in silence for a bit, and my thoughts returned to Steve and the time I'd spent with him at the river. The last night there, Steve and I sat on edge of the dock with our legs dangling, drinking beer and listening to crickets chirp. A three-quarter moon bathed us in silvery light. We were shirtless, and Steve rested his arm on my shoulders. I felt the warmth of his skin on mine.

"I wish you weren't going to Merritt Island. I want you to stay in Pinellas County this summer so we can see each other every day,"

"But I have to go. I owe Ben's dad for my legal fees, plus they need my help over there. Without Ben's brother, they're short-handed."

"If I drive over there one weekend, would you spend it with me? We could get a motel room in Cape Canaveral."

I shook my head. "That's not going to work."

"Why not?"

"It just won't."

Now, as Ben and I walked the shore, I looked at his handsome face and tried to imagine how stricken he'd feel if I went away with Steve for a weekend this summer. As much as I had enjoyed my stay at the river, and as much as I'd enjoy spending a weekend with Steve, I wouldn't dream of hurting Ben that way.

SPRAYING BEEF CATTLE with insecticide had to be one of the nastiest jobs I'd ever performed. The cattle stank like hell, and so did the insecticide.

The process itself was fairly simple. Ben poured several ounces of chemical into a sprayer's tank. He mixed the chemical with water and diesel fuel until the tank was full. We climbed aboard our horses and rode into the pasture until we approached a group of cattle. Then we dismounted. After Ben slipped a lasso around a cow or calf's neck, he handed the loose end of the lasso to me so I could keep the cow or calf in place.

Ben pumped the sprayer's plunger until the tank was fully pressurized. Then he passed the sprayer's wand back and forth, misting the cow or calf with the insecticide mixture. It took a lot of time because every crevice of the animal had to be sprayed, even the insides of ears and under the tail. When Ben sprayed the creature's face, I had to keep its eyelids closed with my fingers. When we were done, Ben used a can of red spray paint to make a large X on the creature's hindquarter so we knew it had been treated.

All of this was performed in treeless pastureland, and the summer sun pounded our shoulders and backs. We both wore straw cowboy hats, long-sleeved shirts, blue jeans, and boots. By 8:00 a.m., my shirt was soaked through and my hair was matted.

"I know the blue jeans are hot," Ben had told me my first day on the job, "but you don't wear shorts on horseback. You'd rub your thighs raw if you did."

Each day, Ben and I used insect repellent we rubbed on our faces and necks to ward off swarms of mosquitoes that dwelled in the pasture.

This was my fifth day on the job, and so far each had been the same. The Stonecipher household rose at 6:00 a.m. Dressed in a robe and slippers, Sarah prepared breakfast for Will, Ben, and me: scrambled eggs, bacon, toast, and grits. We washed the meal down with orange juice and coffee.

I'd never been a big breakfast eater—a bowl of corn flakes was normally all I needed—but with the long mornings I spent in the pasture, I needed a substantial meal to sustain me until lunchtime. By 11:00 a.m., I was already hungry again.

Once breakfast concluded and we'd brushed our teeth, Ben and I saddled our horses. Ben rode Midnight and I rode Penny, who actually seemed glad to see me when I entered the barn in early morning light. I had learned how to place the blanket on her back and how to position the saddle on top of the blanket in just the right spot. I knew how to loop the bridle over Penny's ears and muzzle, and place the bit in her mouth. She submitted to these procedures without protest, and I always fed her a carrot or a few lumps of sugar as a reward.

Before we left the barn, Ben mixed a fresh tank of insecticide and pressurized the sprayer. The stink of the insecticide was always such a contrast to the pleasant odors of the breakfast I'd consumed, and my stomach sometimes churned a little. Ben placed a new can of spray paint in his saddle bag, we both filled our canteens with fresh water, and then we were off to the pasture for another morning of cattle spraying. We processed a cow in about fifteen minutes if we worked quickly.

Ben and I didn't do a lot of talking during working hours. Instead, our thoughts kept us company. I spent a good deal of time pondering how my life had changed since I'd arrived in Gainesville last September. I thought of Ben's emotional meltdown the night he'd told me about Chuck's death in the boating accident. I recalled Ben's description of his near-suicide attempt, something I thought about every time I saw the gun case in the Stoneciphers' den. I remembered how Ben had rejected ATO's pledge bid in favor of our friendship and how much it meant to me. I thought about our Cuba Libre Night and the first time I had sex with Ben in the dorm room. And I pondered the circumstances of our arrest and all the miserable shit that had followed.

Of course, I thought about Steve a lot, and not just the time I'd spent with him at the river, but also the time we'd first had sex in my bedroom and our encounter in Steve's tent at the Sebring race. I thought of our sessions at Steve's aunt's house and the time Steve threw the water pitcher at me. And I recalled the afternoon at my house in St. Petersburg Beach, when Steve had told me he'd fallen in love with me and how miserable he looked until I took him to my bedroom and made things better—at least temporarily.

I spent a lot of time thinking about the proposal Steve had made on the sofa glider at the river. A tempting offer for sure, but I hadn't for one minute considered accepting it. I would live with Ben in the fall, and he'd be my companion in life. That would disappoint Steve—I didn't like hurting his feelings—but it was how things would be.

During our lunch breaks from work, Ben and I held phone conversations with three different rental agencies in Gainesville. They would search for one-bedroom apartments in our price range, units within walking distance of campus. Already we had combed the contents of the Stoneciphers' attic, looking for household furnishings we could take to Gainesville in the fall.

Per Will and Sarah's wishes, I had slept in Chuck's bedroom since my arrival, which didn't really bother me since I was so damned tired at the end of each day that I couldn't even *think* about sex. All I wanted was a shower, the comfort of air-conditioning, a nice dinner, and my bed.

"HEY," BEN WHISPERED while he squeezed my shoulder. "Wake up."

I rolled onto my back and fluttered my eyelids. Sunshine poured into the room from the eastern windows.

When Ben sat on the edge of my mattress, the bedsprings creaked. He wore briefs, nothing else. He clutched a tube of jelly and a towel in one hand. His hair was in tangles and stubble grew on his chin, but to me, he was the most beautiful guy in the world.

"My folks just left for church," he said. "We'll have the house to ourselves for a couple of hours."

I lifted the bed covers and scooted to one side of the mattress to make room for Ben. He slipped in next to me, and I pulled the covers over us. Ben snuggled up to me; his skin felt warm and smooth. He kissed my forehead, the tip of my nose, and my mouth. Our lips parted and our tongues rubbed while Ben ran his fingers through my hair.

This was the first time we'd been intimate since my arrival in Merritt Island, and it felt so nice getting close to Ben again. Between my thighs, I stiffened.

Since it was Sunday, we didn't have to work. The day was ours and we could do as we pleased. No smelly cattle, no mosquitoes, and no insecticide.

We both peeled off our briefs and it wasn't long before Ben's legs were draped over my shoulders and I thrust my hips. The scent of our sex filled the room, and when I reached orgasm, I cried out Ben's name more than once. Ben groaned deep in his throat when he came. His lungs heaved, and his mouth gaped as he spurted his seed.

After we cleaned ourselves up in my bathroom, we returned to the bed and crawled under the covers. Ben lay on his back and I rested my cheek against his sternum. I draped an arm across Ben's belly and listened to his heartbeat.

"God, that was nice," he said.

"It sure was," I replied. "But I really miss sleeping next to you. I mean, this room's nice and all, but I'd rather we were back in the dorm so we could share a bed."

Ben twirled a strand of my hair around his finger. "What do you feel like doing today?"

"Anything that doesn't involve cattle or mosquitoes."

Ben chuckled. "Let's go fishing. I know a shady spot on the Banana River; we can swim there too. What do you think?"

"Let's do it," I said, "but first..."

"What?"

I kissed Ben's shoulder.

"Let's lie here for another half hour. This feels too nice to leave."

Chapter Twenty-Two

DURING THE FIRST week of July, the time came to impregnate the Stoneciphers' cows, either through natural mating or artificial insemination.

"The tough part of the breeding process," Ben told me, "is determining when a cow's in heat. If you spot one cow trying to mount another from behind, that's a sure sign. Or if you see a clear discharge oozing from a cow's vagina, you know. Also, if you see a bull calf sniffing a cow's rear, that's a good sign the cow's in heat."

For natural breeding, a cow in heat was placed in a pen with a single bull. The cow was kept in place with a lasso tied to the pen's fence. Once the bull detected the cow was in heat, he started sniffing her butt. Then his penis emerged, a foot long, pink, and conical in shape. The bull mounted the cow from the rear, slipped his penis inside her, and started humping. The whole thing only lasted a few minutes, and then the impregnated cow was taken back to the pasture.

The Stoneciphers owned six breeding bulls, and they were used in a rotation so that a horny bull was always available whenever a cow went into heat. The first time I watched a bull and cow breed, my stomach roiled, but at least I didn't puke.

I wasn't so fortunate when I watched Will Stonecipher artificially inseminate a cow in heat.

The afternoon before, Ben and I had ridden our horses into the pasture, and right away, we spotted a cow trying to mount another cow. Ben slipped a lasso over the cow in heat, and we led her to a pen, where we left her for the evening.

The next morning, around 7:00 a.m., Ben tied the loose end of the cow's lasso to the pen's fence. Will emerged from the barn with a bucket of warm water that held a glass pipette probably three feet long and equipped with a plunger. The pipette contained bull semen freshly thawed. Will placed the pipette inside his shirt to keep it warm.

Will put on a plastic sleeve that reached all the way to his shoulder, then inserted his arm into the cow's anus, all the way past Will's bicep. Right away, shit spewed from the cow like bullets firing from an automatic rifle. The shit stank like hell, and I couldn't help myself; I walked to the edge of the pen and puked up my breakfast.

After I wiped my lips with my shirtsleeve, I returned to watch the rest of the procedure.

"Dad's massaging the cow's cervix," Ben explained. "He's getting her ready for insemination."

"Doesn't that hurt her?" I asked.

Will looked up at me and shook his head. "In fact, she's probably enjoying herself."

The cow just stood there and stared into space. Her vagina oozed clear liquid that reminded me of Karo syrup.

After a few minutes, Will cleaned the shit off the cow's rear end with a rag. Then he inserted the pipette into the cow's vagina. I gritted my teeth while watching the device disappear. Will's arm remained inside the cow's anus. Once the pipette was deep inside the cow, Will pressed the plunger. Then he removed his shit-coated arm and the pipette from the cow's body.

I don't think I'd ever witnessed a more disgusting event. In fact, I couldn't even eat lunch that day. My stomach was too jittery to keep food down, so I settled for a glass of milk.

Who knew raising beef cattle could be so nasty?

ONCE THE BREEDING and insemination of the Stoneciphers' cows was completed, Ben and I turned our attention to the citrus groves. I'd always thought the groves pretty much took care of themselves, but that wasn't so. Among other things, the trees had to be groomed in order to maximize their fruit output.

On a steamy day in mid-July, Ben operated a tractor-like device with a pair of trimming blades as long as I was tall. The blades were attached to arms that extended from either side of the tractor. The blades could trim trees vertically, to maintain rights-of-way between the rows of trees, or they could trim horizontally to "hedge" trees so they didn't get too "leggy." Right then, Ben was trimming vertically. I followed a safe distance behind him on foot, carrying a long-handled rake. As debris from the trees fell to the ground, I raked it into piles we'd later collect and burn using kerosene as an accelerant.

It was hot and noisy work. We both wore plastic goggles so our eyes wouldn't get struck by flying debris. The whir of the blades and the hum of their cutting actions made it impossible for us to converse, so again, I was left with only my thoughts to keep me company.

As I raked, I pondered a talk I'd had with Sarah Stonecipher the morning before. Ben and Will had gone to Orlando to attend a Florida Citrus Mutual meeting, and I was mucking horse stalls in the barn, another disgusting but necessary task at the Stonecipher property, since their horses produced tons of shit.

The mucking drill worked like this. After removing a horse from its stall and tethering it to a post, I removed the horse's hay, water bucket, and manger. Then I gathered the larger lumps of horse manure using a wood-shavings rake and rubber gloves. I dumped the manure into a metal wheelbarrow, then raked the wood shavings on the stall's floor to the corners and swept the floor clean with a push broom, gathering up smaller clumps of manure with a dustpan and placing them in the wheelbarrow. Then, after I spread fresh shavings in the stall, I returned the horse, the hay, the water bucket, and the manger to the stall. Once the wheelbarrow was filled to capacity, I dumped the manure onto a pile in back of the barn. Some would be used as fertilizer in the Stoneciphers' vegetable garden and shrubbery beds. The rest would be burned.

By midmorning, I had already mucked five stalls and my shirt was soaked in sweat when Sarah came into the barn with a pitcher of fresh lemonade and two plastic tumblers.

"It's hot this morning," she told me. "I thought you could use a break."

We sat on a pair of hay bales, facing each other and sipping from our tumblers. The lemonade was just right— tangy and not too sweet. I pressed my sweating tumbler to my temple and savored the cool dampness on my skin.

Sarah wore capris, canvas sneakers, and a chambray shirt with the tails untucked. She crossed her legs at the ankles and gazed about the barn, surveying the stalls I'd cleaned.

"You're good at this," she said.

"At shoveling poop?"

She laughed and shook her head. "At every job you take on, actually. Will and Ben have both said so."

I sipped from my lemonade and smacked my lips. Then I said, "I never knew caring for cattle and citrus groves was so complicated. It's a never-ending job, isn't it?"

Sarah nodded. "I've been married to Will twenty-three years, and in all that time, we've never taken a vacation."

"Never?"

She pursed her lips and shook her head. "When you marry a citrus farmer and rancher, you marry his land and whatever lives or grows on it. You marry the people who work for him too.

"Mind you, I'm not complaining. I love the life we lead here and the rhythm of the seasons. But sometimes, I wonder how it might feel to spend a week in Miami Beach or Bermuda, lying beside a swimming pool and reading a Jackie Collins novel."

I crossed my knee with a boot. "You could do that this summer while I'm here. Ben and I can look after things, no problem."

Sarah drew a breath and let it out. "It's sweet of you to make the offer—and I'm sure the property would be fine—but Will can't let this place out of his sight, not even for a week. That's just his nature I'm afraid."

"Actually," I said, "I've never taken a vacation myself—my family can't afford travel—but we live at the beach so in a sense we're always on holiday."

Sarah nodded. "Ben tells me your parents are divorced."

"Since I was six."

"Do you stay in touch with your father?"

I shook my head.

"Why not?"

I lowered my gaze for a moment. Then I looked up at Sarah. "We don't even know where he is."

Sarah knitted her brow. "How awful for you, and for your mother and sister as well."

I shrugged.

Sarah said, "My boys have always been close to their father. From an early age, they fished and hunted and camped with Will, and they helped him with chores on the property, even when they were in grade school. I think Will's always been a hero to them."

I moistened my lips. "I don't think I'd have many kind words to share with my dad if he ever showed up at our door. It's often a struggle to make ends meet at my house. Mom does her best, but it's been rough."

I poured myself another glass of lemonade. Then Sarah and I sipped from our tumblers in silence for a minute or so before Sarah said, "I owe you an apology, Johnny."

I crinkled my forehead.

"The night you and Ben were arrested, when we brought you boys home from the jail, I asked Ben if you had led him down the wrong path, as if it was your fault Ben got into trouble. That was wrong of me."

I didn't quite know what to say, but I knew Sarah was making an effort to bridge a gap, so I did my best. "It's okay. We were all upset at the time."

A tiny smile crossed Sarah's lips as she looked at me. "Actually I think you're good for Ben," she said. "Between the day Chuck died and the day Ben left for Gainesville, I never saw him smile or heard him laugh a single time. But now, when I see you and Ben together, he seems almost... happy. Thank you for that, Johnny."

Later that day, when Ben and I took a nighttime walk through the groves, I told him about my conversation with his mom. A fingernail moon hung in the eastern sky and a chorus of crickets serenaded us. I held Ben's hand as we walked.

"I think both my folks are warming up to you," Ben said. "A few days ago, my dad told me, 'Johnny's a fine young man. I can see why you like him so much.'"

"Did he really?"

Ben nodded. "They're not stupid. They see how hard you work every day, and you're always respectful toward them. I know they appreciate it and I do too."

Now, as I trekked behind the hedging tractor in the groves, I looked at Ben as he steered down the right-of-way, and I marveled at the fact I was living in his family's home and sharing my days with Ben and his parents. Yeah, the work was hard and often nasty, but I really didn't mind. After living at the Stoneciphers' property for three weeks, I felt a sense of belonging to the place, as though I was meant to be there.

It was quickly beginning to feel like home.

Chapter Twenty-Three

IN THE THIRD week of July, just after dinner on a Thursday evening, Ben and I loaded the dishwasher when the wall phone in the kitchen rang. Ben lifted the receiver and said hello. Then he said, "Steve, this is Ben. Let me put Johnny on the line."

I hadn't spoken to Steve since mid-June, after our stay at the river, and I furrowed my brow in puzzlement when I spoke into the receiver. "Hey, what's going on?"

"Not much. How's Brevard County?"

"Lots of hard work, but I'm doing fine."

Steve cleared his throat. "My brother and I are spending this weekend in Cocoa Beach. We have a motel room reserved close to the pier. I'm going to rent a board, and Nash said he'd give me a surfing lesson."

I swallowed and didn't say anything in response.

"I was hoping we could get together, at least for lunch or something. Is that possible?"

I looked at Ben, who placed handfuls of silverware into the dishwasher, and then I studied my sneakers. "I work all day Saturday, but maybe Ben and I could drive over to Cocoa Beach on Sunday."

A moment of silence passed. Then Steve said, "I need to talk to you privately. Can we do that?"

"Why? What for?"

"I'll explain when I see you. Please...do this for me."

I chewed my lower lip while shifting my weight from one leg to the other.

"Johnny?"

"Yeah?"

"Will you come?"

Shit.

"All right, Steve. Give me the name of your motel."

"WHY DIDN'T YOU tell me about this sooner?" Ben asked me.

We sat in his bedroom with the door closed, not long after my phone conversation with Steve. I occupied one bed and Ben sat on the other, facing me. I rested my forearms on my knees with my chin lowered and my gaze fixed on the carpet. I had just told Ben about the three nights I'd spent with Steve at the river, and also about the sex I'd shared with Steve at the Sebring race. Now I bathed in guilt, feeling like a guy who had just confessed to a heinous crime.

"I didn't tell you because I didn't want to hurt you."

Ben puckered one side of his face. "While we're at it, is there anything else you'd like to tell me?"

When I looked up at Ben, my eyes were foggy with tears.

"Only that I love you and I'm sorry for what I did. I need to stay away from Steve from now on, and I will, I promise."

Ben scowled. "You just agreed to meet him in Cocoa Beach, remember?"

"I'll call him back and cancel."

Ben shook his head. "You need to go over there by yourself on Sunday. And when you do, you'll need to make it clear to Steve that you're off-limits from now on—that you're my partner and he needs to find someone else to give his affection to. Understand?"

I didn't hesitate to answer because I knew what I had to do.

"All right, Ben, okay."

SATURDAY NIGHT I played gin rummy with Ben and his parents at the Stoneciphers' kitchen table. I partnered with Sarah and she was a cagey player. After four hands, we led Ben and Will by over a hundred points.

All four of us drank highballs—Canadian whiskey poured over ice in a tall glass and topped off with ginger ale. My shoulder and back muscles ached from a long day spent in the groves, scattering granulated fertilizer under each tree and working the fertilizer into the soil with a rake, a slow-moving process involving lots of bending at the waist. And even with the help of two day laborers Will had hired, it would take two weeks before the fertilization task was completed because the groves were so vast.

Now, while he laid down two tricks—four nines and three sixes—Will talked about a pair of young bulls he'd sent for butchering that afternoon.

"As many times as I've done it, I still feel guilty when I see them driven away by the slaughterhouse truck. But they were three years old and their time to leave had come. I can't keep more than six mature bulls on the property."

I drew a jack of clubs from the deck, and Ben hissed when I formed a trick with a ten and queen of clubs that I placed on the table before me.

"You and Mom are *so* darned lucky," he said while he drew from the deck, then discarded.

I felt a bit light-headed from my highball. It was the first liquor I'd consumed since my Cuba Libre Night with Ben, way back in October of last year, and I tried to pace myself. I didn't want to get tipsy around Ben's folks, now did I?

Will looked up from his cards and turned his gaze to me.

"Johnny, I checked my records on the time you've put in since you arrived here in June. A week ago, you'd already put in 250 hours and your debt to me was paid up. I owe you wages for this week, so here you are."

Will reached into his wallet, pulled out three twenty-dollar bills, and handed them to me.

I stared at the bills and crinkled my forehead. "Shouldn't I only get forty dollars?"

Will shook his head. "I'm giving you a raise to a buck-fifty an hour. You're worth every penny of it."

I beamed as my gaze traveled from face to face at the table, and when I looked at Ben, he was smiling too.

"I knew I could make a cowboy out of you," Ben said.

SUNDAY MORNING, AFTER our weekly tryst in Chuck's bedroom, Ben and I showered together and shared a quick breakfast: freshly-squeezed orange juice, corn flakes, and coffee. Sunlight poured into the kitchen through the window above the sink while we studied sections from the Sunday edition of the *Orlando Sentinel*.

Ben scanned the sports page.

I read a story about the opening of the Aswan High Dam and how it enabled the Egyptians to control flooding of the Nile River, but I found it hard to concentrate on the article because thoughts of my upcoming meeting with Steve kept stealing into my head. I was due there at noon, and we were supposed to grab lunch someplace—me and Steve and his brother, Nash. I still had no idea what Steve wanted to talk to me about, but already I had an uneasy feeling about the whole situation.

I would drive Ben's GTO to Cocoa Beach.

When Ben had handed me the keys the previous night, just before we went to bed, he said, "I hope this meeting with Steve clears things up between you and him."

I didn't say anything in response—I only nodded—but I knew what Ben expected of me and I just hoped I'd have the balls to say exactly what I needed to when I met Steve.

Wasn't it time I did so?

THE DAY WAS hot when I pulled the GTO onto the county road and drove toward the Bee Line. I ran the air-conditioning, and cool air wafted from the dashboard vents. I had the radio tuned to WKKO and the disk jockey played "Momma Told Me (Not to Come)" by Three Dog Night. I wore my Ron Jon T-shirt, khaki shorts, and sandals.

I flew past the Stoneciphers' citrus groves while the GTO's mighty engine hummed.

When I reached the Bee Line, I turned east and soon was crossing the Banana River Bridge. At the bridge's apex, I studied the Atlantic's blue expanse and my pulse quickened. This was the first time I had visited the barrier island since Ben took me there months ago. I entered Cape Canaveral with its strip centers and rows of little cinder-block houses, and then I came to Steve's motel, a one-story structure with a weed-and-dirt yard and a pair of scraggly date palm trees.

I parked next to Steve's VW in the motel's crumbling asphalt lot. Then I exited the GTO and knocked on the door of unit number six. Inside the unit, a television played and a sports announcer talked about an upcoming game between the Baltimore Orioles and the Chicago White Sox.

Steve answered the door, wearing a pair of swim trunks, nothing else, and like always, I felt a little weak in the knees when he flashed his one-hundred-watt smile at me. We shook hands and Steve invited me inside. The drapes were drawn so the room was shadowy. It smelled of mildew. There was only one bed, a queen size, and the covers were messed up. A pair of jeans, a pair of briefs, and a T-shirt draped a ladder-back chair that stood in one corner. Steve's sneakers rested on the threadbare carpet, next to the chair. A wall-unit air conditioner blew cool air into the room.

Steve switched off the TV and motioned me to sit on the bed. After I did, he sat down next to me and the bedsprings squeaked.

"Where's Nash?" I asked.

Steve lowered his gaze and moistened his lips, then looked into my eyes. "Nash didn't come. I'm here by myself."

I furrowed my brow. "I don't understand. I thought he was giving you a surfing lesson."

Steve shook his head. "Don't get mad, but I sort of made that up. I was afraid you wouldn't come here if you knew I was alone."

Shit.

"Look, Steve, I—"

He placed a hand on my thigh. "Just listen, will you?"

Like the night at the Gainesville pizza place with Castleman and Steve, I felt ambushed, and my first impulse was to get up and leave. Steve's duplicity rubbed me the wrong way. But he'd driven 160 miles to get there and rented the room, so I decided to stay and hear whatever he wanted to tell me.

"All right," I said. "I'll listen."

Steve kept his hand on my thigh, but he lowered his gaze to study his bare feet. "I accepted the scholarship offer from UF. I'll start classes up there right after Labor Day. Pretty cool, eh?"

"Congratulations," I said.

Steve looked up at me. "I want to live with you this fall, either in a dorm room or a place off campus if we can find something. Just think: we'll be together every day."

I took Steve's wrist and lifted his hand from my thigh; then I rose to my feet. I placed my hands on my hips and looked down at Steve. "Look, I explained things to you when we were at the river. I'm living with Ben this fall. We're already searching for a place off campus, a house or apartment. Nothing you say to me will change that."

Steve looked up at me, and his voice trembled when he spoke.

"Don't you care about me, Johnny? Aren't I important to you?"

"Of *course* you are, and I'll be happy to see you up in Gainesville this September. You can hang out with me and Ben, and we can do things together. It'll be fun."

Steve rose, untied the drawstring on his swim trunks, and dropped them to his ankles. Then he stepped out of them. Already, he was stiff as he continued in a seductive tone. "Why don't you get undressed and lie down with me? We're both here and no one will bother us. It'll be nice."

Don't do it. Stick to your guns.

"Steve, I can't. As beautiful as you are and as much as I care for you, I can't touch you that way anymore. It has to stop."

Steve stepped toward me. He stroked my cheek with a finger while his gaze bored into mine. "You didn't enjoy our time at the river? It didn't mean anything to you?"

I grasped his wrist and pulled his hand from my face. "Of *course* it did, but that's not the point. I can't have two boyfriends at one time. I have to choose, and I've made my decision. My choice is Ben. I'm sorry if that hurts you, but it's how things have to be."

Steve stood there naked with his chin lowered.

"Look," I said, "why don't you get yourself dressed and we'll grab some lunch."

Steve looked up. "I'm not hungry, not after what you just said. So why don't you go back to Merritt Island and I'll drive back to St. Petersburg in the morning. I'm not stupid—I know when I'm not wanted."

I let my gaze travel over Steve's body one more time. "All right then. I'll see you around," I said before turning on my heel and leaving the room.

Tears clouded my eyes when I steered the GTO onto A-1-A. I thought of all the good times I'd shared with Steve over the past three years and how, until I met Ben, Steve had been my closest friend in the world. But now, by choosing Ben as my partner in life, my friendship with Steve was probably at its end. I had mortally wounded the bond between us.

It's over, Darling.

Let him go.

Chapter Twenty-Four

ON A FRIDAY afternoon in early August, Ben and I groomed Midnight and Penny in the barn. Both horses were tethered to posts in the corridor between the rows of stalls. I used a dandy brush on Penny; it looked just like one in my shoeshine kit back at home. I stroked Penny's flank with the brush, and she seemed to enjoy the way the bristles felt on her skin.

The barn doors were open. Off to the west, the sky was the color of charcoal. Thunder rumbled and a metallic scent of approaching rain hung in the air. A breeze swept through the barn while we worked. Ben's portable radio was tuned to WKKO, and right then, the DJ was playing "In the Summertime" by Mungo Jerry, a kicky tune that made me rock my shoulders to the beat.

That night, Ben and I would drive to Orlando to attend a concert at the Tangerine Bowl. The headliner act was the jazz/rock group Chicago. Ben had bought their double LP back in June, and since then, we'd listened to it almost every day in Ben's room. I liked all the songs on the album, but my favorite was "Where Do We Go from Here?", a powerful anti-war song and a plea for peace.

When I finished using the dandy brush on Penny, I switched to a soft brush to groom her face, and just as I cleaned her muzzle, Sarah called to us from the back door of the house. Her voice sounded frantic.

"Ben, Johnny, please help me," she cried. "Something's wrong with Will."

Ben and I dropped what we were doing and ran to the house, where Sarah led us to Will's office. Will lay on his back on the carpet. His eyes were glassy and one side of his face sagged. He was dressed as I last had seen him an hour ago: cowboy shirt, jeans, and boots.

"I found him like that, just a few minutes ago," Sarah said. "I've already called for an ambulance."

Ben got on his knees next to Will. He ran his fingers through Will's salt-and-pepper hair. "Dad, what's wrong? What happened?"

Will didn't answer; he only stared at the ceiling and breathed.

"Can you hear me, Dad?"

No answer.

Ben looked up at Sarah. "What's wrong with him, Mom?"

Sarah's arms were crossed beneath her breasts and her mouth was a thin line. "I just don't know. It could be anything."

It seemed like forever before the ambulance arrived, and when it finally did, two guys in white uniforms knelt on the carpet. They took Will's vital signs: pulse, temperature, all of it.

One guy shone a penlight into Will's eyes. Then he said to the other guy, "I'm guessing it's a stroke. Let's bring the gurney in here. The sooner we get him to the hospital, the better."

Ben stood with his arm around Sarah, whose eyes glistened with tears. "I told him he was working too hard," she said to no one in particular, "but he wouldn't listen. I was afraid something like this might happen."

Sarah and Ben rode to the hospital in the ambulance. I would drive the GTO to the hospital after I put the horses in their stalls and closed up the barn. The ambulance siren wailed as I walked out the back door of the house. Lightning snaked across the darkening sky, and when thunder rumbled, the ground shook. I untied Penny from her tether and led her to her stall, then followed suit with Midnight. Both horses seemed a little unnerved by the approaching storm. Their ears twitched.

I fed each a lump of sugar to calm them. "Don't be afraid. It's only a storm."

After latching the barn doors shut, I entered the house and grabbed Ben's keys from his bedroom desk, and when I did so, I studied a framed photograph of me sitting on Penny and Ben on Midnight, both of us wearing cowboy clothes. Sarah had taken the photo a few weeks before, just after my conversation with her in the barn, the day she'd brought out the pitcher of lemonade.

That little talk, I knew, had been a turning point in my relationship with Ben's parents. More and more I felt like I'd become a member of the Stonecipher family.

At the hospital, I found Ben and Sarah seated in the emergency room's waiting area, a cramped space full of plastic chairs and Formica tables bearing stacks of dog-eared magazines. Overhead fluorescent ceiling fixtures hummed. A clerical worker sat at a desk behind a wall opening, tapping away on a typewriter, seemingly oblivious to the misery Ben and Sarah were enduring.

Ben held Sarah's hand. Sarah's eyes were swollen and red-rimmed, and her normally squared shoulders sagged as though she carried a twenty-pound weight on them. She looked like she'd aged five years in the space of forty-five minutes.

Ben pointed to a pair of swinging doors with little windows in them. "They took Dad back there as soon as we arrived. Right now, we don't know what's going on. I guess we'll just have to wait until someone comes out here to tell us."

"Johnny," Sarah said, grasping my wrist. "I know there's a cafeteria somewhere on this floor of the building. Would you be an angel and get me a cup of coffee?"

"Of course," I told her.

Then I looked at Ben. "Want something?"

He shook his head.

Moments later, I strolled down a brightly lit corridor, passing doors with labels like X-Ray, Linens, and so forth. The linoleum floor gleamed like a mirror. I encountered nurses in crisp white uniforms and stockings, doctors in scrubs with stethoscopes hanging about their necks. An orderly pushed a gurney with a gray-haired man lying on it who was seemingly asleep.

The cafeteria was as quiet as a tomb and virtually devoid of patrons. Only a few tables were occupied. The coffee urn was self-serve, and I filled a paper cup for Sarah. After I added a packet of sugar and a dash of cream, I paid at the cashier's stand.

Back in the ER waiting room, I found a middle-aged man in a suit and tie conversing with Sarah and Ben.

"Johnny," Sarah said, "this is Doctor Heinzmann, Will's physician."

The doctor didn't extend his hand; he only nodded before returning his attention to Sarah.

"I believe your husband suffered a hemorrhagic stroke; bleeding in his brain deprived certain brain cells of oxygen to the point where they died. It's caused paralysis on the left side of his body—the face, arm, and leg."

Sarah's eyes glistened as she brought her fist to her mouth and bit her knuckles.

"Sometimes the paralysis is only temporary—it can often be alleviated through physical therapy—but other times, it's permanent. In your husband's case, it's too early to tell."

"Is he awake right now?" Ben asked.

The doctor shook his head. "I've sedated him so he'll remain calm. This was a traumatic event and he needs complete rest."

"What brought this on, Doctor?" Sarah said.

"Most likely hypertension."

"What's that?" Ben asked.

"High blood pressure usually caused by stress. The pressure causes blood vessel walls in the brain to weaken and ultimately burst. We call that sort of event an aneurysm."

"When can I see my husband?" Sarah asked.

"Right now, if you'd like, but I'm afraid he won't know you're there."

"Can I see him too?" Ben added.

Sarah turned her gaze to Ben. "Stay here with Johnny. I need to visit your father by myself."

Only after Sarah left with the doctor did I think about the cup of coffee I held. I figured by the time Sarah returned, the coffee would be cold, so I poured it into a water fountain's drain and tossed the empty cup into a trash can.

Ben and I took seats beside each other. Ben closed his eyes and rubbed his temples with the tips of his fingers. "I can't believe this is happening. Dad's always been so healthy. He never smoked cigarettes and rarely drinks. And he gets plenty of exercise with all the work he does."

"You heard the doctor," I said. "It's probably all the stress he's been under. A person can only take so much before something gives."

Ben shook his head. "This is my fault. It never would have happened if Chuck were still alive. He could've helped Dad with things."

I put a hand on Ben's shoulder. "You don't know that's the case—you shouldn't blame yourself."

Ben's eyes were teary and red when he looked at me.

"It *is* my fault, Johnny. Like I told you before, I'm just a miserable fuckup."

TEN DAYS AFTER his stroke, Will came home via ambulance. Because he was unable to walk or to stand for more than a few seconds, two attendants had to bring him into the house employing a gurney. The left side of Will's face still sagged. His left arm hung lifelessly, and his left leg wobbled when he was wheeled into the master bedroom and lifted into the king-size bed. When he talked, he mumbled because only the right side of his mouth could move.

Earlier in the day, when Ben and I had shared breakfast with Sarah, she offered specifics on what to expect in the days and weeks ahead. "Doctor Heinzmann says Will's recovery will be slow."

Ben knitted his eyebrows. "Define slow."

"Many months. It seems the stroke did significant damage to Will's brain. If he's ever to walk again and speak normally, he'll need intensive physical therapy to strengthen his muscles and joints."

Ben's chair squeaked when he rearranged his limbs. "I'm going to take a leave of absence from the university. I'll skip fall quarter and try to keep this place running while Dad recovers."

Sarah didn't say anything; she only looked at Ben and nodded.

"I'll take a leave of absence too," I said to Ben. "The two of us should be able to handle things."

Ben looked at me and shook his head. "I can't let you do that. I appreciate your offer, but this place is not your responsibility. It's mine. Plus, you need to get your education; it's important for your future."

"School can wait till January, I—"

"Johnny, no."

I lowered my gaze and fingered the rim of my coffee cup. I tried to imagine returning to school without Ben being there. How would I stand it and who would I live with? I'd be right back where I was the night Ben ate dinner at the ATO house: lonely and depressed. How would I survive without his touch every day?

Now, as Sarah, Ben, and I gathered around Will's bed, Will sat propped up by pillows stacked against the headboard. His gaze traveled to each of us as he mumbled his words.

"I'm sorry this happened," he said. "I don't want to be a burden."

"You *won't* be a burden," Sarah answered. "If you follow doctor's orders and do your physical therapy every day, you'll be on your feet in no time."

Will shook his head. "The groves and the cattle. How—"

"I'm taking time off from school, Dad. Of course, you'll need to tell me what to do each day, but I'll get it done, whether it's supervising the migrant workers or bookkeeping or whatever. I'll keep things going while you recover."

Will lowered his gaze, then looked up at Ben. "I'm afraid if you don't go back to school this fall you'll never go back. I've seen that happen with too many young men."

"I'll get my degree," Ben said, "but right now, school's on hold. The property's more important than textbooks."

Will lowered his gaze again and nodded. "All right, son. And thank you."

HOURS AFTER WILL returned home from the hospital, and right after Ben and I finished cleaning up the kitchen after dinner, I asked Ben to take a walk in the groves with me.

"We need to talk," I said.

Outside, the night was a warm and humid. We both shed our shirts and draped them over our shoulders. A three-quarter moon illuminated the grove. Crickets serenaded us while the resident hoot owl sang his ghostly tune. Our sneaker soles scuffed the sand as we ambled between two rows of trees, holding hands. A thousand stars twinkled overhead.

"I don't want to go back to school without you," I told Ben. "I should stay here and help with things."

"Do you know what would happen if you did?"

"What?"

"You'd lose your student deferment. Selective Service would draft your ass and send you to Vietnam, and *that* wouldn't be good, now would it?"

Shit.

"Won't they do the same to you?" I asked.

Ben shook his head. "I spoke with my local board. I explained my circumstances, and they told me I'll qualify for a hardship deferment because of my dad's health condition and the fact I'm my parents' only son."

I felt like I was sinking into a tarpit. All summer long, I'd assumed Ben and I would live together this school year and I'd fall asleep in his arms every night. But now it wasn't going to happen, was it?

"I know you're disappointed," Ben said, "and so am I. Believe me, I'd like nothing better than to share an apartment with you this fall. I was so looking forward to it. I had all these visions of us cooking meals together and lying on the sofa in our underwear, watching TV at night. It would have been amazing."

I squeezed Ben's hand. "Maybe by January, your dad will recover. He could run things again, and you could go back to school for winter quarter."

"Maybe," Ben said, but his tone told me he didn't think that would happen.

Chapter Twenty-Five

ON AUGUST 20, a Gainesville rental service phoned me and Ben. They had a one-bedroom apartment available, two blocks from campus, in the College Park neighborhood.

"It's partially furnished," the agent told us. "The rent's $100 per month. I'll need first and last plus a $50 security deposit to hold it. You'd pay the electric bill. They'd cover the water, garbage, and sewer. This won't last long, so if you're interested I'd suggest you pounce on it."

Later that night, I lay in my bed in Chuck's room, staring at the ceiling while my thoughts spun. The College Park apartment was just what Ben and I had hoped for, only now Ben wouldn't be able to share it with me. So if I took the apartment, I'd need to find a roommate.

And I already knew who the roommate would be.

THE WEDNESDAY BEFORE Labor Day weekend, Ben drove me to St. Petersburg Beach with my belongings. The sky was overcast, and I-4's roadbed shone from recent rainfall. We passed by cattle ranches, farmland, and billboards advertising tourist attractions like Six Gun Territory and Cypress Gardens. An Orlando radio station played "Signed, Sealed, Delivered I'm Yours" by Stevie Wonder.

I felt lousy as hell. Back at Merritt Island, when Will and Sarah Stonecipher had told me goodbye and wished me well, I felt like I was abandoning them at the worst of times.

I paid a last-minute visit to Penny in the barn and fed her a carrot. "Bye, girlfriend," I whispered while she munched and I stroked her neck.

When Ben steered us onto the county road, I turned in my seat and studied the cattle in their pasture. I gazed at the rows of citrus trees and wondered how long it would be before I saw them again. And I tried to imagine how Ben would be able to manage it all on his own.

Now, as we cruised I-4 and the GTO's engine purred, I wondered to myself how my absence from Ben's life in the months ahead would affect his depression. Would it worsen?

We had agreed that we would talk on the phone at least twice a week, on Wednesday and Sunday nights. Ben would call me at exactly 9:00 p.m. But phone calls would be a poor substitute for our nightly walks in the groves and our Sunday-morning intimacies.

Our lives would change in a major way, and there was nothing Ben or I could do about it.

Two days before, when I'd phoned Steve about the College Park apartment, his first remark was "What about Ben?"

I explained events at Merritt Island. Then I said, "I don't want to spend another school year in the dorms, and this apartment's perfect for us. The rent's cheap and we can walk to campus. Between you and me, we can scrounge up things we'll need for the kitchen and all. What do you say?"

A few seconds passed before Steve responded. "I was going to live in the jock dorm on campus, so I'll need to discuss things with my folks. But it sounds good to me."

Afterward, when I discussed the situation with Ben, he scowled and shook his head.

"What is it?" I said.

"You know what'll happen once you two live in the same place, right?"

"I'm not *going* to let it. I belong to you, and no one—not Steve or anyone else—is going to touch me. Twice a month, I'll ride the bus over to Merritt Island on Friday afternoon. We can spend the weekend together. Then you can drive me back to Gainesville on Sunday. We'll make it work."

But even as I spoke those words, I wondered in the back of my mind if I could resist Steve's advances once we were in residence at College Park. We'd share a bedroom, for god's sake, and how long would it be before something happened?

Now, on our trip to St. Petersburg Beach, Ben and I visited a rest stop outside of Haines City to use the toilets and buy sodas from a vending machine, and then we were back on I-4, passing by towns like Lakeland and Plant City.

"My dad wants to hire an assistant to help me with things," Ben said. "I objected—I don't want to spend the money—but Dad overruled me; he said, 'I don't want you running yourself ragged. You'll just make yourself sick like I did.'"

"I think it's a good idea," I told Ben. "You deserve rest and a little time to relax each week. Life's not all about work."

"True," Ben said, squeezing my hand in his, "but who will I spend my free time with now that you're gone?"

Ben's words tore at my heart. I couldn't stand the thought of him feeling lonely and depressed.

I squeezed his hand back. "I wish things weren't the way they are. If I could change our circumstances, I'd see to it we were never separated."

Ben looked at me and nodded. "Don't worry, Johnny—things will be okay."

But would they be?

Chapter Twenty-Six

ON THE SATURDAY before Labor Day, Mom and I drove northward on I-75, doing sixty-five miles per hour. Steve followed us in his VW. The day was hot and sunny, and swarms of insects called love bugs hovered over the highway. They splattered Mom's windshield and plastered the front grill of her car.

My possessions crammed her back seat and trunk, including boxes full of kitchenware, plates, silverware, glasses, blankets, and linens, some garnered from friends' closets and attics, others hastily purchased by me or Steve at thrift shops. None of the stuff matched, but who cared? We even had a portable black-and-white TV with a rabbit-ears antenna we'd bought through a newspaper classified ad for twenty dollars.

Despite my angst over the separation from Ben, I felt a sense of excitement about returning to school and moving into the apartment with Steve. I'd never furnished a dwelling or kept house before. I'd never done much cooking either. Steve was in the same boat, so we were sailing into uncharted waters. Living in our own place would be a challenge, but one we'd deal with together.

So far, Steve had not made a single pass at me or said anything suggestive in the many hours we'd spent together in the days since my arrival from Merritt Island. It seemed he knew I meant what I'd said back in the motel at Cocoa Beach, and I believed he had finally accepted the fact I belonged to Ben.

When we arrived in Gainesville, the whole town buzzed with students moving into dorms and various dwellings surrounding campus.

Our apartment building was called Gator Manor. A three-story cinder-block structure with exterior staircases and corridors, it failed to live up to its grandiose title. But forty-foot pines and live oaks cast pleasant shade over the crabgrass lawn, and azalea shrubs as big as Steve's VW hugged the exterior walls. The unit Steve and I had rented was located on the second floor, so we had to tote everything up a flight of stairs. The day was hot and humid, and we sweated as we lugged boxes from the cars.

Our corner-unit apartment was maybe 800 square feet with plaster walls, venetian blinds at the windows, and linoleum tile floors. The living/dining area had a vinyl-upholstered sofa, a plaid Barcalounger with multiple cigarette burn holes in the arms, a coffee table with a broken leg, and a chrome-and-porcelain dining table with two metal chairs. An electric heating unit hulked in one corner. The kitchen featured wooden cabinets, an electric range, and a rusty fridge. The bathroom was equipped with a tiled shower, a wall sink, a medicine cabinet with a cracked mirror, and a toilet with rust stains in the bowl. The bedroom was furnished with two twin beds bearing suspicious-looking stains on their mattresses, two Formica bureaus, and a closet with sliding doors.

Okay, the place was a dump, but still...

Sunlight poured into every room through the casement windows, and outside, a blue jay tootled on a live oak limb. So despite its drawbacks, the apartment was much better than the dorm room I'd shared with Ben the previous year.

After my mom carried a stack of my hang-up clothes into the bedroom and put them in the closet, she walked through the apartment with her arms crossed under her breasts. She glanced at cobwebs in ceiling corners and mildew growing in the shower grout. She peered into the kitchen cabinets and drawers.

"You boys need to give this place a thorough cleaning. And you'll have to buy a shower curtain right away. Did you think to bring toilet paper?"

Mom treated us to lunch at a fried chicken place on Thirteenth Street, where a sign said the restaurant was looking to hire a part-time busboy. I spoke to the assistant manager, who told me to come around Tuesday after 5:00 p.m. when the head manager could talk to me.

Back at Gator Manor, Mom waved as she drove off toward I-75 for the trip back to St. Petersburg Beach.

Steve and I spent the better part of the afternoon unpacking, and by four thirty, everything was put away. A stack of *Time* magazines rested on the coffee table and the cupboards were stocked with canned vegetables and boxes of breakfast cereal, macaroni-and-cheese, and spaghetti noodles. We'd made our beds with sheets, blankets, and pillows, and bath towels hung on a bar in the bathroom. Plates and glasses perched in the kitchen cabinets, and our mishmash of silverware resided in a kitchen drawer. The place was starting to look like a real dwelling.

Steve and I visited a supermarket in the VW. We bought milk, juice, eggs, hamburger, lunchmeat, cheese, bread, and other perishables. We purchased paper goods too. And heeding my mom's advice, we stopped by a five-and-dime for a shower curtain.

Saturday night, after we bathed, I cooked dinner—spaghetti with meat sauce and an iceberg lettuce salad with Italian dressing. We cleaned up the kitchen, then walked to a sketchy gas station where they sold me a six-pack of beer without asking for my ID. Back at our apartment, we sat on the sofa with our bare feet resting on the coffee table and sipped from our beers. A battered floor lamp we'd found next to a dumpster in St. Pete cast its glow, reflecting in Steve's pretty eyes.

"I can't believe we're actually living here," he said, "just you and me."

I nodded while reflecting on the weird turn of events that had brought us there. I thought of Will Stonecipher, lying in his bed with half of his body lifeless and limp, and of Ben going through his days without me beside him. Did he miss me as much as I missed him?

Steve showed me his schedule of classes for the week and the subjects looked all too familiar: English, American Institutions, Logic, and of course, my nemesis—physical science.

"I'll have track practice every weekday at 5:00 p.m., for ninety minutes. And there's a meeting at the field house tomorrow afternoon I'll need to attend. They take the sport seriously up here."

At nine, we turned on our little TV to watch *NBC's Saturday Night at the Movies*. That night's offering was *True Grit* with John Wayne and Glen Campbell. The film was okay, but halfway through I found myself yawning.

"It's been a long day," I told Steve, "and the beer made me sleepy. I'm ready to turn in."

"Let's do it," Steve said.

We used the toilet and brushed our teeth, side by side at the bathroom sink. We locked the front door and extinguished light fixtures. In the bedroom, we undressed. The night was still and warm, and I switched on a box fan to help keep us cool. We crawled into our respective beds, and I lay on my back, staring at the ceiling and listening to the hum of traffic on University Avenue.

Glow from a nearby streetlamp entered the room through the venetian blinds, enough so I could make out Steve's facial features. He also lay on his back. His fingers were gathered behind his neck and his elbows jutted.

"My bed's pretty comfortable," he said. "How's yours?"

"It's fine."

"I think this place is going to work out really well," Steve added. "I like it here."

I didn't say anything.

"Johnny?"

"H-m-m-m?"

"I know you'd rather be sharing this apartment with Ben because he means so much to you. But I hope living here with me counts for something too. I still consider you my best friend, and having you here each day will make my first year of college much easier. Thank you for this."

"Hey, I'm glad we're here together," I responded.

"Are you really?"

Am I?

"Of course," I said. "Now let's get some sleep."

FRIDAY AFTERNOON ARRIVED, and the first week of classes had ended. The courses I took that quarter differed radically from those I'd endured the previous year. I had a five-hour class in humanities, a precalculus class, a course called Introduction to Journalism, and another in geology. All but the precalculus class were pretty interesting. I didn't want to take precalculus, but to obtain my associate's degree at the end of the year, I *had* to take at least one advanced math class, so there I was, struggling to understand derivatives and variables.

I had seen little of Steve since classes started. Each morning, after a hasty breakfast, we were both out the door. Steve had track practice every afternoon. Weekdays, he ate lunch and dinner at the training table provided by the team, so on those days, I didn't see him till he arrived home around eight in the evening. By then, I was immersed in my studies, and next thing I knew, bedtime was upon us.

Four days before, I had interviewed with the manager at the fried chicken place and landed the busboy job. Already I had worked two shifts, four hours on Tuesday and Thursday, and I'd work another Saturday evening. The pay was $1.65 per hour plus a share of the tips left by diners, which was pretty good money for part-time labor. After taxes, I would clear about twenty-five bucks a week, and the extra money would really help with expenses that school year.

Wednesday night, Ben had phoned me exactly at nine, and we talked for nearly an hour. It felt so good to hear Ben's voice, but then I had to tell him about my new job and how it wouldn't allow me to leave Gainesville on weekends to visit Merritt Island.

"I'm sorry," I said, "but I really need the cash to make ends meet."

"It's okay, Johnny. You have to be practical."

"Maybe you could drive up to Gainesville some weekend soon. You can stay with me and Steve in the apartment. I'll have to work Saturday night, but otherwise, I'll be free to spend time with you."

"You don't understand," Ben said. "This is the time of year when we start preparations for the migrants' arrival in late October. I'll work twelve-hour days between now and then."

Shit.

I asked Ben if he'd hired an assistant yet.

"I'm working on it," he said, "but it's not easy finding someone who's willing to work as hard as me or my dad."

"And how's Will doing?"

"He started physical therapy this week. Right now, the therapist comes to the house three days a week. He gets Dad out of bed and has him using a walker with wheels on it. But the muscles on Dad's left side are so weak he can't do much other than shuffle around."

I talked about my classes and also about the Gator Manor apartment. "It's nothing fancy but much better than the dorm. You'll like it when you see it."

A few moments of silence passed before Ben spoke again.

"How are you and Steve getting along?"

I shifted my weight from one leg to the other while twisting the phone cord around my finger. "I haven't seen much of him this week. He's busy with classes and the track team."

"Have you guys...?"

"What?"

"Had sex?"

I blew air out my nostrils. "Of *course* not, that's something I save for you and me."

Ben's voice shook a little when he spoke. "Thanks for saying that, Johnny. It means a lot to me."

Now, in my apartment's kitchen, I fried hamburger, boiled noodles, and heated a can of green beans. The sun had already disappeared behind buildings to the west of Gator Manor, and the color of the sky in that direction was a mix of orange, yellow, and robin's egg blue. Crickets chirped in nearby trees, and traffic rumbled on University Avenue. The temperature was probably around eighty-five, and my shirt felt damp in the armpits. Sweat beaded on my upper lip.

Between my classes and the two shifts I'd worked at the fried chicken place, this was the first time I was able to relax and forget about my responsibilities. The night before, prior to going to bed, Steve and I had agreed that we would see a film on campus at the student union, a foreign production called *Zabriskie Point*.

Steve arrived home, just as I was cleaning up the kitchen and putting my leftovers in the fridge. He wore khaki shorts and a blue T-shirt with the UF track team logo on the chest. His hair was neatly combed, and he smelled of soap and shampoo from his evening shower at the field house. He carried a stack of books under one arm and also a zippered canvas bag containing his running gear.

When I asked him how his day had gone, he drew a deep breath and let it out while his shoulders sagged. "I'm beat. Our training schedule's wicked—I ran thirty-five miles this week. And I'm already behind on my reading assignments. I'll have to study tomorrow and Sunday to catch up."

I glanced at my wristwatch. "The movie starts at seven. Let me grab a quick shower and then we can get going."

Steve groaned.

"What is it?" I asked.

He plopped onto our sofa and put his feet up on the coffee table. "Is it okay if we skip the film? All I want to do is buy a six-pack and maybe watch a little TV."

I raised a shoulder and let it drop. "That's fine."

In the bedroom, I undressed and tossed all my clothes into my hamper, then hit the bathroom and climbed into the shower. I turned the handles, and warm water pounded my shoulders and upper back. I scrubbed my limbs with soap and a washcloth and shampooed my hair.

After I dried off, I returned to the bedroom, where Steve lay on his bed with his hands joined behind his neck. Light from the ceiling fixture reflected in his eyes. He had kicked off his shoes, and his legs were crossed at the ankles. His gaze traveled over me like a clothes iron pressing a pant leg, and a little shiver ran through me because I knew exactly what he was thinking as he viewed me naked.

I slipped into a pair of cotton briefs. Then I stood before my bureau mirror, combing my damp hair into place. I tried to maintain a calm demeanor, but already my knees quivered.

"Johnny?"

"Yeah?"

"Don't put on any more clothes, okay?"

I stared at myself in the mirror. There was no question what Steve wanted, and I knew how much I'd enjoy an hour of tenderness with him. But once again, I faced the same crossroads I'd come to multiple times since finding out Steve was gay. Each time I'd had a choice, and on most occasions, I acceded to Steve's will.

Should I now?

I turned to look at Steve, just as he pulled his T-shirt off his shoulders and over his head. He looked at me with his eyebrows raised as he tossed the shirt aside.

"It's been a long week. So can we?"

I looked into Steve's pretty eyes, and then let my gaze travel over his smooth torso. He was so beautiful he was almost like a dream. Between my thighs, I stiffened. I lowered my gaze and licked my lips, then returned my gaze to Steve.

"All right, but why don't we move our beds together first?"

Chapter Twenty-Seven

ON SUNDAY MORNING, I woke to find Steve's cheek resting against my shoulder. Sunlight poured through an open window and outside birds tweeted in the pines and live oaks. The morning air felt cool and fresh on my face.

We hadn't bothered to separate our beds since Friday evening, and why should we? Now that I'd given myself to Steve again, what was the point of pretending we wouldn't have sex on a regular basis in the days and weeks ahead? After all, Ben was 165 miles from Gainesville, and I wouldn't likely see him until Thanksgiving. But I'd spend time with Steve every day, and I might as well make the most of our situation. In our Gator Manor apartment, we had complete privacy; we could do whatever we wanted, and no one would know.

The night before, when I'd come home from the fried chicken place, the time was around 10:00 p.m. Steve lay on the sofa watching an episode of *Mannix*. He wore cotton briefs, nothing else. I smelled of grease and cigarette smoke, so I showered. Then I sat alongside Steve with my damp towel wrapped around my waist. I put my feet up on the coffee table and clasped my hands behind my neck. On a windowsill, the box fan blew cool air into the room.

Steve put his hand on my thigh. Then he kissed my cheek. "How was work tonight?"

I shrugged while gazing into the TV screen. "It's an easy job, really, except for the fact I'm on the move the whole time. I should buy a better pair of shoes so my feet don't hurt at the end of the night."

"Want me to rub them for you?"

We changed position so that my head rested on one arm of the sofa and my feet were sitting in Steve's lap. He worked on one foot, massaging the arch, the ball, and then my toes. It felt so heavenly I groaned.

"You're good at this," I said.

Steve nodded while he worked his finger between my toes and rubbed the finger back and forth. "My mom taught me. She'd always give me a massage after cross-country practice when my feet were hurting like crazy."

After a few minutes, Steve switched to the other foot, and I groaned again at his attentions. He kneaded the arch with his thumbs, applying just the right amount of pressure.

"Want to do something tonight?" he asked.

I shrugged again. "I'm fine with this until it's time to hit the bedroom."

"Works for me," Steve said while he continued to work on my foot. "I spent most of tonight catching up on my reading for school. Now I just want to relax and enjoy spending time with you."

I shifted my ass on the sofa cushions while I thought about Friday night and how Steve had grunted as I thrust inside him and gazed into his eyes. The backs of his knees rested on my shoulders. His hot breath swept my face, and when he came his muscle squeezed me like a vise. My orgasm was so intense I cried out, and the sound of my voice bounced off the walls.

Now, as lay next to Steve on Sunday morning, I recalled our sex session on Saturday that might have been even better than Friday's. We had tried a new position, with me on my back and Steve straddling me. He lowered himself onto my erection, and I felt him stretch. Then he raised his chin and gazed at the ceiling while he clenched his jaw.

"You okay?" I asked him.

He nodded. "Just give me a minute to relax."

Ten minutes later, he scattered my chest with sticky pearls while I bucked my hips and chills ran through my body as I unloaded inside Steve. After he dismounted, he lay beside me, and we both stared at the ceiling, breathing.

"That may have been the best ever," Steve finally said.

I looked at him and waggled my eyebrows. "It *was* special, wasn't it?"

Now, as I lay in bed on Sunday morning, I listened to Steve breathe and wondered where things between us were headed. It seemed pretty clear that we'd sleep together each night, just as Ben and I used to in the dorm. Only we wouldn't even have to move our beds apart each morning because we had our privacy.

It's all so easy, isn't it?

BEN CALLED ME at exactly 9:00 p.m. on Sunday night, and his voice sounded tired.

"I spent most of today cleaning two barracks and placing linens and blankets on each bed. Oh, and I hired a new assistant; he starts tomorrow."

"What's he like?"

"Typical Brevard farm and ranch hand—a twenty-one-year-old from Cocoa who quit high school when he was sixteen. He's not the sharpest tool in the shed, but he surfs at Sebastian Inlet so we have that in common. I think we'll get along okay."

Ben asked about my new job, and I told him what I'd told Steve earlier, that it was easy work and the money was good. "Including my share of the tips, I cleared almost thirty bucks this week."

We talked about my classes and also about the apartment and how it was working out so far. Then Ben asked about Steve. "Are you two guys getting along all right?"

I glanced into the bedroom where Steve lay on our conjoined beds, on his belly, studying a textbook. He wore a pair of tight-fitting briefs that showed off his butt cheeks.

I licked my lips before I answered. "Everything's fine."

"I sure wish I could pay you a visit in Gainesville," Ben said, "'cause I'm missing you like crazy. But it's just not possible right now."

"I'd ask for a Saturday off so I could visit Merritt Island, but I just started the job and I don't think asking would sit well with my boss, not right now. Maybe in a month or so, I'll approach him on it."

When our phone conversation concluded, Ben said, "I love you, Johnny."

"Same here," I told Ben.

"Say it, please—I need to hear the words."

My voice squeaked a bit when I said, "I love you too, Ben. I really do."

After we hung up, I sat on the living room sofa and stared into space while my brain churned. I *did* love Ben, more than I'd ever loved anyone. But he was so far away, and I was a weak-willed bastard who would soon crawl into bed with Steve.

What kind of man was I?

OUR SECOND WEEK of school seemed to last forever. Between classes, studying, and my job I had little time for anything else. Just like the week before, I saw little of Steve until he got home from the field house around 8:00 p.m. We'd both spend a couple of hours on the sofa with our textbooks, and then it was time for bed. When we crawled between the sheets, we were both too tired for sex. All we wanted to do was hold each other and sleep.

Wednesday night when Ben called, he didn't sound as tired as he had Sunday.

"My new assistant—his name is Brian—helped out on spraying the cattle with insecticide this week. He's a good worker and doesn't complain. I think I made a good choice."

"How's your dad doing?"

Ben paused before answering.

"The physical therapy is going slowly. I mean, it's been less than a month since the stroke, so I guess I shouldn't expect improvement right away, but Dad still spends most of his day in bed."

I shifted my weight from one leg to the other. "Think there's any chance you'll be able to come back to school in January?"

"Doubtful, but we'll see."

Around eight on Friday night, Steve entered the apartment with his books and canvas gear bag. He tossed his belongings onto the Barcalounger, and after he flopped down next to me on the sofa, he raked his fingers through my hair while a chill ran up my spine.

"I need a kiss," he said.

He brought a hand to the back of my neck and pulled my face to his. Our mouths met, our lips parted, and our tongues rubbed. I tasted the spaghetti Steve had eaten for dinner. Little smacking sounds filled the room while the two of us slobbered like kids at an after-prom party.

I was already as hard as a stone.

When we finally parted, Steve eyes glittered and his cheeks were flushed. His chest rose and fell with his breathing. "What'll we do with our evening?"

I shrugged.

"We should get out and do something," Steve suggested.

We decided to play foosball at a tavern on University Avenue. We could even walk there from Gator Manor. The day's heat had lessened, and it actually felt pleasant outdoors while we ambled down a sidewalk, passing storefronts. Traffic on the avenue whizzed by us, and headlights shone their glares into our faces.

I squinted while Steve talked about track practice.

"We ran nine miles today at seven-minute-per-mile pace. Some of these guys on the team are unbelievable; they weren't even breathing hard at the end."

"Do you think you're keeping up?"

Steve rocked his head from side to side. "I guess, but this is NCAA Division 1 stuff. I'll need to work on my training if I want to keep my scholarship."

The Bench & Bar tavern was owned by a local attorney. The place was poorly ventilated, and a scrim of cigarette smoke hung in the air. Furnishings included a bar with stools, a few booths, and several table-and-chair combinations. Rock music blared from a jukebox. Most patrons were university students wearing blue jeans and T-shirts. We bought a pitcher of beer, and the bartender gave us two plastic cups.

A separate room housed two pool tables and two foosball tables, all in use. We placed a quarter on one foosball table where four boys in fraternity jerseys competed. Then we sat on stools and sipped from our beer cups, watching the guys play and waiting our turn.

It didn't take long before the fraternity boys' game ended. The winners were pretty good, and Steve and I knew we'd have our work cut out for us if we wanted to be competitive. We shook hands with our opponents and took our positions. I played goalie, Steve forward.

Steve's family owned a foosball table they kept in the breezeway at their St. Petersburg home. I had played on that table, as Steve's teammate, scores of times, usually with our friends Stewart and James as opponents, so we were seasoned teammates.

Steve and I played well, and quickly took a lead over the fraternity boys. The ball spun and cracked against the table walls; it skittered between the little men on the stainless-steel poles and made a clunk when a team scored a point.

When I looked across the table at the fraternity boys, I wondered what they might say if they knew Steve and I were lovers, and what they'd think if they could see what we often did in our bedroom. They'd probably call us perverts or some other insulting name.

Then I thought about the night the year before when the ATO guys came to the dorm room to recruit Ben as a pledge. Ben had tossed his pledge pen into a trash can, and the memory brought a smile to my lips. Now, I wondered what Ben was doing at the moment, and then I realized how much I missed him.

All right, for the past week, I had slept beside Steve every night. We had shared sex twice and would likely do so again that night, and I had enjoyed our intimacies a whole lot. But I also knew this: if Ben were to return to school the following day, I would immediately break things off with Steve, no doubt about it.

I asked myself if I should feel guilty about that. Was I simply using Steve as a surrogate for Ben since Ben wasn't available right then? Was I nothing more than an opportunist?

Now, at the Bench and Bar, the faggots—me and Steve—won the foosball game 7-3. The fraternity boys asked for a rematch, but Steve and I declined.

"We just want to drink our beer and relax," I told them. Then, after Steve and I found an empty booth to occupy, we poured ourselves fresh cups of beer.

Steve gazed about the room with a smile on his lips. "It's still hard for me to believe I'm here."

"In this tavern?"

He hissed. "I mean in *Gainesville,* running track, going to classes, and living with you in our own apartment." He lowered his voice, and his gaze drilled into mine. "And I'm still amazed we're sleeping together. It's cool waking up next to you each morning and knowing I can touch you whenever I want to."

I lowered my chin and studied the tabletop. I took a sip of beer and moistened my lips with my tongue. Then I looked at Steve. I wanted to tell him what I'd been thinking about during the foosball game: that when the time came, I would choose Ben as my partner in life, and that our present situation—Steve's and mine—was only temporary. But I refrained from saying those words just then because I knew when our beer pitcher was empty, we would walk back to Gator Manor. We'd enter the bedroom, get undressed, and our bodies would entwine.

Don't say anything, Darling—don't spoil the evening.

Just...shut up.

Chapter Twenty-Eight

WEEKS PASSED. BY then, Steve and I had fallen into our routines. For me: classes, my busboy job, and studying. For Steve: classes, track practice, and studying. I did my best to keep up with my precalculus class. All my other courses were a piece of cake, as long as I finished my reading assignments and didn't skip class.

Steve was cruising academically, now that he'd adopted a study schedule and kept to it.

When mid-October arrived, the evening temperatures cooled, so now we I slept under a blanket.

The Florida Gators football team was playing well, their record 5-1, with their only loss to Alabama. Our new head coach was a guy named Doug Dickey whom nobody seemed to like, not the players, the fans, or the sports writers for Florida newspapers. Arrogant was the word I normally heard when Dickey's name was mentioned, either in conversation or in print.

Ben and I continued to speak over the phone Wednesday and Sunday nights, but I sensed he and I had grown a few degrees apart, due to the fact we hadn't seen each other in over six weeks. How could we possibly maintain emotional intensity between us when 165 miles separated us?

Meanwhile, I had shared intimacies with Steve on a daily basis. We didn't have sex every day, of course. Often we were just too tired for it. But we traded kisses and put our arms around each other's shoulders when we watched TV on the sofa. We slept naked and spoon-style every night, with my hips pressed against Steve's ass and my chest touching his shoulder blades.

Things came easily between me and Steve now; we never quarreled. Sunday was our special day because Steve didn't train and I didn't work at the fried chicken place. We had the day to ourselves. We liked to have sex in midafternoon while light streamed into our bedroom through the windows. And Sunday was the one night of the week when we shared an evening meal. I liked to cook, but Steve didn't, so I prepared dinner and he cleaned up afterward.

It all worked, and I knew Steve loved me deeply. He had told me so several times in recent weeks, and of course I had told him the same.

But was I acting like a total shit, carrying on an affair with Steve behind Ben's back?

And what would I do when Ben returned to Gainesville?

THE FIRST WEEKEND in November, my boss gave me Saturday off so I could ride the bus to Merritt Island and spend the weekend with Ben. Midday Friday, I asked Steve to give me a lift to the Greyhound depot in his VW.

During the ride to the depot, Steve said, "Are you going to tell Ben that you and are living as a couple up here?"

I gazed into my lap and shook my head. "He'd be so disappointed if he knew."

"Maybe you shouldn't even make this trip," Steve suggested. "Maybe you ought to break things off with Ben."

I shook my head again. "I can't do that to him; he counts on me for emotional support. You don't know how important those Wednesday and Sunday phone calls are."

When we reached the depot, I grabbed my overnight bag from the back seat. Then I squeezed Steve's shoulder.

"Thanks for the ride. I'll see you Sunday afternoon."

He gazed into my eyes and nodded, but I could tell he wasn't happy about my departure.

The bus took me to Orlando, a three-hour trip because we made stops in Ocala and Leesburg to pick up passengers. Then I had a forty-five-minute wait before I could board another bus that would take me to Merritt Island. We traveled the Bee Line Expressway, passing by cattle ranches, pine forests, and swampland, and by the time we reached Merritt Island, shadows had grown long. The sky to the west glowed in shades of red, yellow, and green.

Sarah Stonecipher waited for me when I departed the bus. She looked careworn. Her hair was slightly disheveled and her shoulders sagged, but she greeted me with a hug and a tiny smile.

"Ben would have come for you himself," she told me, "but the migrants are already picking and the fruit has to go to the sorting barn right away. Ben and Brian have hauled orange crates since sunup."

After we climbed into Sarah's car and she started the engine, I asked about Will.

Sarah gripped the steering wheel while she let out her breath and stared through the windshield. "He's making progress—he's able to walk better than he could six weeks ago—but still has a long way to go."

We passed by familiar terrain on the way to the Stoneciphers' property: orange groves, squatty houses with screened porches, dense tropical forest. The top on Sarah's car was lowered, and the wind tossed my long hair about. Already my pulse quickened at the thought I'd soon see Ben.

Once we reached the house and I stowed my bag in Chuck's room, I visited the horse barn to greet Penny and stroke her muzzle. She pawed her stall floor and nickered while I fed her a lump of sugar from a jar on a nearby shelf.

"I'll give you a nice grooming this weekend," I told her.

When Ben arrived at the house in the pickup truck, my heart leapt into my throat. I had almost forgotten how handsome he was, and it seemed to me, after he exited the truck, that his muscles had thickened a bit since I'd last seen him. He wore a plaid cowboy shirt, dusty blue jeans, and cowboy boots. He'd had a haircut recently, and the trim looked good on him.

A big grin crossed Ben's face when he approached me and we shook hands. "I'm so glad you're here. Thanks for coming."

Another guy exited the truck from the passenger side. His blond hair reflected the fading afternoon sunlight. He was as tall as Ben with broad shoulders and a slender waist. Ben introduced him as Brian Conover, and we shook hands. His grip was firm and warm, and his ice-blue eyes crinkled at their corners when his gaze met mine.

"I hear you guys have been working long hours," I said.

"We're always on the go around here," Brian responded, his voice a raspy baritone flavored with a drawl. "Ben's a darned slave driver."

Ben looked at Brian and chuckled. "I work just as hard as you do, Bubba."

"I won't deny that," Brian said, "but look—I'm beat. Mind if I call it a day?"

"It's fine," Ben agreed. "I'll see you around seven tomorrow."

Brian climbed onto a Honda motorcycle with a split in the vinyl seat and a cracked headlight. He kicked the starter a couple of times before the engine turned over, then gave us a wave as he drove off toward the county road.

"So," I said, "I guess he's turning out okay?"

Ben nodded. "He's a hard worker, plus we get along well. I could have done a lot worse."

I followed Ben into the house and then to his parents' bedroom, where Will sat in a chair, reading a *Time* magazine. When he saw me, the right side of his face smiled, and he spoke with a mumble.

"Hi, Johnny. Welcome."

We shook hands.

Ben looked at me. "I'm filthy and I'll need to shower before dinner. Why don't you keep Dad company while I do that?"

I took a seat on the bed, facing Will, and asked how he was feeling.

He shrugged his right shoulder. "I'm not doing cartwheels at the moment. How's school?"

I talked about my classes, my job, and the apartment I shared with Steve. "I stay really busy, but I don't mind. The days fly by."

Will nodded. "I was hoping Ben could return to school in January, but now it doesn't seem possible—not with my health like it is—and I feel terrible about it."

I moistened my lips. "Maybe by spring quarter, he'll be able to come back to Gainesville. That's five months from now."

Will lowered his gaze and didn't say anything.

SARAH SERVED A delicious seafood stew for dinner, with shrimp, chunks of fish, crabmeat, clams, oysters, and assorted vegetables, all floating in a creamy broth flavored with sherry. Like always, an extra place setting appeared before a chair at the dining room table.

After Ben and I cleaned up the kitchen, we took a walk through the orange groves. A half moon was up, and it bathed us in silvery light. The night was cool and still, and crickets chirped in the trees. Over in the barracks, a radio played a James Brown song, "Give It Up or Turn It a Loose." I didn't often listen to funk music, but Brown's number had a catchy beat I kind of liked.

Ben took my hand in his as we ambled along, and our sneaker soles scuffed the sand.

"I can't believe you're here tonight," Ben said. "It feels so good to touch you and hear your voice. And I'm not waiting for sex till Sunday morning. Tonight, I'm sneaking into Chuck's room after my folks go to bed. I have plans for you, Mr. Darling."

I squeezed Ben's hand. "Sounds good to me."

"Every night when I go to bed, I think of how much I miss you. It's hell being apart like we are right now. Some days, I don't know how I stand it."

A wave of guilt washed over me when I thought of how, up in Gainesville, I fell asleep every night holding Steve while Ben went to bed alone.

"How about a kiss?" Ben asked.

We turned to each other in the moonlight. My heart chugged and a shiver ran up my spine. Ben toyed with my ear while our lips made smacking sounds. I felt so happy I wanted to weep. How had I stood my separation from Ben for so many weeks? And how would I handle watching him drive away from Gator Manor on Sunday? Already I dreaded that moment.

"Do you mind helping me and Brian out tomorrow?" Ben asked. "There's so much to do, and we could really use an extra pair of hands. Dad will pay you for your time."

"Not a problem," I said. "And you don't need to pay me. I'm just glad I can be of use."

Two hours later, around 10:00 p.m., I lay in Chuck's room, staring at the ceiling with my fingers interlaced behind my neck. Moonlight entered through the open windows. The hinges on the door squeaked when Ben stole into the room, wearing only his briefs. After he placed a tube of jelly and a few hand towels on the nightstand, he sat alongside me on the mattress and ran his fingers through my hair.

"We'll have to be quiet," he whispered. Then he pulled the bedcovers aside and slipped in next to me. I felt the warmth of his skin, inhaled his familiar scent. Our bodies came together, and instantly I was as stiff as a dowel. Ben reached between my legs and gave me a squeeze.

"Ditch your briefs," he told me. "I'll do the same."

Moments later, we were naked and I was atop Ben. I rolled my tongue around in his ear and listened to him sigh.

"God, Johnny, how I've missed this."

A little while later, after we'd both reached orgasm, we lay side by side in the moonlight, breathing, and I marveled at just how wonderful I'd felt when I came inside Ben. It was almost like that first time with him when I cried my eyes out.

For a moment, I considered telling Ben about my life with Steve in Gainesville. I liked being honest with Ben; I didn't want to hide things from him. But I was afraid that explaining things would only hurt him, and he'd already endured enough sadness in his life.

Why add to his emotional burden?

Saturday morning, I woke up alone in Chuck's room. But I could smell Ben's scent on my skin and the sheets. Sunlight poured in, and a blue jay sang on a laurel oak branch just outside the windows. The all-too-familiar aroma of horse shit wafted from the barn out back. I buried my cheek in my pillow and recalled my lovemaking with Ben the night before, when everything had seemed just right.

A thought entered my head. If I were to quit my job at the fried chicken place, I could visit Merritt Island every weekend. And if I worked for the Stoneciphers ten hours every Saturday, I'd earn about two-thirds of what I did at my present job. Sure, it would mean less money in my pocket, but I could get by, no problem. And then I could spend two nights and two days with Ben each week.

At the breakfast table, I discussed my idea with Will, Sarah, and Ben.

"That's a lot of time spent away from school," Ben said. "Won't your grades suffer?"

I shook my head. "If I quit my job, I'll have two more weekday nights free when I can get most of my studying done. And I can hit the books Sunday nights when I get back to Gainesville."

All three Stoneciphers exchanged glances.

Then Will told me, "We know what a good worker you are, and we'd be glad to have you here on weekends, if that's what you want to do."

Ben, Brian, and I spent most of our Saturday in the groves, loading full citrus crates into the pickup truck's bed, then driving them over to the sorting barn, where a half-dozen women picked through the fruit, setting aside the best oranges for the Stoneciphers' retail outlet in Cocoa Beach. We also drove emptied crates back to the groves and stacked them so they could be refilled.

The weather was close to perfect: sunny, still, and cool. I wasn't even breaking a sweat as I hefted crates.

Like always, it amazed me how agile and quick the migrants were as they scaled their ladders and plucked fruit from the trees. They conversed among themselves in their curious patois as they worked, cracking jokes and laughing. Sometimes, they sang together, sad little tunes about love gone bad or pretty gospel numbers that required a bit of harmonizing.

Already, I could see why Ben was pleased with Brian's performance. More muscular than Ben or me, Brian slung full crates of citrus around as if they were matchboxes. Like the migrants, he moved swiftly. He took a cigarette break maybe once an hour, and that was the only time he stopped moving.

When we drove the full truck to the sorting shed, the three of us sat in the cab with me in the middle. As we rocked along and the gears grinded, my knees and shoulders rubbed against Ben and Brian, and I had to admit it felt kind of sexy getting sandwiched between two cute guys.

Brian was good-looking, and not just because of his athletic physique. His blond hair glistened in the sunlight, and his blue eyes twinkled when he cracked a joke. His chin was square, and when he smiled, his big teeth reminded me of piano keys.

No wonder Ben liked working alongside him.

Sarah served the three of us a hot lunch at the house, and then we were back in the groves until sunset. By dusk, my back, shoulders, and arms ached from my labors, but the good kind of ache, one that let me know I'd accomplished something meaningful with my day.

Saturday night, Ben and I visited a movie theater in Cocoa to watch *Tora, Tora, Tora,* a film about events leading up to the 1941 Japanese attack on Pearl Harbor. The movie was a nonstop action production and very entertaining, but I still found myself yawning during the last half hour of the film. On the drive home, I held Ben's hand in mine as he steered the GTO down a county highway. The windows were lowered, and cool air rushed through the car.

Ben squeezed my hand.

"In the morning, as soon as my folks leave for church, I'll come to Chuck's room."

I felt a tingle in my briefs. "Perfect."

Ben said, "Tomorrow, we'll have a few hours to fill before I drive you back to Gainesville, so figure out what you'd like to do with our time."

I recalled the Cocoa Beach Pier and the surfers we'd watched there during my first visit to Brevard County. How long ago had that been?

"Let's go to the beach and take a walk along the shore," I suggested.

Sunday morning, after a nice lovemaking session, Ben and I showered together. Then we slipped into swim trunks, T-shirts, and sandals. Another beautiful fall day greeted us when we stepped outside. The sun shone and the air was cool. The GTO's engine roared as we cruised eastward on the Bee Line.

I felt about as relaxed as I'd ever been, despite my achy muscles. I had fifteen dollars in my pocket, money Will had insisted on paying me for my Saturday labors. I sipped from a cold bottle of 7-Up while I stared out my passenger window at a marina where sailboats rocked. Wind rushed through the car, fluttering my long hair.

"You know," I told Ben, "I like your short haircut—it looks good on you. I'm thinking I might get mine cut too. What do you think?"

Ben looked at me and touched my cheek with a fingertip. "Leave it long, will you?"

I smiled and said, "Whatever you want, Lover Boy."

After we fed a parking meter at the pier, we took off our sandals and walked along the shore. Wet sand oozed between my toes. A hundred yards to the east, a dozen surfers bobbed on boards, waiting for waves. I felt an urge to take Ben's hand in mine, and how I wished I could have done so. But I would have to satisfy myself with looking at him and listening to his voice instead.

"I'm really happy you're quitting your job," he said. "It'll be great having you here every weekend; almost as nice as when you lived at Merritt Island full-time."

"You're sure you won't mind driving me to Gainesville every Sunday? That's six hours in the car."

"True, but three of those hours, I'll be with you, so I'm fine with it."

Ben's remark made my spirits soar.

I bought us lunch at an open-air beachfront bar and grill. We dined on cheeseburgers, fries, and sodas, and once we'd finished our meal, Ben glanced at his wristwatch.

"We'd best get back to the house. I want to hit the road by one so I'll be home in time for dinner tonight."

I nodded while my mood sank, and for a moment I pondered whether or not I should skip classes tomorrow and stay another day. But no, I needed to get back to school and my responsibilities there. As much as I loved being with Ben, I needed to exercise self-discipline. School had to come first, right?

The drive to Gainesville seemed like it took only an hour. I held Ben's hand during the entire trip, and we talked nonstop, about all that we'd done that weekend and about the future weekends we'd spend together. We made plans for the next Saturday night. Ben wanted to attend a Crosby, Stills, Nash & Young concert in Orlando's Tangerine Bowl. I was a huge CSN&Y fan—I must've listened to their album,

Déjà Vu, a hundred times—and the thought we'd see them live had me all excited.

By the time we reached Gainesville, the sun was already low in the western sky. The air was much cooler than in Merritt Island, and I shivered in my T-shirt. I grabbed my overnight bag from the back seat, and Ben followed me up the stairs to my apartment.

Inside, Steve sat on the sofa; he studied his physical science text with his bare feet resting on the coffee table. He rose to greet Ben and shake his hand.

Ben's gaze traveled about the living room. Then he looked at me. "Give me a tour, will you?"

I showed him the kitchen and bathroom.

"Not bad," he said.

But when we entered the bedroom, I saw I'd forgotten to separate Steve's bed from mine before I left on Friday. Our pillows lay side by side and our double blanket covered the mattresses and sheets.

Uh-oh.

When I glanced at Ben, a vertical crease appeared between his eyebrows. He stared at the beds, then turned his gaze to me and narrowed his eyes.

"I need to get going," he said.

"Already?"

He pointed to the beds. "I'm sure you guys have plenty of things to do."

"Ben, I..."

"You don't have to explain, Johnny. Actually, I'm not surprised."

Ben turned on his heel, walked to the front door, opened it, and entered the corridor without even speaking to Steve. I followed him down the stairs to the GTO, and in the fading sunlight, I placed a hand on his shoulder while he unlocked his driver's door.

"Don't be angry," I said.

He shook off my hand and turned his gaze to me. "You told me this wouldn't happen—you said sex is something you only share with me—but that's clearly not true."

Shit.

"Please don't let this ruin our weekend," I said. "I'll separate my bed from Steve's right after you leave. Then I won't touch him again, I swear."

Ben hissed and shook his head. "Save your empty promises for someone else, Johnny. I'm tired of hearing them."

Ben climbed into the driver's seat and started the engine with a roar. Then he backed into the street without even saying goodbye. I watched him drive away while my brain fluids boiled.

You've fucked up everything, Darling.

Congratulations.

When I returned to the apartment, Steve looked at me with a puzzled expression. "What's going on? Ben didn't even say *adios* before he left."

I shook my head. "I forgot to move our beds apart before I left on Friday. I should have known Ben would want to see the apartment. Why didn't I prepare for the situation?"

Steve set his text aside. "Is he mad at you?"

"Majorly pissed is more like it."

After I sat down next to Steve on the sofa, I stared at the coffee table and rubbed my temples with the tips of my fingers. Right then, because of my carelessness, I knew it was possible I'd just destroyed my relationship with Ben, and facing that awful fact seemed devastating.

Shaking started in my feet and traveled up my legs. Pretty soon, I trembled all over and my stomach was in knots. There on the sofa, I buried my face in my hands and sobbed like a kid whose dog had just been run over by a car. My shoulders shook like a sapling in a gale.

Steve put his hand on the back of my neck and squeezed.

"Shhh, it'll be okay, Johnny."

But I kept on wailing because, in truth, I *didn't* think things would be okay.

Would I ever hold Ben in my arms again?

Chapter Twenty-Nine

THE NEXT THREE days passed so slowly I felt like I was swimming in molasses. Whenever I looked at a clock, the hand movements seemed to have stalled. I couldn't concentrate on my studies worth a damn, and at work I dropped an entire tub full of dirty dishes. Several items shattered and my boss scowled.

I hadn't touched Steve a single time since the blowup with Ben. Sunday night, I'd moved our beds apart, and thereafter, we each slept alone. Steve did not protest —he knew how upset I was—so he kept a respectable distance from me.

Wednesday evening, I felt so nervous I couldn't even eat my dinner. I just sat there staring into my plate of food, which looked about as enticing as chunks of cardboard covered in ketchup. After dinner, I lay on my bed, studying a cobweb in one corner of the ceiling, and listening to traffic pass on University Avenue.

Would Ben call me?

Would he?

When 9:00 p.m. arrived, the phone on our kitchen wall remained silent. I paced the kitchen floor while chewing a hangnail. I had a terrible headache and my stomach hurt. My vision was even a little blurry.

Come on, Ben—call me.

By 9:30 p.m., I knew it wasn't going to happen.

Do something, Darling.

I reached for the phone and dialed the Stoneciphers' house. After three rings, Ben's mom answered.

My voice quivered when I said, "Hi, Sarah, it's Johnny. Can I speak with Ben, please?"

A few seconds passed before Sarah responded. "He told me you might call tonight, but I'm afraid he doesn't want to talk with you right now."

Shit.

"What's going on between you two? Ben won't tell me. Was there a quarrel?"

"Worse than that. I've acted very stupidly during the past couple of months. I haven't been faithful to Ben, and he discovered that Sunday when he drove me up to Gainesville."

"I see..."

I kept pacing the kitchen floor. My pulse pounded inside my head and my feet felt like cinder blocks. "I need to talk with Ben. I have to make him understand a few things."

Sarah let out her breath. "I can't force him to speak on the phone if he doesn't want to."

"I know, but could you do me a huge favor?"

"What's that?"

"If I ride the bus over to Merritt Island Friday afternoon, will you pick me up at the Greyhound office and take me to your house?"

More silence ruled the line before Sarah finally spoke.

"Are you sure you want me to do that?"

"I'm positive. Ben can't very well avoid me if I'm there in person."

Sarah let out her breath a second time. "All right, Johnny. What time will the bus arrive here?"

Moments after I concluded my phone conversation with Sarah, Steve cruised through the front door with his gear bag and books. He tossed those items onto the Barcalounger and sat on the sofa, dressed in a hooded UF Track & Field sweatshirt and blue jeans.

I stood in the kitchen, feeling dazed.

"What's going on?" Steve asked.

Go on: do it.

"We have to talk—I mean right now."

Steve shifted his weight on the sofa and the seat springs squeaked. "All right."

I drew a breath and let it out. The room seemed to shrink, and my voice sounded funny. "I can't live with you anymore, and you know why. If we keep sharing this apartment, I will lose Ben and I can't let that happen. One of us needs to move out really soon."

Steve lowered his gaze and moistened his lips, then looked up at me. "Are you sure that's what you want? Are you positive?"

I kept my gaze locked onto Steve's and nodded.

Steve's chest rose and fell while we looked at each other. Then he said, "Okay, I understand. I'm not going to keep on fighting a battle I know I'm going to lose. So I'll tell you what: you can keep the apartment. I'll talk to my coach tomorrow after practice. I can probably move into the jock dorm and won't even have to pay rent if I do."

My shoulders sagged in relief. "Thanks, Steve. I'm sorry about this—you know how much I care for you—but I can't have two boyfriends at once. It just won't work."

"Will we still be pals? Can I see you sometimes? I don't mean for sex but just to spend time together."

I nodded. "We'll always be friends. You can count on that."

MY BOSS WASN'T happy when I told him needed Saturday off again.

"This is two weeks in a row. Look, if you can't show up when you're supposed to, then I'll have to find someone else, understand?"

The bus ride to Merritt Island seemed to last forever. Again, we stopped in Ocala, then Leesburg to take on more passengers. An old man seated next to me ate a pork chop from a paper bag; he dropped the bone onto the floor when he'd gnawed all the meat off it. The smell from the chop made my stomach churn. I stared out the window next to me, at palmetto and pine forests and pasture land, trying to think about what I would say to Ben when I saw him that evening.

Would he even listen to me?

We finally crossed the bridge that arced over the Indian River, and then we entered Merritt Island. When we reached the Greyhound office and I disembarked with my overnight bag, Sarah wasn't waiting for me. I glanced all about me, looking for her convertible, but didn't see it. My heart started beating faster, and I felt a sense of panic inside me. What if Sarah didn't show? Maybe she'd told Ben about my plans to visit, and he told her not to pick me up. If she didn't come, where would I sleep tonight, behind a gas station?

But then I spotted Sarah's car approaching. She had the top down. She wore sunglasses and a head scarf that fluttered in the breeze. When she saw me, she gave me a wave and pulled to the curb.

"I'm sorry I'm late," she told me when I climbed into the passenger seat. "Will needed help bathing, and it took us longer than I thought it would."

"It's okay," I said. "I've only been here five minutes or so."

Sarah pulled from the curb, and very soon we flew by pastures and tropical forest. The sun was low in the western sky; clouds there were aglow with color. The air seemed cooler than it had the previous weekend, and I shivered a time or two before putting on a sweatshirt I retrieved from my bag.

"Does Ben know I'm coming?"

Sarah shook her head. "I thought it best if you took him by surprise."

When we reached the house, the sun had already set, and a few stars appeared in the eastern sky. After Sarah parked in the garage, she turned to me and said, "Ben should be home very soon. Where would you like to wait for him?"

I pointed to the barn. "I'll pay Penny a visit."

Penny nickered when she saw me. I petted her muzzle and fed her a sugar cube. Then I groomed her flank with a body brush, making long strokes while she shifted her weight from left to right. I talked to her about my bus ride and how long it had taken, and I didn't even hear Ben enter the barn until he spoke.

"What are you doing here, Johnny?"

I turned to find Ben leading Midnight into his stall. He was dressed in cowboy clothes and hat, and like always he looked handsome as hell, even though right then he scowled. He removed Midnight's bridle while I talked.

"I came because you wouldn't take my phone call and I need to speak with you."

Ben glanced at me for a brief moment. "Why, so you can make me more promises you don't intend to keep?"

I chewed my lips and flexed my fingers.

"I finally figured something out," Ben said while he hung up the bridle on a wall hook.

"What's that?"

"Steve's more important to you than I am."

Ben unbuckled the belt on Midnight's saddle. He removed the saddle and draped it over a saddle rack in Midnight's stall.

"That's not true," I said.

Ben cocked his head to one side. "*I* think it is."

"Well, you're wrong. I came to tell you something—Wednesday, I told Steve I couldn't live with him anymore, that either he or I had to give up the apartment. He's decided he'll live in the athletic dormitory starting this Sunday."

Ben looked at me for a long moment before returning his gaze to Midnight. He removed Midnight's blanket, folded it in half, and hung it over a railing.

"Won't you be lonely without him?" Ben asked.

"A little, but I can handle it as long as I know I'll have you, and that we'll see each other every weekend. What we have between us is more important than anything else to me."

Ben looked at me and raised his eyebrows. "How can I be sure you won't get together with Steve again?"

I lowered my gaze and shifted my weight from one leg to the other, then returned my gaze to Ben. "Because I'm giving you my word that it won't happen anymore. Look, I know I've given you plenty of reasons not to trust me in the past, but you have to believe what I'm telling you right now. I will never touch Steve that way in the future."

Ben lowered his gaze and his face crumpled. He brought his forehead to Midnight's shiny flank. His lips quivered, his shoulders shook, and a tear dribbled from the corner of his eye. He sniffled a time or two before wiping snot away from his upper lip with his shirtsleeve. Then he looked at me with bloodshot eyes.

"Johnny Darling, you'd better mean what you just said. I'm serious—don't fuck with me."

"I'm *not* fucking with you. If I was, I wouldn't be here right now. Listen, whenever I'm on this property, I'll spray cattle with insecticide, no matter how bad everything stinks. I'll launder linens till my hands turn red and blistered. And I'll even stick my arm up a cow's butt if it's necessary. I'll do all of that for you, Ben, because I love you and want to be a part of your life. I want to be a part of this place too. It's where I belong."

Penny snorted in agreement.

Ben looked at Penny, then me. "You know, sometimes that horse is a lot smarter than you."

"True, I've made mistakes, just like you did in your boating accident with Chuck. But if Chuck were here today, I know he would forgive you, and right now, it's your turn to do the same for me. Is that possible?"

Ben lowered his chin and worked his jaw from side to side. Then his gaze met mine again. "Of course it's possible. I can't imagine my life without you in it."

Shit.

Now *my* eyes fogged with tears. I went to Ben and wrapped my arms around his neck. I pulled him to me, and we sniffled with our chins resting on each other's shoulders.

I felt like we'd stepped back from a precipice.

After we calmed down, I followed Ben into the house. We found his folks seated on the living room sofa, reading sections of the *Orlando Sentinel*. An aroma of roasting meat wafted from the kitchen, and I suddenly realized that I was very hungry.

Ben cleared his throat. "Dad and Mom, we need to talk with you for a few minutes about something very important."

"All right, son." Will motioned us to a pair of armchairs.

Ben and I sat down. Ben gazed into his lap for a minute, and I knew he was deciding exactly what he'd say next. He finally lifted his gaze and looked at Will.

"It's been six months since Johnny and I were arrested and you both found out we are a couple. Our probation ends in another week, and we've stayed out of trouble; we always will from now on. But I need to know that you accept my love for Johnny and my need to have him as my partner. Can you do that?"

When Will looked at Sarah, she nodded. Then Will said, "Of course we can. Your mother and I think the world of Johnny, and we know how deeply he cares for you. If he makes you happy, that's all that matters."

Ben made a thin smile and looked at Sarah. "One more thing—Johnny shouldn't have to sleep in Chuck's room any longer. He and I are adults. We should be able to share a bed at night, just like the two of you do."

Sarah looked at Will, and he shrugged his right shoulder. Then Sarah's gaze traveled to Ben. "It's fine if Johnny shares your room with you. There's a queen-size bed in the attic you can bring downstairs if you'd like. It won't be such a tight fit for the two of you."

Minutes later, Ben and I occupied his bedroom with the desk lamp lit. The door was closed, and we lay on Ben's bed, holding each other and not saying a word. Outside, the sky had darkened and crickets in the trees chirped like crazy.

Was I floating? So much had happened over the past week since Ben had seen my bed joined with Steve's up in Gainesville: Ben's blowup, my futile attempt to phone Ben, my announcement to Steve that I could not live with him any longer, my bus ride to Merritt Island, and my pledge of fidelity to Ben when we'd spoken in the barn.

Now it seemed Ben's parents had accepted me as their son's partner, and each night, when I went to sleep under the Stoneciphers' roof, I would hold Ben in my arms.

What more could I ask for?

Chapter Thirty

THE WEDNESDAY AFTERNOON before Thanksgiving, Steve and I drove to Pinellas County in Steve's VW. The day was cool and sunny, and traffic on I-75 was thick with holiday travelers. We passed by cow pastures and horse ranches. Billboards advertising retirement communities were numerous. Chilly air rushed through the car, tossing our hair about. We both wore blue jeans and sweatshirts to keep warm.

I had seen little of Steve since he'd moved out of Gator Manor. Weekdays, he was busy with classes, track, and studying. And I spent my weekends at Merritt Island now, so the only times we'd spent together were a couple of Sunday evenings when I cooked dinner for us after Ben dropped me off at the apartment.

Steve seemed a bit distant during those visits. We limited our conversations to impersonal matters. He talked about life in the jock dorm and some new friends he'd made there. I talked about the work I'd performed at the Stoneciphers' property and a Jack Nicholson film Ben and I had seen called *Five Easy Pieces*. There was no physical touching, and no suggestive remarks were made. And even though it would have been easy for me to invite Steve into the bedroom for a round of sex, I wouldn't even allow myself to consider it.

My two-timing days were over.

Now, on our trip southward on I-75 we didn't talk much. Instead, we listened to the radio. In the course of our journey, we probably heard "Voodoo Chile" by Jimi Hendrix at least four times.

When we reached my home in St. Petersburg Beach, Steve parked in the driveway and engaged the emergency brake. By then, the time was past 4:00 p.m. and the sun was low in the western sky. I handed Steve two bucks for my share of the gas we'd burned, and while he pocketed the money, I asked what his plans were for the next few days.

"Stewart and I may camp at Ft. De Soto Park Friday night, and I spoke on the phone with Castleman a few days ago. I might spend an evening with him while I'm here."

The mention of Castleman made my stomach muscles tighten. "I thought things were over between you two."

Steve gazed out the windshield. "When I broke things off with him, I believed I had a decent chance at becoming your boyfriend, but now I know that's going to happen, so why not see Castleman?"

Like always, the thought of Steve and Castleman in bed together made me jealous, which was exactly the reaction Steve wanted from me. But by then, I knew Steve's tactics all too well. He was fishing for sex—he knew Ben was 160 miles away—but this time, I wasn't taking the bait.

"Well," I said, "you'll do what you have to do, I guess."

Steve moistened his lips with his tongue and stared into his lap. "I miss falling asleep with you holding me."

"I know. I miss it too."

"Do you?"

"Of course—how could I not—but we aren't kids anymore. I have responsibilities to Ben I need to honor. It's the way things have to be, so please respect that."

Steve drew a breath and let it out, then looked at me.

"Have a great Thanksgiving. I'll pick you up on Sunday, right after lunch."

Also Available from NineStar Press

Connect with NineStar Press

Website: NineStarPress.com

Facebook: NineStarPress

Facebook Reader Group: NineStarNiche

Twitter: @ninestarpress

Tumblr: NineStarPress